THE VICTIM came visiting—but didn't even get to say hello before the killer struck.

THE SUSPECTS were several—and most of them were lying about *something*.

THE DETECTIVE was a disbarred lawyer who could still run rings around the cops.

THE SOUND OF MURDER combines "an expertly constructed plot" *(Saturday Review of Literature)* with "a slick snoop and entertaining fellow" *(New York Herald Tribune)*—Rex Stout's most oddball detective, Alphabet Hicks.

THE SOUND OF MURDER

(Original title: ALPHABET HICKS)

REX STOUT

PYRAMID BOOKS ▲ NEW YORK

THE SOUND OF MURDER
(Original title: ALPHABET HICKS)

A PYRAMID BOOK—published by arrangement with the author

Farrar & Rinehart edition published 1941
Pyramid edition published January, 1965
Second printing April, 1967

PYRAMID BOOKS are published by Pyramid Publications, Inc.
444 Madison Avenue, New York, N. Y. 10022, U.S.A.

One

IF JUDITH DUNDEE HAD NOT GLANCED AT THE NAME OF the taxi driver, there before her on the framed identification card attached to the panel, she might eventually have found some other way out of her trouble. Or she might not.

What caused her to glance at the name was a little incident that occurred when the taxi, with her in it, stopped for a red light at 50th Street and Park Avenue. Three or four pedestrians eyed the cab to make sure it was going to stop, and the face of one of them, a well-dressed and dignified gentleman who might have been on his way to a directors' meeting, lit up with pleased recognition. He stepped from the curb to the side of the cab, thrust a hand in to the driver for a shake, and offered a greeting in the tone he would have used to a fellow director:

"Hello, Hicks, how are you?"

That was the first and last appearance of the well-dressed gentleman in Judith Dundee's life, but in that brief moment he did her a valuable service. Her mind jostled momentarily from its concentration on the stew she was simmering in, she glanced at the framed card on the panel and saw the name, "A. Hicks." The "A" pushed speculation further and aroused memory, as the cab started forward and rolled on uptown.

She remembered the yellowish brown eyes which, by their glint and the configuration of their lids, looked like a cat's or tiger's eyes . . . and the magazine article she had read about him a year or so ago, a Profile in the *New Yorker* . . . Harvard Law School . . . his melodramatic disbarment during his first year of practice . . . submerged years not revealed . . . night watchman . . . subway guard . . . the famous Harley case . . . the girl with clothespins on her fingers and toes. . . .

Preoccupied as she had been when she entered the cab at 40th Street, she had had no glance for the face of its driver. Now, when it stopped in front of her apartment house in the

Seventies on Park Avenue, she did not step out though the
halberdier with no halberd opened the door. Instead, she
leaned forward to the opening:

"Mr. Alphabet Hicks?"

The driver's head turned, came around to her, and she saw
his face—and the eyes. They were fully as remarkable as
she had remembered them to be. She asked inanely:

"So you're driving a taxi now?"

"No," Hicks said.

She laughed nervously. "It was a stupid question." She
shook her head at the halberdier and he closed the door and
retreated across the sidewalk. She resumed, "Of course you
don't remember me. About a year ago—you were working
for a tree company then—I read that article about you—I
wanted you for the lion at a dinner party and you wouldn't
come—"

"Dundee," Hicks said.

"Then you do remember?"

"No, I was just guessing. There's a car behind that wants
to get in here."

"Let them—" She glanced back; and the impulse that
had been fluttering in her took control. "Look," she said
decisively, "I want to talk with you. Not to persuade you to
come to a dinner party. I'm in trouble."

One end of his wide mobile mouth curved upwards and
made him look sardonic. "What kind of trouble?"

"I can't tell you—it's a long story. You can park around
the corner and come up to my apartment. Will you? Please?"

"Okay." He eased the gear in.

Judith Dundee wasn't forty-five years old, but in a few
months she would be. Whether she looked it or not depended
on the time of day or night, the lighting, the state of her
mind and nerves, and who was doing the looking. As far as
physical details were concerned—the smooth well-kept skin,
the large dark eyes, the brown hair still brown, the throat
nicely curving from a chin that was her daintiest feature—
she was quite capable of being taken for under thirty, when
the conditions were ideal.

On that Wednesday in September, however, the conditions
were apparently far from ideal. She looked distinctly draggy
as she sat on a divan in a corner of the slightly grandiose living room of her duplex apartment high above Park Avenue.

"The trouble I'm in," she said, "is very—intimate."

The taxi driver merely nodded. There on a chair, he looked less than ever like a taxi driver, even disregarding the details that his face was too clean and his clothing not greasy enough.

"I mean," Judith said, "that I wouldn't want anyone to know about it. But I have to get help from somebody. I was thinking of going to a detective agency this afternoon, but I don't know any, and it would be so distasteful—" She made a face. "Not that it isn't already distasteful. Then I saw you and remembered what I had read about you . . . and the marvelous things you had done . . . and your eyes were the cleverest I ever saw. . . ." She stopped and looked embarrassed.

"You'll have to make the sale," Hicks said dryly. "I just accepted your invitation to come up and listen."

"I know you did." She sat and looked at him a moment, then said abruptly in a new and harsher tone, "My husband has gone crazy."

Hicks grunted. "I've never handled a maniac—"

"No, no," she said impatiently. "But he has. It's simply insane. We've been married twenty-five years. Our life together hasn't been exactly continuous bliss—for one thing, I'm extravagant, I always have been—not to mention any of his faults—but we've done fairly well. We've raised two children, which is what marriage is for, I believe, and we've never tried to poison each other. I imagine our friends would say that our marital happiness rating is well above the average. And suddenly one day last week, Tuesday, a week ago yesterday, he came home from the office and confronted me with a perfectly terrible look in his eyes and asked me how often I had been to see Jimmie Vail!"

She halted. Hicks looked uncomfortable. He muttered, "Jimmie Vail?"

"Yes!"

"What's that, a man?"

"Certainly he's a man. I was dumfounded. When I could speak I said that if at my age I went in for clandestine meetings with a man I would pick a better specimen than Jimmie Vail. With the same eyes and voice he said, 'I don't mean that. You know what I mean. I mean how often have you been to his office to betray the secrets of my business. I have proof. You might as well tell me.' That left me speechless again. Before I could speak he said, 'Who did you get it from, Brager? Did you worm it out of Brager? And did you pay him what he wanted? And how much did Vail pay you? Did you get a good price?' "

"I asked him if he was crazy. He said it was useless for me to try to deny it, he knew I had done it, all he wanted was the details, the full story, so he could decide what to do. It was impossible to get him to talk sense. We were here in this room. Somebody came, and he left and didn't return that night. The next day, towards noon, he came, and started all over again, just the same gibberish. It was awful. Finally he said if I would go to his office at four o'clock that afternoon he would prove it to me, and I said I would go, and he left. I really thought he was unbalanced. Around three o'clock he telephoned and told me not to come to the office, just told me that and hung up. I went anyway, and was told he wasn't there. That evening he came home late—and absolutely refused to discuss it! He still refuses to discuss it! If I try to, he leaves. Before people, he treats me—he tries to act as if nothing had happened. When we're alone—we just aren't alone. We have adjoining bedrooms, and he keeps the connecting door locked. When I went into his room by the hall door a few nights ago—well—he simply won't discuss it! Did you ever hear of anything so utterly senseless? Now did you?"

"It sounds pretty odd," Hicks admitted. "What kind of business secrets does he think you sold?"

"I suppose manufacturing secrets for making plastics. That's the only—"

"What are plastics?"

"Why—plastics!" She looked as if he had asked what were apples. "Everything is made of plastics, or soon will be—fountain pens, clocks, furniture, dishes—Ford is experimenting with them for automobiles. They come in all colors—"

"Does your husband manufacture plastics?"

She nodded. "His firm is one of the largest. R. I. Dundee and Company. The office is on 40th Street and the factory is at Bridgeport, and that's about as much as I know about it. He never discusses business with me—or very little." Her voice took on a sudden edge, a note of metallic hardness. It was all the more noticeable because it was a distinctive and attractive voice, with richness and color, and a slurring of the hard consonants and a fullness of the soft ones that made it warm and pleasing. The abrupt change was slightly shocking. "How," she demanded, "could I betray secrets if I didn't know any? And have never had an opportunity of learning any? And anyway, it's idiotic! What if your wife suddenly accused you of—of—"

"Never had one." Hicks's tone did not indicate that a filling of the vacancy was contemplated. "But I see your point. Who is Jimmie Vail? Does he make plastics too?"

"Yes, he's the head of the Republic Products Corporation."

"A competitor?"

"Very much so. He and my husband used to be friends, but not any more. My husband says he's a crook and a thief. I don't know much about it, but apparently Vail has been getting Dundee formulas in some underhand way—or my husband thinks he has. That's been going on for two or three years."

"How well do you know Vail?"

"I used to know him rather well. I haven't seen him for a long time."

"Have you been to his office recently?"

"I never have. I don't even know where it is."

"Your husband asked if you had wormed it out of Brager. Who is Brager?"

Judith Dundee's lips curved in a little smile, whether of disdain or pure amusement could not be told. "Herman Brager," she said, the R's fuller and the G softer in her attractive voice than they were in Hicks's twang. "A scientist. According to my husband, a genius; and perhaps he is, I don't know. He does experiments and makes amazing discoveries. He has been with the company for several years. He wouldn't work at Bridgeport, said there were too many people around, so my husband fitted up a laboratory for him up in Westchester, near a place called Katonah." Her lips smiled again. "He's what is called a character."

"Do you know him?"

"Oh, yes. Not so well personally, if that's the way to put it, but I've seen him often. My husband often has him here. He comes into town twice a month and dines here and they spend the evening talking business. And by the way—I said I never had an opportunity to learn a secret—but perhaps I did. Once Mr. Brager left his brief case here overnight, and possibly it was full of secrets. I can't say, because I didn't look. It must have been important, because my son drove in especially the next day to get it."

"How long ago was that?"

She pursed her lips. "About a month ago."

"Is your son with the company?"

"Yes, indeed. He's twenty-four years old." Her tone acknowledged the difficulty of crediting her with a son of so advanced an age, and to do her justice, it was rather surprising. "He finished a postgraduate course at M.I.T. in June, and now he's up there with Mr. Brager." She shifted her position on the divan, with a gesture of impatience. "But that's irrelevant, isn't it?" She made another gesture, of appeal, and smiled at him. "Won't you help me? It's so preposterous, and I feel so darned helpless! I went to a lifelong friend—he was best man at our wedding—and he has been to see my husband twice. That's where I was this morning, at this friend's office—he says that my husband absolutely refuses to discuss it and there's nothing he can do. So I thought of going to a detective agency, and then I saw you, and remembered what that article said."

She put out a hand, palm up. "You will help me, won't you? Of course, since you despise money—but I can afford to pay whatever you ask—" She ended on a note of embarrassment.

"I don't despise money." Hicks surveyed her, and the glint in his unblinking eyes was more than ever the lazy but watchful insolence of a cat's eyes. "In spite of what that article said, I'm not a nut. I admit one thing. It would be a lot of fun to find out if you really did sell your husband's business secrets and what you're really after is to learn what kind of proof he's got hold of. Also I admit I could use about—" he paused a moment— "about two hundred dollars."

She met his eyes. "I've told you the truth, Mr. Hicks."

"Okay." His eyes didn't change. "I'll take a crack at it. As I say, I need some cash. And I want a picture of you—a nice handsome picture. And maybe you can tell me a few more things."

It appeared that she couldn't, at least nothing useful or significant, though for another half an hour she answered his questions. When, a little later, he left, in his pocket was a check, and in an envelope under his arm was a large photograph of Judith Dundee, quite good-looking, even striking, with a gay tilt to her head and a provocative smile on her lips. There had been no explanation of his need for that. Down on the street, he returned to his cab and got in and started the engine.

On Madison Avenue in the Forties, a patrolman new to the beat was speaking in a grieved tone to his precinct sergeant, through the police phone box:

". . . I was here on the sidewalk and this taxi stops right by me and the driver gets out and says, 'How do you do, Officer,' and hands me this piece of paper. I unfold it and look at it and it says—here, I'll read it—'Kindly phone Sheridan 9-8200 and tell Jake, the checker, to send a driver for the cab. I have no time because the police are after me.' It's signed, 'A. Hicks,' and that's the name on the identification card in the cab. The writing's hard to read, and then I look around and he's gone. Nowhere in sight. I started—"

"What did he look like?"

"About thirty-five maybe, medium height, kind of slow-moving—at least I thought he was—big wide mouth, funny eye like a Chink—no, not like a Chink—"

The sergeant cackled. "That's him. Alfred Hicks, alias Alphabet Hicks. Save that paper for me, I want to keep it."

"Maybe I can pick up his trail if I—"

"Forget it. Kindly call the number he asked you to."

"Do you mean," the patrolman's voice shrilled with indignation, "it was just a prank?"

"Prank hell." The sergeant cackled again. "He saved a nickel, didn't he?"

It would be a pleasure to record that during the ensuing hours of that Wednesday afternoon swift strides were made toward the solution of Judith Dundee's problem, but it would be contrary to fact. Though Hicks performed various errands, the only perceptible progress was toward the disappearance of Judith Dundee's money, beginning with cashing the check. The major expenditures were as follows:

Suit of clothes	$ 65.00
Pocketknife	2.50
Two-pound box of chocolates	2.25
Postal money order for British War Relief	100.00
Photographs of Myrna Loy, Bette Davis, Deanna Durbin and Shirley Temple	4.00
	$173.75

At seven o'clock that evening Hicks was eating spaghetti and arguing about Mussolini at the family table in the kitchen of an Italian restaurant on East 29th Street. At nine o'clock the table was cleared and a pinochle game was started. At midnight Hicks went upstairs to the furnished room for which he paid six dollars a week.

In yellow pajamas piped in brown, he sat on the edge of the bed and opened the box of chocolates and smelled it with a long deep inhalation.

"I'll earn it and then I'll eat it," he muttered. If he had known how much of a chore the earning was to be, he might have added, "If I'm still alive."

Two

IN THE RECEPTION ROOM OF THE EXECUTIVE OFFICES OF the Republic Products Corporation high above Lexington Avenue, the receptionist sat at her desk and tried not to yawn. Losing the struggle, she covered her mouth with a palm. It was five minutes past nine, Thursday morning. Life presented a dreary outlook. Her feet hurt. Dancing till after one o'clock, and less than six hours' sleep, and standing up in the subway . . . no more, she just couldn't take it, not at her age . . . that was all right when she was younger, but now she was twenty-three, nearly twenty-four—

"Good morning," said a twangy voice.

The voice irritated her. Her tired eyes saw a man in a new-looking brown suit, and a face that was new to her, with a large envelope under his arm.

"Who do you want to see?" she asked. Ordinarily she said "Whom," but, feeling as she did, that was beyond her.

"You," the man said.

That old gag deserved, and usually received, chilly disdain. But the idea that anyone on earth could want to see her then, the way her face felt and the way her feet hurt, was so perfectly excruciating that she had to laugh. She burst into laughter.

"No," the man protested. "Really. I want to ask if you'd like to take a trip to Hollywood."

"Sure," she said scornfully. "Does Garbo need a double or what?"

"You'll never get anywhere," said the man severely, "with an attitude like that. Here's opportunity knocking at your door and listen to you." He placed the envelope on the desk, opened the flap, extracted a large glossy photograph, and held it in front of her. "Who is that?"

With one glance she said sarcastically, "John Barrymore."

"Very well," he said reproachfully. "You'll live to regret it. There's four more pictures of movie stars in here. If you can identify all five, you get a year's subscription to the *Movie Gazette*. Free. Then you write an article of a thousand words and send it to our contest editor—"

"I don't know any thousand words." She glanced at the photograph again. "But if they're all as easy as that. Shirley Temple."

"Right." He pulled out another one. "Now watch your step."

She snorted. "Those eyes? Bette Davis."

"Two right. This one?"

"Deanna Durbin."

"And this?"

"Myrna Loy."

"Good for you. Four down and one to go. This last one?"

She squinted at it. She took it from him and peered at it from different angles. "Huh," she said, "I thought there was a catch in it. This is probably some dame that sat on a wagon in 'Gone With the Wind' when they fled from that town in Virginia, I think it was—"

"Atlanta, Georgia. But you wrong me. I think you ought to recognize her without straining your brain beyond its capacity. Dressed differently, of course. For instance, imagine her getting out of the elevator and walking up to you here at your desk—with a hat on, remember, and some kind of a wrap probably, and sort of nervous, and saying for instance that she wanted to see Mr. Vail—"

The girl hissed at him.

He followed her glance and saw a man approaching—a large man, well fed and well shaved, with a broad nose and a thin mouth. He had been headed from the elevator for the corridor leading within, but swerved and was approaching. . . .

"Good morning, Mr. Vail," the girl said as brightly as though her feet were perfectly all right.

His "Good morning" sounded more like Bulgarian. "What's all this?" he demanded, stopping at the desk. He frowned at the photographs, at the stranger standing there. "I heard you mention my name—"

"Just accidentally, Mr. Vail," the girl said hastily. "He was only telling me—only showing me—"

She stopped because something queer was happening. Vail had glanced at the photograph she had put down, the unidentified one, had bent over to look at it, and then had abruptly straightened up; and the expression on his face frightened her, though it was directed not at her but at the stranger. Though she had seen him angry before, she had never seen his lips as thin as that, nor his eyes drawn so narrow.

"Ah," he said. Then suddenly he smiled, but it was not a smile to reassure anybody, least of all the man it was aimed at. "There is some explanation of this, I suppose? This picture of a lady—an old friend of mine?"

The stranger smiled back. "I can make one up."

Vail took a step. "Who are you?"

The other took a wallet from his pocket, fished out a card, and offered it. Vail took it and looked at it:

A. HICKS

M.S.O.T.P.B.O.M.

He looked up, unsmiling. "This—this hash?"

The other gestured it away. "Unimportant. One of my titles. Melancholy Spectator of the Psychic Bellyache of Mankind. The name is Hicks."

"Who sent you here?"

Hicks shook his head. "I didn't come to see you, Mr. Vail. Some other time, maybe." He reached for the envelope and photographs.

"Leave those things here and get out!"

But Hicks gathered them up with one swoop of his hand and made for the elevator. In a moment a down car stopped for him.

As he emerged from the building no sign of the smile was

THE SOUND OF MURDER

on his face. He was beginning to suspect that he was in for something nasty. It seemed likely, considering how startlingly Vail's narrowed eyes had been those of a wary and malevolent pig, that some one was going to get hurt.

He sat on a bench in Bryant Park and thought it over.

The office of R. I. Dundee and Company was on 40th Street near Madison Avenue, a mere five-minute walk from that of its hottest competitor, Republic Products Corporation. At eleven o'clock that Thursday morning, anyone seeing R. I. Dundee seated at his desk would not have guessed that only ten minutes ago a phone call from the Chicago branch had brought the glad tidings that a $68,000 contract for plastics had just been closed with Fosters, the biggest manufacturers of loose-leaf binders in the country. Dundee sat staring at a corner of the rug with an expression of mingled dejection and choler. With his regular precise features and his well-fitting conservative gray coat, he looked like a man intended by both nature and himself to be neat and personable, but with his disarranged hair and his bloodshot eyes, the intention was shockingly impugned.

He shifted in his chair and groaned, and when there was a knock at the door he yelled in a tone of extreme exasperation, "Come in!"

A boy entered and handed him a card:

A. HICKS
C.F.M.O.B.

Beneath was written in ink, "Have just seen Mr. James Vail. It might interest you."

Dundee straightened up and gave the card another look. He rubbed it with his thumb and forefinger, and looked at it again.

"What does this man look like?"

"He looks all right, sir. Except his eyes maybe. They're kind of gleamy and menacing."

"Send him in here."

The boy went. When, a moment later, the visitor entered, he got a cool reception. Dundee stayed in his chair, offered no greeting, and stared up at the newcomer. Hicks stood on the other side of the desk and returned the stare, then circled around to a chair, sat, and said:

15

"Candidate for Mayor of Babylon. Not Babylon, Long Island. Babylon."

Dundee blinked with irritation. "What the devil are you talking about?"

Hicks pointed to the card which the other still held in his fingers. "Those letters. That's what they stand for. To save you the trouble of asking. Sometimes they help to open a conversation, but in this case of course Jimmie Vail's name would have been enough. Wouldn't it?"

"What about Vail? What do you want?"

Hicks smiled at him. "First I'd like to get acquainted a little. If I bounce it right back at you, what I want, you'll probably tell me to get out, as Vail did, and then where are we? The way you look, on edge the way you are. And with that stubborn mouth you've got. But I guess I can lead up to it. Yesterday afternoon your wife paid me two hundred dollars."

"My wife!—" Dundee goggled at him. "For what?"

"For nothing. That's the sad part of it. It happened that I needed the money, so I took it. If you made the money and it's being wasted, it's your own fault. I've never heard of anything dumber than a man accusing his wife of treachery and claiming to have proof of it, and then refusing to produce the proof or even to discuss it. Whether she's guilty—"

"Get out!" Dundee said. His voice trembled with rage. Hicks shook his head.

Dundee stood up. His hands were shaking. "Get out!"

"No," Hicks said, not moving and not raising his voice. "You ought to see yourself in a mirror. Your wife thinks you're out of your head and she may be right. If you handled your business problems the way you're trying to handle this one, by simply having a fit, you'd have been bankrupt long ago. I've come here to make you an offer, and I'm going to make it before I leave."

"I don't want any offer—"

"How do you know till you've heard it? If you'd let your brain cool off a little, you'd realize that I'm in a position to get you what you want. Your wife has paid me money. She has confidence in me. You told her it was useless for her to try to deny she had sold your business secrets to Vail, you knew she had done it; what you wanted from her was the full story so you could decide what to do. What if I can get that out of her? Wouldn't that help?"

"I see." Dundee's lips worked, and he clamped his jaw to make them stop. He gazed down at the other's face.

"That would be worth something, wouldn't it?" Hicks argued. "But of course you'd have to give me something to work with. For instance, that proof you were going to show her—I'd have to know what that was—I'd have to know enough of what you know to be able to impress her—"

"Ha," Dundee said derisively. "You would?"

"Certainly."

"Where did you see Vail?"

"At his office."

"Did my wife send you to him?"

"No. I was just poking into holes."

"Do you expect me to believe that?"

"I think it's fairly credible."

"I don't. What are you, a lawyer?"

"No. I'm just a guy. A sort of a freak. You might say, an outlawyer." Hicks gestured it away. "I understand your reluctance. You don't know whether I'm enough of a philosopher to double-cross your wife, or whether I'm trying to pull a fast one on you. That's a risk you have to take. However, I can prove that I was disbarred from practicing law, and that ought to be a point in my favor. You can check that."

Dundee had stopped trembling. His blood, obviously, was under control again; he had no longer the aspect of a man about to clutch a throat or pick up a chair and hurl it. He asked in a hard, even tone:

"Where did my wife get hold of you?"

"That's a long story. I have a—I've had some notoriety."

"I don't doubt it. Of course you're working for Vail."

"No. I never saw Vail before today."

"I don't believe it." Dundee's nostrils bulged and subsided again. "I'd like to wring your damned neck. Get out of here."

"I don't think—"

"I said get out."

Hicks, his lips pursed into an O as if he were going to whistle, sat for five seconds gazing up at the stubborn jaw and mouth, the cold fury of the contracted pupils in their bloodshot whites. Then he heaved a sigh, lifted himself to his feet in no haste, got his hat from a corner of the desk, and walked out.

After the door had closed, Dundee stood there without

any change of expression, slowly rubbing his palms up and down the sides of his thighs. He kept that up a while, then sat and pulled his phone over and told it.

"Get me the Sharon Detective Agency."

Three

HICKS SAT ON A BENCH IN BRYANT PARK AGAIN, WATCHING a pigeon strut. It was an utterly disgusting and sordid mess, and he was in for it. Not its least disgusting aspect was that he had only twenty dollars left of Mrs. Dundee's two hundred. He could take the subway downtown and borrow a hundred and eighty from old man Harley and pay Mrs. Dundee back. He sat and watched the pigeon and considered that, and finally decided to eat lunch first.

But it was significant that instead of making for Third Avenue, where a plate of stew, with bread and butter, was twenty cents, he went to Joyce's on 41st Street, got comfortable in one of the leather-upholstered booths, and ordered a double portion of baked oysters.

And it was there that he found a short cut to a trail which otherwise he would have reached only after long and laborious twists and turnings. He was spearing the last oyster when something so abruptly caught his attention, by way of his ear, that the oyster on his fork was halted in mid-air. He had been so preoccupied with his own concerns that he had been oblivious to the murmur and clatter of the restaurant, and probably would have remained so had not a sudden lull in the general noise cleared the way for an instant, so that he heard the voice quite plainly. It came from directly behind him.

It said, ". . . going now, and you can't stop me!"

It was the voice of Judith Dundee.

The oyster still brandished on his fork, Hicks twisted his

18

head. The voice went on. Enough reached his ear to confirm his recognition of it, and to tell him that it came from the booth adjoining his, over the back of the upholstered seat, but in the renewed surrounding noise no more words were audible. He could hear, or thought he could, a low urgent masculine voice replying to her, and was straining his ear to recognize it, when he became aware of swift and impetuous movement. Were they leaving? He slid to the edge of his seat and peered around, and got a view of a female figure, the back of it, in a gray woolen suit and a fur neckpiece, darting down the aisle. Alone. On sudden impulse he acted. Tossing a dollar bill on the table and grabbing his hat, he followed. As he passed the adjoining booth a glance showed him that it was occupied by a man about his own age, with a sharp pointed nose incongruous in a face white and puckered with distress.

By the time Hicks got to the sidewalk Mrs. Dundee was thirty paces away, headed east. He kept his distance. There were people—Inspector Vetch of the Homicide Squad, for instance, who would have richly appreciated the situation. Absolutely typical Hicks, Vetch would have said, tailing the woman who had hired him.

But he would have been wrong, as Hicks soon discovered for himself, when the gray woolen suit turned left on Madison Avenue and he caught a glimpse of its wearer's profile. It was not Mrs. Dundee!

He stopped short. Then he went on again, impelled by logic. That voice had come from the booth behind his or he would cut off his ears. And that woman had come from that booth and there had been no other woman in it. At least he would hear her speak again. He closed up. She turned right on 42nd Street and entered Grand Central Station, and when she headed across the concourse for a ticket window he was only ten paces behind. There was a man ahead of her at the window, and as she stopped she turned for a look at the clock.

It certainly was not Mrs. Dundee. She was something more than half Mrs. Dundee's age, but not much. She was fair, extremely fair; and when her glance, leaving the clock, rested on Hicks's face for an instant, his eyes dropped, away from the pain and distress in hers. It came her turn at the window and she spoke through the grill:

"Round trip to Katonah, please. There's a train at one-eighteen, isn't there? Track twenty-two? Thank you."

It was the voice he had heard in the restaurant. Hicks stared incredulously at the back of her head. The resemblance to Judith Dundee's voice was startling, little short of amazing. Even so, that might be dismissed as none of his business, as merely one of nature's rare slips in her monumental task of differentiating two billion two-legged creatures one from the other; but what about Katonah? She was going to Katonah!

That was too much. When she had moved away he bought a ticket to Katonah, hurried to the track entrance, and reached the platform in time to see her enter a coach. Inside he took a seat behind her, three seats removed from hers, and presently the train started. She had removed her hat and neckpiece, and he could see the back of her head. It was a well-shaped head, and her hair was fair and soft-looking. . . .

Beyond White Plains the train was a local, and the ride consisted mostly of jolts, stops, starts, and more jolts, but at least it kept to schedule, and Hicks's watch told him it was 2:39 when the trainman opened the door and called Katonah. He followed the quarry down the aisle to the vestibule, descended at her heels, and paused to light a cigarette as she looked uncertainly around. Three cars were backed up to the platform extension, with men standing by them calling "Taxi!" and she headed for one. Hicks was there close enough to hear when she spoke to the driver:

"Dundee's? On Long Hill Road? Do you know where it is?"

The driver said he did, and opened the door for her, and they were off.

Hicks felt his blood moving. That was totally unreasonable; the mere fact that a woman whose voice resembled Judith Dundee's was bound for Dundee's laboratory brought home no bacon; but it is not reason that pumps blood. He addressed another driver standing there:

"If I'd been quicker on the trigger that lady might have been willing to save me a quarter. I'm going where she is."

"You'd have saved more than a quarter, brother. It's three miles. One buck. Hop in."

Hicks got onto the front seat with him. As they rolled away from the station the driver asked, "Which do you want, the house or the laboratory?"

"Why, is there a house?"

"Sure there's a house." The driver explained, as one who

likes to explain, encouraged by questions. The people who worked in the laboratory—Mr. Brager, young Dundee, and Miss Gladd—lived in the house. Likewise Mrs. Powell, who looked after the house. The outside man didn't live there.

"Was that Miss Gladd who got off the train?"

"Her? No."

"Who was it?"

"Don't know." He slowed the car, which had been speeding along the highway, swung it sharply to the right onto a narrow graveled road, and accelerated. "Never saw her before that I remember."

A little farther on the car had to swerve onto the grass to meet and pass the other taxi, returning, and in another minute it slowed to a crawl as it approached an entrance to a drive on the right.

"Here's the house," the driver announced. "The drive goes on around some woods to the laboratory—"

"This will do." Hicks climbed out, got rid of a dollar, and stood there while the car backed, got turned, and sped off in dust. Then he walked up the curving drive toward the house.

The age of the trees and shrubbery showed that the place was an old one, but the house had been modernized. Instead of a covered porch in front there was a flagged terrace open to the sky, the walls were stucco with a plain trim of a greenish material which Hicks suspected of being a Dundee plastic, and the windows had metal casements. No one was in sight. Hicks pushed the button beside the door, and when it opened and a florid-faced woman appeared, he asked for Mr. Brager.

"He's over at the laboratory."

"How do I get there, by the drive?"

"You've got a car?"

"Taxi. I sent it back."

"Then it's shorter this way."

She bustled out to show him, off to the left, where at the edge of the lawn a path entered a strip of woods and undergrowth, and he thanked her and made for it. In the woods was a cool damp smell, and he had gone not more than forty paces when he came to a little bridge over a brook. That stopped him. There were not many things in life that he ever felt the need of, but among the few people who knew him well it was notorious that he needed a brook. He had, off and on, and here and there, looked at dozens of brooks.

Now he halted on the bridge and looked at this one, and listened to it. His thoughts, however, for the minutes he stood there, were more ironic than idyllic. The aimlessness of the brook was only apparent; his own aimlessness in following that voice. . . .

"Looking for somebody?"

The footsteps on the soft dirt path, not yet carpeted with autumn leaves, had not been audible. Hicks whirled, startled, and was looking at a young man clad in soiled white coveralls, hatless, with sober bluish-gray eyes set deep in a bony but well-arranged face.

Hicks nodded and moved on off the bridge. "I'm looking for Mr. Brager."

"He's at the laboratory. I doubt if he can see you—we've got the furnace going." The youth stepped onto the bridge and turned back. "I'm Ross Dundee, his assistant. Will I do?"

"I don't believe so. It's just a little personal matter."

"Righto." He was off the way Hicks had come.

Hicks went on. In another hundred yards or so the path emerged from the woods, and there, across a small meadow, was a low unadorned concrete building flanked by two venerable oaks. He approached. A graveled drive extended the length of the front and curved around either corner, evidently encircling it. From open windows came a low steady hum as of a gigantic motor. Toward the left was a door, and since no push button was there, Hicks turned the knob and entered.

No space was wasted on a hall. This, evidently, was the office, a medium-sized room which at first sight made you blink on account of the riot of colored plastics. There was a purple desk, a row of blue filing cabinets, a mottled gray and yellow table covered with an assortment of gadgets, and chairs of all colors; and at another desk, that one pink, with a green typewriter and a red microphone perched on it, a girl sat crying.

The scene was altogether so chaotic as to be grotesque, with the subdued hum of machinery from beyond walls providing a background like the rumbling of a dragon from the depths of a cavern—but it had competition from another dragon. Though no man was visible, a man's voice filled the room, uttering strident and mysterious incantations:

"Six eighty-four! Twelve minutes at five one oh, nine minutes at six three five! Vat two at three-ten, less tendency to streak and more uniform hardening! Shrinkage point oh three millimeters. . . ."

And the girl sat with her fingers dancing on the keys of her typewriter, typing away like mad, while tears ran down her cheeks and made dewdrops on both sides of her chin. Hicks gazed at her in consternation. Suddenly the man's voice stopped, and immediately the girl, peering through her tears at the sheet in her machine, read off what she had typed into the red microphone. She spoke clearly and distinctly, stopping twice to catch her breath with spasmodic gasps.

Then the subdued humming dragon had the field.

"Mother of waters!" said Hicks in a tone of astonishment. "Do you have to splash on it to make it work?"

The girl did not reply. She was using her handkerchief, removing dewdrops and streaks. Hicks noted with approval that her nails were not painted and her lips were her own— or at least not obtrusively chromatic. Her eyes, when they finally came to him, were clear and candid and direct.

"I wasn't splashing," she said with spirit. "What do you want?"

"That's rude," Hicks said firmly. "You shouldn't be rude."

"Neither should you. You bust in here when I'm crying and make that crack about splashing."

"Okay. I'd like to see Mr. Brager."

"I'm afraid you can't." Her lungs' urgent demand for oxygen spoiled her dignity. The air rushed in with little hissing gasps, shaking her shoulders and breasts. She gulped and recovered. "He's very busy."

Hicks nodded. "I met Mr. Dundee on the path, and he said they've got the furnace going. Will it go all day?"

"I don't know. Sometimes it does—"

"What was the pressure on Lot Six from eleven to twelve?"

It was the voice again. This time Hicks localized it as coming from a grill set in the wall at the girl's right. She spoke into the microphone:

"I haven't that, Mr. Brager. Mr. Dundee wasn't using the speaker, he recorded it, and it isn't typed yet."

"Run over the plates and get it."

Hicks sat down in a yellow chair and took a newspaper from his pocket, but watched the ensuing performance instead of reading. The girl reached to a contraption at the end of her desk and pulled it closer, and from a rack attached to it selected one of a row of disks like phonograph records, except that they were the color of weak tea. She put it in place on the player and flipped a switch, and in a moment a voice sounded, the voice of Ross Dundee:

"Thirty grams of Formula K give no result. Fifty grams increase the viscosity. . . ."

When the third plate she tried gave her the desired information, she relayed it to Brager through the microphone, pushed the machine out of the way, and sat in readiness for another sortie by the dragon.

She sighed deeply.

Hicks asked, "Are you Miss Gladd?"

"Yes." She sighed again. "That's me. Why?"

"I just wondered. I happened to know there was a Miss Gladd here, and when a young woman got off the train I was on and I heard her tell the driver to bring her here, I jumped to the conclusion she was Miss Gladd. She was about your build, but a few years older. And by the way—" Hicks glanced around as though the thought had just occurred to him—"where is she? Didn't she get here?"

"Not—not here. She's over at the house."

"Oh, then you know her?"

"She's my sister."

"Then I was right about her name anyhow. She is Miss Gladd."

"Not any more. She married—her name is Mrs. Cooper."

"Cooper? I knew a—"

The voice filled the room again, and the girl began on the typewriter. Hicks unfolded his newspaper, but still did not read. He was not in a mood to read. His blood had tricked him. It had begun to pump, he had felt it, when that woman had told the driver to take her to Dundee's; and now she was only coming to see her sister! He had never been fooled like that before, by his blood or nerves or whatever it was, and he didn't like it.

Nor, obviously, did he accept it as final, for he continued to sit there. Parallelograms of the afternoon sun through the windows crept slowly across the floor. During the intervals between the dragon's incantations he made efforts at conversation with Miss Gladd, but she was preoccupied and laconic. When his watch said ten minutes past four he decided, from pure obstinacy, that he wouldn't go without a talk with Brager.

But there was an intervention. Hearing a sound outside, Hicks stretched his neck to look through a window, and saw a car pull up on the drive and stop directly in front of the door. The man driving it popped out, and Hicks knew the man. It was R. I. Dundee. Just as the doorknob turned Hicks hunched over with his elbows on his knees, his head down, myopically intent on his newspaper. That way he could see nothing but Dundee's feet passing in front of him, and his face could not be seen at all. Dundee's voice sounded:

"Good afternoon, Miss Flagg—that's not your name. What's your name?"

"Gladd, Mr. Dundee. Heather Gladd."

"No wonder I couldn't remember it. Where's Mr. Brager, inside? I hear the furnace, don't I?"

"Yes, sir. Shall I tell him—"

"No, I'll go in."

Dundee's feet were moving, receding, and Hicks was congratulating himself on having escaped an embarrassing encounter when suddenly the hum ceased and an instant later came the sound of a door opening, and Dundee spoke:

"Hello, Herman."

"Hello, Dick." It was the strident voice that had been coming intermittently from the grill for the past hour. "I saw you passing the windows. Ross told me you were coming out. He went over to the house—"

"I saw him. I want a talk with you."

"Of course. But the furnace—excuse me. Who is that man, Miss Gladd. if you please?"

"He's waiting to see you, Mr. Brager."

That ruined it. Hicks arose and faced them. The incredulous and irate stare of R. I. Dundee gave Hicks an opportunity to observe that Brager was a flustery little man with a flat head and protruding eyeballs, somewhat ludicrous in a faded and spotted brown apron that reached below his knees.

"What the devil," Dundee blurted, "are you doing here?"

Hicks, in a tone of most emphatic and unalloyed disgust, said one word.

"Nothing."

And made for the door.

Four

HICKS SAT ON THE NARROW LITTLE FOOTBRIDGE, FACING downstream, his feet dangling, watching the brook gurgling around the stones.

He had been there only a matter of minutes when his head jerked sharply to the left. Footsteps from the direction of the laboratory—glimpses of a figure on the path, through the undergrowth—then he saw who it was. Heather Gladd was moving slowly, as though reluctantly, long-legged and something to watch, with a hint of youthful awkwardness in her grace like a two-year-old thoroughbred.

She got to the bridge and Hicks twisted his neck to look up at her.

"Can you get by?"

"Sure."

But she stood there, and after a moment said, "What I ought to do is go back and tell Mr. Dundee you're here."

"Why?"

"He told you to get off the place, didn't he? And he told Mr. Brager not to let you on again. Also he told him your name. Hicks."

"Right."

"Alphabet Hicks."

"Dundee didn't tell Brager that."

"No, but I know." She stepped onto the bridge. "I've seen your picture and read about you. I read the *New Yorker*. I'm a very smart girl."

"Good for you. Knocking off for the day?"

"Yes. Mr. Dundee chased me."

"So you're going to see your sister?"

"Yes." She grimaced. "And I don't want to."

"Why not?"

She made no reply to that. Instead, she moved to the center of the bridge, and before he knew it was sitting there beside him, deftly flipping her skirt over her knees as her

26

legs swung over the edge. Her shoulder, with a narrow white strap crossing it, visible through her thin green blouse, was inches lower than his, but her feet hung almost as far down as his did. Her length was mostly below her waist.

"I'm not smart at all," she said dismally.

"Oh, come," he reproved her. "Blow on it. Keep the home fires burning."

"But I'm not! Two days ago I was much older and much smarter than I am now."

"How old are you now?"

"Twenty-three." She gestured impatiently. "That's not the question. If I were as old as you are that wouldn't necessarily make me as smart as you are. Nor as romantic as you are either. Are you really romantic? I mean, in your heart are you romantic?"

"Sure I am. Head to foot."

She looked sidewise at him. "You're not kidding anybody. When I say I'm not smart I don't mean I'm dumb. The way you wouldn't do what that man wanted you to, and you quit the case, and then you went to the courtroom and made them put you on the stand, and told all about it, and you knew it would mean the end of your career—that was romantic! I'd love to do something like that. And the way, when they took that woman to jail, what's-her-name—"

"This is sweet," Hicks interjected gruffly, "but I'm on a diet. I can wiggle my ears, too. Why were you so much smarter two days ago than you are now?"

She looked at him again, not sidewise, but turning her head to face him, and demanded, "Were you ever in love?"

"Certainly. I'm never out."

"I'm being serious."

"So am I. I fall in love an average of twice a week. I can fall in love with a girl your age, even younger, and anything from that on up—well, not indefinitely—"

She shook her head. "Please," she pleaded. "I mean the kind of love that—" She stopped for a word. "The desperate kind. The awful kind."

"Why, is that the kind you've got?"

"Lord no, not me. Me in love?"

"You can't rule it out as contrary to nature."

"Well, I'm not. This is serious, terribly serious. Say you were in love with a girl, desperately in love, and you shouldn't be. Say she didn't love you, and anyway you were

27

already married. Wouldn't there be any way in the world to make you stop it?"

"You might shoot me."

"No." Her chin quivered. "Please don't be flip. I'm serious. I really don't know anything about love, not that kind. But you're a man and you're smart. Isn't there anything I can—I mean, if a man falls in love like that, is it just simply incurable? You don't need to think I'm dumb. There aren't many girls my age who do know anything about love, the kind I'm talking about. I want to know what can be done about it."

"Well." Hicks pulled at his nose. The brook beneath their feet gurgled happily. "If you mean the man makes a nuisance of himself and the problem is to get rid of him . . ."

"No. I mean how to make him stop."

"Stop being in love?"

"Yes."

"Shoot him or marry him."

"You're a lot of help," she said bitterly. "It isn't anything to be cynical about. I didn't stop here to ask you about it. I didn't even know I was going to until I realized I was sitting down by you. There's nobody else I can ask. There simply isn't any sense in it, two people unhappy and miserable just because one of them gets a crazy idea in his head. If it is in his head. He acts more as if it was in his stomach."

Hicks grunted. "Tell him that."

"Tell him what?"

"That it's in his stomach. Tell him anything like that you can think of. Make him hate you. At your age the instinct to cruelty is still fairly intact. Turn it loose on him. Or eat raw garlic—no, that's no good. He'd eat some too and then he wouldn't notice it."

She tried not to laugh, but first a sputter forced a way out, then she was laughing. For a moment she chortled along with the brook, and then abruptly stopped.

"I didn't want to laugh," she said resentfully, her cheeks flushing.

"That's all right. It only proves what I said about your instinct to cruelty."

"It does not! I'm not cruel! But you are! And I didn't think you would be! I thought you'd be wise and—and helpful. . . ."

"You expect too much." Hicks was looking at her face. "I've got a stomach too. I don't like garlic, but I see now

28

that there might be a good reason for eating it." He added hastily, "Hypothetically, I mean. Anyway, I doubt if any wisdom except your own could be of any help to you. If all you wanted was to avoid annoyance, that would be simple, but you're thinking of the happiness of two other people, and that depends on them more than it does on you. I don't know them and you do. Of course it's your sister, isn't it?"

Heather made no reply. She leaned forward with her elbows on her knees and stared down at the water, her legs swinging to and fro. The fringe of tiny hairlets at the back of her neck was so nearly the same color as her skin that it was doubtful where it ended. Hicks was considering the matter as a problem in optics when presently she asked, without changing her position:

"What did she look like?"

"Huh?"

"Martha. My sister. You said you saw her on the train."

"Oh. She looked all right. Maybe a little distressed."

"Of course." Heather sighed with a catch in her breath. "What a terrible mess—simply terrible. I would have been so happy to see her. I haven't seen her for nearly a year."

"No?"

"No. She married George and went to France with him. He was the Paris correspondent for the *Dispatch*. When the Nazis came they had to leave, and finally they got to Lisbon and got on a ship. They came back just a few days ago. I didn't even know they were back until Monday evening, when he—" She stopped. In a moment she went on, "She didn't even telephone me. I would have been happy to see her, and so would she, I'm sure she would, because we loved each other more than most sisters do. And now she's there waiting for me, and I sit here dreading to see her because I don't know how to act, I don't know what to say to her—it doesn't seem posible that I could be dreading to see Martha—but it's going to be awful—"

She jerked up straight, stiff and alert.

The voice, the cry in a man's voice, repeated, though muffled by the woods, yet had reached their ears. . . .

"It sounded like a man calling Martha," Hicks said.

She scrambled to her feet. "But it couldn't—it was George!"

She stepped around Hicks and off the bridge, and swung into the path. Hicks got up and followed her, and found that he had to step lively to keep up. When he emerged from the woods she was already a third of the way across the lawn, streaking for the house. From there a voice came, agonized and importunate:

"A doctor! Call a doctor! . . ."

Hicks supposed it came from open windows of the house, but it didn't. On account of shrubbery screening the side terrace, he didn't know the terrace was there, but Heather led him to it. She was running now, and so was he, at her heels as she bounded through a gap in the shrubbery onto the flagstones.

A man was kneeling there, with a face like a gargoyle. He saw them and seemed to think the noises he was making were words. Heather ran to him, or rather to the figure prostrate before him, and went down to it—

"Sis!" she cried from her heart. "Sis dearest—"

"Don't!" the man blubbered. "Don't pull at her! She's dead."

Five

AT THE OFFICE AT THE LABORATORY BUILDING THE LATE afternoon sun flooded in through the windows, and the colored plastics fought back and made a hubbub of it.

Herman Brager sat in a chair frowning at R. I. Dundee. The fact that he was popeyed gave his frown an air of ferocity which was probably misleading. Dundee, paying no attention to him, was absorbed in an activity which, if not mysterious, seemed at least pointless. He was seated at the purple desk, with the contraption like a portable phonograph in front of him, and beside it was a carrying case, made of the ubiquitous plastic, with the lid open, containing dozens of the disks resembling phonograph records. A stack of the disks was there on the desk, and Dundee was taking them one at time, playing the first few words of each, and returning them to the case.

"Resume on number four—"

"Vat two is now—"

"Viscosity disap—"

"Coefficient of all—"

The voice coming from the disks on the machine was Brager's. As the stack was nearly exhausted, Brager started from his chair, offering:

"I'll bring another case."

"I'll get it myself," said Dundee shortly. "You understand, Herman, I'm going to make sure—well, damn your nerve!"

The door had opened and Hicks was there.

Brager shifted his frown to the intruder. Dundee switched off the machine, shoved back his chair, nearly toppling it over, and came around the desk.

His voice trembled with fury. "Look here, I told you to get—"

"Can-it!" Hicks said peremptorily. "No time for comedy. The cops are coming. Police. Gendarmes."

Dundee stared. "What kind of—"

"Crime." Hicks's eyes, their glint more insolent than ever but the laziness gone, went from Dundee to Brager and darted back again. "Assault and battery. A woman over here on the terrace has been assaulted and battered—"

"A woman? What woman?"

"I'm telling you. Martha Cooper. Mrs. George Cooper. Miss Gladd's sister. Do you know her?"

"Certainly not! Never heard of her! What was she doing—"

"Do you know her, Mr. Brager?"

"No." Brager looked more popeyed and flustered than ever. "And I assure you I did not assault her and batter her."

"Nobody said you did. But there she is. She's lying on the terrace in front of an open window. The top of her skull is crushed in. On the window sill is a heavy brass candlestick, and it looks as if a corner of its base would fit the hole in her head, but I didn't try it because the police are touchy about things like that, and also I didn't have time. I wanted—"

"You mean she was hit with the candlestick?"

"It's a bet."

"Is she badly hurt?"

"She's dead."

Dundee's jaw fell. "Good God." He stood, looking foolish. "This is a fine situation," he said somewhat inadequately. He looked at the paraphernalia on the desk, and at Brager.

"You'd better get over there, Herman. I'll lock up here and come along."

Brager arose, protesting, "The vats have to be cleaned—"

"They can wait. Go ahead. Tell Ross I'll be right over—"

"Just a minute," Hicks interposed. He spoke to Dundee. "I may detain you a little. I suggest that Mr. Brager ought to forget about your little display of temper a while ago when you arrived and found me here. As I remember it, it was like this: I was sitting here waiting to see Brager when you entered and said you wanted to speak with him privately, so I went outside to wait. Wasn't that it? You see, Brager couldn't tell the police what brought me here even if he wanted to, because he doesn't know. But they'll want me to tell them, and I guess I'll have to. I'll have to admit that you hired me, that I came out here on a confidential job for you—which they'll have to ask you about, and you can tell them what you please."

Brager was regarding Dundee with an expression of mingled reproach and bewilderment, but the latter was looking not at him but at Hicks, thoughtfully and warily.

"I don't know," said Hicks, "whether I've made it plain that that woman was murdered. And we're all going to be put through the wringer and hung out to dry. My suggestion may be a little complicated, and if you don't understand it—"

"I understand it perfectly," Dundee snapped. He turned to Brager. "Herman, this is going to be damned unpleasant. Please go over there. If you find the situation isn't as Hicks describes it, phone me. If it is, I suppose you'd better notify the police—"

"They're already there," Hicks said. "I took to the woods and waited till I saw them come."

"Good God." Dundee looked from Hicks to Brager and repeated, "Good God. Herman, get over there. And please forget my display of temper when I found this man here. I wished to speak with you privately, and he went outside to wait. You understand."

Brager, slipping off his apron and dropping it on a chair, did not look happy. "I don't understand at all," he declared. "Not at all. But very well. And I am no good at taking charge of a murder. And the vats, as you know. . . ."

They got him out. Hicks opened the door for him and closed it after him. Then he sat down and said:

"All right, let's have it. Where's your proof that your wife sold your secrets to Vail?"

Dundee looked at him with no friendliness. "So that's it."

Hicks nodded. "That's it. With no palaver. Unless you want the police trying to tie it up to a murder."

"It has nothing to do with a murder."

"That won't keep them from trying."

"I know it won't. If there was a murder. It's incredible—"

Hicks pointed to the phone. "Call up the house. Ask your son."

Dundee took the chair at the desk, but he didn't reach for the phone. "Who the devil," he demanded, "could have done such a thing? How did she get there? Did she come alone?"

"Yes. Who did it will have to wait. I'd advise you to quit stalling, because we might be interrupted. Let's see the proof you told your wife about."

"I haven't got it."

"You told her you had it."

"I did have it. It's gone."

"Gone? You mean lost? Stolen? Burned? Dissolved?"

"I don't know."

"What was it?"

Dundee scowled at the phone, reached a hand for it, stopped the hand in mid-air and after a second withdrew it, rested his elbows on the desk, and stared at Hicks with his mouth drawn tight.

"Suit yourself," Hicks said as if he wasn't interested. "The cops won't like it that I went for a walk. If one of them drops in here, say two minutes from now, and starts asking me questions, I'll answer by the book. I came out here to try to earn the two hundred bucks your wife gave me. That will certainly make him curious, and I have nothing to conceal."

Dundee's mouth stayed tight.

Hicks twisted his head around for a glimpse of the meadow path through the window, and then shifted his chair so that he could keep an eye on it without twisting. "My mouth isn't watering," he declared. "I'd prefer to catch the next train back to town and forget it, but that isn't practical."

Dundee snapped, "It was a sonotel record of a conversation between my wife and Jimmie Vail."

Hicks met his angry eyes. "What's a sonotel record?"

"A sonotel is an electric eavesdropper. I had a detective agency plant one in Vail's office over a year ago. I had reason to believe that Republic was getting some of our formulas, and I knew that if they were it was Vail who was working it. For a year I got nothing—at least, I didn't get what I was after. Then I did get something." Dundee looked grim. "I got more than I bargained for. A record of my wife in Vail's office talking with him, telling him she hoped he'd be pleased with what she'd brought him, and him saying he would if it was anything like carbotene. The damned crook. In 1938 we had developed a formula to the patent stage, and found that a patent had already been applied for by Republic, the identical formula and process. They called it carbotene, and they're going to make millions on it."

"What date was it? The conversation."

"September fifth. Two weeks ago today."

"How sure are you it was your wife's voice?"

"I've been listening to it for twenty-five years."

Hicks nodded. "Long enough. What does a sonotel record look like?"

"It's a plate. Like these sonograph plates." Dundee indicated the stack of disks on the desk. "They're made from one of our plastics. That's what I was doing, looking for that record—"

Hicks shook his head. "Go back a little. Where and when did you see it last?"

"I only saw it once. In the testing room at my office. I thought I took it—"

"When was that?"

"Tuesday. A week ago Tuesday."

"But you said the conversation took place on the fifth, and a week ago Tuesday was the tenth."

"What of it?" Dundee was not making friends. "I had paid for so damned many of those records from Vail's office without any result that I had lost interest in them. I had them stacked in cases in the testing room. Once in a while I ran through a batch. I was doing that, that afternoon, and there I heard it—my wife's voice and Vail's. I was stunned. I was absolutely stunned. I ran it through again, and right in the middle of it somebody came in. I stopped the machine and took the plate off and put it at the end of the case. Other men came. We had a conference scheduled, among other things to test results on variations of the formula on this plastic. We're selling it for all kinds of sound reproduction. They came from Bridgeport, from the factory, for the conference. I stayed with them a while as long as I could stand

34

it, and then I got the plate from the end of the case and took it to my room and locked it in a drawer of my desk, and went home and—spoke to my wife."

"Why didn't you take the plate with you?"

"That's what I'd like to know," Dundee said bitterly. "I didn't want to hear the damned thing in my home—and the servants—and it was a business matter. My wife denied it—"

"I know that part."

"Very well. I spent that night at a hotel. The next day I asked my wife—"

"I know that too. She was to go to your office at four o'clock to hear the proof, and at three you phoned her not to go."

"Yes. Because I got the plate from my desk and went to the testing room and started it on the machine, and it wasn't the one. I supposed someone had put another plate at the end of the case, though I thought I had kept my eye on it. And all the others were gone, case and all. After the conference they had taken everything from the testing room, some to the factory and some out here. I sent instructions to both places to return all JV plates to me—"

"JV for Jimmie Vail?"

"Yes. That's how Sharon's man marked them, JV and the date, in pencil. This plastic takes either pencil or ink. I got them back and ran them through, but it wasn't there."

"Did you get back the same number of JV September fifth plates as there had been originally?"

"I don't know. I hadn't counted them."

"Didn't Sharon have a record of the number he had turned in?"

"No. His man gets paid by the day, not per plate."

"Does he hear the sounds—the conversations—as they are recorded?"

"No. The way it works—"

"I wouldn't understand it. Does Sharon run the plates through, listen to them, before he sends them to you?"

"No."

"Then no one but you ever heard that record?"

"I suppose not. I hope not. But *I* heard it."

"Sure, I know you heard it. Have you done any more searching?"

"Yes. The factory and here, both. There are thousands of these plates filed away, tens of thousands, but no more of the JV plates were found. So I—"

Dundee stopped abruptly.

Hicks nodded. "So here you were having a go at every plate in the place, no matter how it was marked. Suspecting that someone had deliberately changed the marking?"

"Suspecting nothing," Dundee snapped. "But I want that plate."

"So do I," Hicks said sympathetically. "I've been paid two hundred dollars for it. Were Brager and your son present at the conference that afternoon?"

"They—" Dundee bristled. "My son," he said, and stopped as if he had completed a sentence. Possibly he would have gone on to furnish the remainder of it if there had been no interruption, but Hicks's eyes had left him to concentrate suddenly on the view through the window. Dundee turned his head to look, and saw that it was Heather Gladd approaching, trotting across the meadow. It was more of a shuffle than a trot, her feet and legs betrayed into clumsiness by the urgency that impelled them; and as she got to the edge of the graveled drive in front of the building she stumbled and nearly fell, regained her balance, came on to the door, and entered.

She was panting, which was incongruous and even startling, because her face, which should have been flushed from an effort that made her pant, was gray with no color at all except for a smudge of dirt that streaked from a corner of an eye toward a corner of her mouth.

Dundee said something, but disregarding him, she opened a leather handbag she was carrying, fumbled in it, and took out something which, unfolded, proved to be a ten-dollar bill. She held it out to Hicks and said:

"That's for a retainer. I need some advice."

Six

DUNDEE REPEATED WHAT HE HAD SAID BEFORE.

"We're busy," he said sharply. "Go back to the house."

Hicks was out of his chair. He took a folded white handkerchief from the breast coat pocket of his new brown suit, held it by a tip and flipped it to open it out, and with it wiped at the smear on the girl's face. He was as impersonal about it as though he were cleaning a windshield.

"What is it?" Heather asked.

"Dirt. It still shows, a couple of scratches."

"I fell down in the woods."

"Damn it—" Dundee sputtered explosively, and stopped abruptly as his eye caught something through the window. The others looked too, and saw a six-footer in the uniform of the State Police, having emerged from the woods, striding across the meadow.

"Oh!" Heather gasped. "I wanted—"

Hicks had her by the arm. "Come on," he commanded. He spoke rapidly to Dundee, "Engage him. Take him to the house in your car—be busy with those plates—tell him we're on our way back through the woods—"

He was moving, with the girl, to the door that led to the inside, to the lair of the dragons that had rumbled and bellowed that afternoon; and, ignoring Dundee's expostulations, he opened it and pulled Heather through and closed the door behind them.

He stood there with her, motioning her for silence, and surveyed the place with his eyes. It was a long and spacious room, and appeared to be indeed the lair of dragons, with great vats and furnaces, arrays of benches and retorts and mysteriously complicated paraphernalia, and intricate networks of metal tubing like nests of entwined snakes. The walls and floor were of plastic.

Straining his ears, he could barely catch the opening and closing of the outside door, and the voices that followed were but the faintest of murmurs. Apparently the soundproofing was good. He put his lips to Heather's ear and whispered:

"Back door?"

She nodded. He signaled to her to lead the way, and she did so on tiptoe, past the long row of cluttered benches and cabinets to the rear, where he cautiously opened a door, and found to his surprise that here was another large room, a jungle of packing cases and cartons and various kinds of materials. He let Heather thread the maze ahead of him, and when they came to another door, a wide one of heavy metal, he noiselessly turned the knob of the Hurley tumbler lock and pulled the door open, passed through after the girl, and closed the door. They were on a concrete landing platform at the rear of the building, and a glance showed him that to the right the woods were only twenty paces away. He paused a moment to listen for the sound of Dundee's car but heard nothing. They descended the concrete steps and made the woods. Here there was no path and the ferns and undergrowth were dense, but after a little they came to an open spot with an enormous boulder in the middle of it.

"Sit down," Hicks said.

"I want—"

"Sit down."

She sat on an edge of the boulder. On her upper cheek two thin red lines were the scratches the smudge had covered and were vivid on the gray of her skin. Hicks sat on an angle of the boulder facing her and said:

"You'd better put that ten bucks back in your purse or you'll lose it."

She looked at the bill still clutched in her fingers as if in an effort to make out what it was. "Oh," she said. "That's for you."

She looked at him. "I remembered what that article said, that you like to pretend you do things only as a matter of business." The hand she held out with the bill in it was trembling.

Hicks took the bill from her fingers, got her handbag from where she had laid it on the rock, put the bill in the bag and placed it back on the rock. When his eyes returned to her face he saw that her eyes were shut.

"What am I supposed to be doing?" he asked.

Heather didn't reply. After a silence she said in a dull dead voice, "All of a sudden I see her. The way she was—

her head. Then I shut my eyes, and then I see her plainer than ever."

"Sure," Hicks agreed. "It wasn't anything to look at. What am I supposed to be doing?"

"Somebody did that to her. Didn't they?"

"Yeah, somebody killed her."

"George didn't do it." Her eyes opened. "It wasn't George. He said he didn't. And he had only just got there—Mrs. Powell told him she thought she was on the terrace and he found her there—"

"You say he had just got there?"

"Yes, he came in his car."

"Even so." Hicks shook his head. "Do you want to make a deal? I'll make a deal with you. Dundee has decided he made a show of himself there in the office, when he came in and saw me. In case you're asked about that, you can forget about him ordering me off the place. Just say he wanted to speak privately with Brager and I went outside to wait. It's a small detail, but if you'll do that I'll forget you were crying when I first saw you, and also I'll forget what you said there on the bridge. Isn't that what you wanted to retain me to do?"

Heather was staring at him. "How did you know?"

"That was pretty obvious. Was there anything else?"

"No."

"There ought to be." Hicks stared back at her, not with approval. "Naturally you're all shot to pieces, but that only makes it worse if you're going to try to conceal the tangle George's emotions had got into. For instance, there on the bridge you started to tell me something he did Monday evening, and then stopped. What did he do, phone you?"

"No." She tried to swallow. "He came out here and talked with me."

"Did anyone else see him?"

"Yes. Mrs. Powell and Ross Dundee—and I guess Mr. Brager too. I don't know."

"Then you can't conceal the fact that he was here. Have you already lied about it?"

She shook her head. "They didn't ask me anything like that. They didn't ask me hardly anything."

"They will before they're through. Have you had a talk with George and agreed on what you're going to say about his visit Monday evening?"

"Of course not, how could I? At first—you saw how he was—and then they came, the doctor and the police—"

"Then don't be silly. This isn't for matches. Don't you realize your sister was murdered?"

"Yes. I shouldn't—" Suddenly she stood up and held her head up. "I'm sorry," she said, "I shouldn't—" She started off.

In two steps Hicks had her arm and headed her back. "You sit there and decide what you're going to do," he said gruffly. "Or decide who to get to decide for you. Do you know a lawyer?"

"No."

"Where's your father and mother?"

"They're dead."

"Brother?"

"No."

"Fiancé?"

"No."

"Have you got any money?"

"I've got three hundred and twelve dollars in Postal Savings."

"My God." Hicks was glaring at her. "What did you do there at the house, skip out and dive for the woods?"

"I didn't skip out." Heather's voice was no longer from a constricted throat. "They wouldn't let me stay there on the terrace and I went inside. One of them was talking to George and another one to Mrs. Powell and Ross Dundee. Then Mr. Brager came and wanted to ask me things, but I couldn't talk, and I went up to my room, but after a while I decided to see you and I came down and went out the back door—"

She stopped and turned her head to listen. The sound of a car engine came from the direction of the laboratory. It grew faint, then was louder again, loudest when they could also hear the noise of the wheels on gravel as they passed on the near-by road through the woods, and they caught one glimpse of the car.

"That guy may have come for Dundee and me," Hicks observed, "but if he was after you they'll be starting to yell in a minute. Of course you can stall them for today at least by being overcome by shock, but sooner or later you'll have to talk."

Heather wet her lips with her tongue, and the tongue stayed there, visible, its red tip quivering. It disappeared and she said, "She was murdered."

"Yes."

"Murdered!"

"Yes. About what you told me there on the bridge, was that straight? I mean about George's emotions. Sure you weren't in love with him too?"

"Of course I'm sure. That's not it."

"What's not what?"

"George didn't do it, I know he didn't, but I'm thinking about Martha." Her lip trembled on the name, and she halted to control it. "I suppose I'm thinking about myself too, but anyway Martha wouldn't want—"

She buried her face in her hands.

Hicks looked at her in silence, and finally shook his head. "One thing certain," he declared, "the cops are going to be partial to George, no matter when he got there. He could have—are you listening to me?"

She nodded without uncovering her face.

"He could have come twice, the first time without knocking. I advise you to go back to the house and go up to your room and be overcome. You are, anyway. I'm a good lawyer, probably the best disbarred lawyer in the country. They have no legal right to any information from you about anything, but it isn't a good idea to go dumb. By tomorrow morning your wits may be good enough to stand them off. You can take it for granted that they already know about George's visit Monday evening, since Ross Dundee and Mrs. Powell saw him, and when they ask you what he came for, say you prefer not to tell them. Then they'll jump on you, but just keep your head and stay polite, and above all don't try to invent anything or they'll tie you in a knot. If you get a chance alone with George, don't try to cook up a story. That's impossible. By the way, do you happen to know whether your sister knew a man named Vail? James Vail? Jimmie Vail?"

Heather shook her head.

"Sure?" Hicks insisted. "Did you ever hear her mention him? It may be important."

Heather's face came up, grayer than ever. "Why would it be important?"

"It might be. Have you ever heard her mention that name, Vail?"

"No."

"Did Brager or either of the Dundees know your sister?"

"No, how could they? She was in Europe."

41

"She only went to Europe a year ago. Didn't she ever come here to see you?"

"Just once—no, twice. I've only been working here a little over a year. I went into town oftener when she was there."

"The twice she came, didn't Brager or Ross Dundee meet her?"

"Mr. Dundee wasn't here. He came in June, just three months ago. And Mr. Brager—I'm sure he was away both times. He often goes to town in the evening to confer with Mr. Dundee Senior."

"Have you ever met Mrs. Dundee? Dundee Senior's wife?"

"No."

"Have you ever talked with her on the phone?"

"No, I haven't, and I don't know what you think you're doing, unless you think I need practice answering questions, and I don't think—"

"Call it practice," Hicks conceded. "But you seem to be convinced that Cooper didn't do it, and in that case who did? There's only Mrs. Powell and the two Dundees. You can't count you and me and Brager, because we were at the laboratory all the time. Unless someone sneaked in from the road and then sneaked out again. What did your sister do before she married Cooper?"

"She was an actress. You must have heard of her."

"I'm not much up on actresses."

"She was good. She wasn't a star, but she would have been. That's another thing—she gave up her career for him—" Heather's chin started to tremble, and she clamped it.

"Did she know anyone connected with the Dundee outfit? Or with Republic Products? Anyone at all?"

"Not that I know of. I'm sure she didn't, because I knew everyone she did. I had a job in New York then. Even then George was trying to make a fool of himself, and I got a job out of town because I thought that would be better, and then I got to like it out here, and the pay was good. . . ."

"Well." Hicks stood up. "We'd better make an appearance. At least I had, and you can take to your room."

A shudder ran over her. "I hate that house now. I'm going to stay here a while."

He looked at her keenly. "What about you?"

"I'm all right."

"You're not considering anything childish like running away from it?"

"Certainly not."

"Okay. Can I cut through that way to the path?"

"It would be better to go by the road."

He went, diving into the undergrowth, and in a moment was hidden by it. The sound of his progress, slashing through it, grew fainter in Heather's ears, then abruptly ceased and was replaced by the barely audible crunch of his steps on the graveled road, which soon was gone too. Heather remained motionless on the boulder for long minutes, then her head dropped forward until her chin touched, her eyes closed, and she was motionless again.

Suddenly her head jerked up and her eyes came open startled. A noise—something in the brush—I'm silly, she thought, it's just him returning. But as the noise grew louder and she realized it was from the wrong direction, she leaped to her feet and stood peering toward it, all her muscles tensed. I'm afraid, she thought. That's ridiculous; there's absolutely nothing to be afraid of, but I'm afraid. I'm a hot one, I am. . . . Then abruptly her muscles went loose as she saw and recognized him, when nothing intervened but brush lower than his shoulders.

Ross Dundee emerged into the open spot and encircled the boulder to get around to her side. He had discarded the soiled white coveralls, but was scarcely more elegant in flappy gray slacks and an old gray sweater. He was hatless, and a limp tuft of his brown hair slanted down to a corner of his eye and was ignored, as he stopped six paces short of Heather and stood gazing at her.

"I'm alone here," Heather said.

Neither of them appeared to be cognizant of the fatuity of that. In fact, Ross matched it.

"Excuse me," he said. He took a step and stopped again. "I was looking for you. Dad said you started back to the house. I heard voices and saw you, but I didn't want to intrude. I waited until he had gone— Who is that fellow?"

"If you don't want to intrude, then don't."

The young man's cheeks flushed, but if from resentment, there was no flash of it in his deep sober eyes. "Now look here," he protested, "you might as well forget you don't like me, at least temporarily. Petty things like that at a time like this. What do you know about that fellow Hicks? You never saw him before. It might have been him—"

"I never said I didn't like you—Oh, go away!"

Ross sat down on the angle of the boulder that Hicks had occupied and said firmly, "I'm not going to go away."

"Then I will."

"All right, I will too when you do."

A ridiculous silence ensued. Heather shut her eyes. Ross sat and gazed at her, with his arms folded, while the flush gradually left his cheeks. At length he broke the silence.

"Not that it is of any importance under the circumstances," he said stiffly, "but you did say that you don't like me. I heard you say it to Mrs. Powell. But I have a right to say I am sorry about your sister—I mean I'm very very sorry—and if there is anthing I can do and if you will let me do it—"

He stopped. After a moment Heather opened her eyes and said:

"Thank you."

"You're welcome. And also, as a business associate and living in the same house with you, I have the right to see that the same thing doesn't happen to you that happened to your sister. How do I know it wasn't that fellow that did it? Anyhow, I'm not going to leave you here alone in the middle of the woods, and if you start off I'm going to follow you. If you regard that as merely obnoxious, I'm sorry. You may have forgotten about telling Mrs. Powell you didn't like me. It was on the front terrace one evening about a month ago." He unfolded his arms to make a gesture of dismissal. "Anyway, you've made it plenty obvious enough without that."

Heather had nothing to say. She sat with sagging shoulders and no muscle in her, looking not at the young man but vacantly at a chipmunk perched on the end of a log. Ross gazed at her steadily.

He broke the silence again. "Since I'm here, and there's nothing I can do about your trouble, or if there is you won't let me, I'll try to do something about a trouble of my own. I hate to ask you, but I've got to. It's very humiliating, but I've got to. I've lost a sonograph plate."

He paused, but Heather said nothing and didn't move.

"I've got to ask you about it," he went on, "because it's important. Maybe you know where it is. It may have got into one of the racks I've taken to you from the laboratory, among the other plates. When you were running them off, have you come onto one that was—well, peculiar?"

Heather's face turned to him. "I don't know what you're talking about," she declared.

Her eyes met his, and Ross's face was suddenly flushed again, redder than before, in a wave of embarrassment. "It's hard to explain," he said, half stammering, "because it's complicated by those other plates. I don't mean one of them. I don't even know whether you played them through. This plate wasn't marked, and I thought maybe I put it in the rack through carelessness, and you thought it was the same as the other plates that weren't marked, and you didn't put in on the machine at all and for that reason didn't find out that it was different. You see?"

"I certainly don't see."

"But you must," he insisted. "It's a question of where those unmarked plates are, because I'm almost sure it's among them. God knows I wouldn't be asking you this if I didn't have to. I never intended to mention them if you didn't. And all I want now is just to get them so I can run them through and find the one I'm looking for. I don't suppose you kept them, but you couldn't destroy them because they won't break and they won't burn. I know you didn't put them in the waste, because I looked. So I suppose you just threw them away. Will you tell me where?"

"I have no idea what you're talking about."

Ross stared at her. "Certainly you have."

"I have not."

"But my God—I'm talking about the unmarked plates that I—that you have found in the racks mixed in with the others! I admit I was an ass! I know you don't like me and never will! But there's no reason why you shouldn't tell me what you did with them—"

He stopped abruptly because Heather had buried her face in her hands. A shiver ran over her, all over her body.

Ross's jaw fell. He got up and started for her, then dropped back again and sat there with his clenched fists at his sides on the rock.

"Don't do that!" he implored her. "For God's sake—"

"Go away," she said from behind her hands. "Oh, go away. . . ."

"I will not go away," he said doggedly. "I won't talk any more. I won't say anything, but I won't go away."

After a minute the chipmunk appeared at the end of the log again, then ran to the middle of it and perched there for a good look at them. A last ray of the setting sun found its way through the foliage of the trees and brush and made his coat a spot of golden fire.

At the house Hicks found about what he expected to find. A jumble of parked cars filled a large graveled space in front of the garage. Through a rear window he caught a glimpse of the florid face and large form of Mrs. Powell, in the kitchen. Encircling the house to the side fronting the woods, he came to the side terrace with its screen of shrubbery. A glance showed him that the body of Heather Gladd's sister was no longer there; but a rough outline in chalk showed where it had been. A man in a Palm Beach suit and a battered Panama hat stood at the edge of the terrace staring thoughtfully at the sky as if to read the weather, and in chairs against the house two other men sat. One wore the uniform of the State Police; the other was George Cooper. When Hicks had first seen that face with the sharp pointed nose, in a booth in Joyce's restaurant, it had been white and puckered with distress; now it was a deadpan, drained of all expression by shattering disaster.

Hicks started for the door to the living room.

"Hey," the cop growled, "back up! Who are you?"

"The name is Hicks."

"Oh. Where've you been?"

"Sitting on a rock. I'd like to see Mr. Dundee."

"He's inside with the lieutenant. Don't go in there. You can wait here."

"Then I'd like to see Mr. Brager."

"He's in with the district attorney."

"Is anybody interested in me?"

The cop nodded. "You'll get attention. Have a seat— Hey, where you going?"

Hicks, who had started off, turned to say distinctly without elision, "I am going to the kitchen to get a drink of water," and, without waiting for written permission, retraced his steps around to the rear of the house, opened the door and entered.

A saucepan dropped from Mrs. Powell's hands and clattered on the floor.

Hicks stepped across and retrieved it, but when he straightened up to present it to her, he found that she had backed clear against the wall and was regarding him with an expression of terror that was unmistakable. She was paralyzed with fear.

"Scream," Hicks told her encouragingly. "Go ahead and scream."

The woman flattened herself against the wall and made no sound whatever.

Hicks put the saucepan on the table. "It's like this," he explained. "Even if you're correct in concluding that I'm the murderer, your conduct is unreasonable. Even if I killed Mrs. Cooper it doesn't follow that I want to kill you too. The fact is that what I want is a drink of water." He crossed to the sink and opened the faucet, got a glass from a shelf, filled it, and drank. "That's good water. Above all, you should have screamed. If I had intended violence, your failure to scream would practically have made you an accessory." He refilled the glass and drank again. "In an assault case in Brooklyn in 1934, the judge held that—"

"You get out of here!" Mrs. Powell squeaked.

"I would like to ask if you ever—"

"Get out of here!"

"But I want to know. Have you ever met Mrs. Dundee Senior?"

"Get out of here! I *will* scream! I *can* scream!"

"Oh my lord," Hicks muttered in disgust. He had his pick of two doors, not counting the one he had entered by, and chose the one on the left, which was a two-way door, and found himself in the dining room. It was uninhabited. Here again was a choice of two doors. The one at the right was closed; the one opposite him stood open, and through it could be seen a stair, which was what he was looking for. Making for it, and entering the hall where it was, he was confronted by another policeman in uniform.

"Where you going?"

"Bathroom," Hicks said, and detoured around him and started up the stair.

With no pause on the landing at the top, he proceeded with a confident step down the hall, though he was not particularly confident about anything. Certainly he was by no means confident that the sonotel plate of the conversation between Mrs. Dundee and Jimmie Vail was concealed in that house, but there was a fair chance that it was, and if it was, he wanted it. From the seven doors which were disclosed to a quick survey, he selected one at random, turned the knob, and opened it. One glance at its interior was enough to identify it; the array of toilet articles on the dresser would alone have sufficed; it belonged to Heather

Gladd. And it smelled like her. He backed out and closed the door and tried another down the hall. It too was unlocked. He opened it and passed through, with no special caution.

■■■

Seven

■■■

TO A SWIFT GLANCE AROUND NO ONE WAS VISIBLE. HICKS had rather hoped to hit on Ross Dundee's room for a start, regarding that as the most likely for his purpose, but a dozen details revealed to a hasty inspection made it evident that the hope had not been realized. More than half of the books in shelves that covered an entire wall were in German, and letters under a paperweight on a large flat-topped desk were addressed to Mr. Herman Brager.

Hicks moved rapidly and silently. None of the drawers of the desk was locked, and none had a sonotel plate among its contents. It was the same with the drawers of a chiffonier, and with the shelves of a large clothes closet. Shelves in the room displayed neat stacks of scientific journals, and he peered at them for a gap anywhere in their edges, but saw none. He looked at the bed, and shook his head; and went to the books and began sliding them out and tipping them for a peep behind. Suddenly he stopped, muttered to himself, and went and sat in the chair at the desk.

He was, he thought, making an ass of himself. In the first place, there was no reason to suppose that Brager had the plate hidden in his room, and in the second place, a search should be conducted with the head rather than the hands. For instance, if he wanted to conceal a thin flat round object in that room, what would he do? He looked around, and after a little consideration discovered that the answer was right there under his hand, which was resting on the desk pad. There were three thicknesses of blotter on it. Remove the top blotter. Cut a hole in the two bottom thicknesses the size of the plate, and put the plate in it. Replace the top blotter. Tell Mrs. Powell to touch nothing on your desk. Perfect. The plate would be immediately available if wanted, and yet secure against accidental discovery. It was so good that it was a shame that there had been no reason for Brager to swipe the plate and hide it.

He got hold of the edges of the top blotter and pulled its corners out and lifted it; and stared in utter astonishment.

"I'll be doggoned," he said. "That's what he did do!"

Not that the plate was there. The hole that had been cut in the two bottom blotters was not round but rectangular, and the object nesting in it was a photograph mounted on cardboard, and the photograph was of Judith Dundee—a replica of the one Hicks had used that morning for his experiment with the receptionist at the Republic Products office. On the cardboard border at the bottom was written in ink, in a fine precise hand:

> *To die for you? I would not aim so high.*
> *Your smile I had, and oh, my love, for that*
> *My heart is proud, and would be proud to die*
> *To feed the worm that you have shuddered at.*

"Holy smoke," Hicks said in a tone of dazed incredulity.

He read it again. It was appalling. It made him a little sick, but only for an instant, for there were its practical implications to consider; and he considered them, meanwhile replacing the top blotter, tucking its corners in and smoothing it out neatly. For if, however preposterously, the flustery, popeyed Brager was possessed of such a passion for Judith Dundee, it was quite possible that he had intervened to save her from the consequences of her folly, and there was an excellent reason to suppose that the sonotel plate was hidden in this room. He might, of course, have destroyed it . . . but he might not . . .

Hicks stood up and looked around. Behind the books? The mattress? Then suddenly he sat down again, as quick footsteps outside in the hall stopped at the door; and by the time the door swung in and Herman Brager entered, Hicks was leaning back in the chair with his arms extended and his mouth wide open in a yawn.

Brager stopped short and goggled at him.

"I beg your pardon," Hicks said amicably. "I guess you're surprised to find me here."

"This is my room," Brager asserted truculently.

"Yeah, I know it is."

"But I am not surprised. I am no longer surprised no matter what happens." Brager walked to the bed and sat on its edge. Suddenly he exploded bitterly, "I would not work in that factory! Oh, no! I would have a place of peace and quiet where I could work! And now this! In the evening I sit on that terrace where I can hear the brook!"

Hicks nodded. "And now there's blood on it. But I doubt if it was bloodied up just to irritate you."

"I don't say it was. What are you doing here in my room?"

"Waiting for you. There's a question I want to ask you."

"I won't answer it. Down with that man I have answered a thousand foolish questions."

"Mine isn't foolish, it's just a plain question. What was in your brief case the night you left it at the Dundee apartment?"

Brager scowled at him. "My brief case?"

"Yep. About a month ago. Ross drove to town especially to get it the next morning."

"You ask me what was in it?"

"Yep."

"Who told you to ask me that?"

"Mrs. Dundee."

"You are a liar."

Hicks's brows went up. "Maybe I am at that," he conceded. "She told me about it yesterday, and we discussed the matter, but I guess she didn't tell me in so many words to ask you what was in it. Despite which, I ask. I'm working for Mrs. Dundee."

"No," Brager said.

"No what?"

"You are not working for Mrs. Dundee. You are working for Mr. Dundee."

"So are you. It's all in the family. I'm just trying to straighten out a little misunderstanding. You know about that."

"I do not know about it!" Brager jumped up and flapped his arms. "My God," he blurted, "all I ask is peace to work! All I expect is a little sweetness! A little sweetness from people to people!" His eyes were popping with indignation. "Above all I must work! And what happens in these places where I work? Dark things and perhaps ugly things! Suspicions!" He hissed. "Suspicions! Now that woman dead, dying there where I sit in the evening and can hear the brook! Can I sit there now and hear the brook? And I come to my room and find you here—"

The door opened and a policeman was on the threshold, the one whom Hicks had encountered in the lower hall. He looked at Hicks and said curtly:

"You're wanted downstairs."

The lights had been turned on in the living room, though it was only the beginning of twilight outdoors. It was a large and pleasant room, with comfortable chairs and sofas still in gay summer covers. Two men in the uniform of the State Police were there, in addition to the one who accompanied Hicks, and seated around a large table with a reading lamp were three in civilian clothes. One of these, with dark skin and hair pasted down, was armed with a stenographer's notebook; the other two, Hicks was acquainted with. The one with little gray eyes and a jaw displaying more expanse than his forehead was Manny Beck, chief of the Westchester County detectives, and the one with a pudgy round face and scarcely any mouth at all was Ralph Corbett, the district attorney. Corbett half rose to his feet and extended a hand across the table for a shake.

"Hello there, Hicks! How have you been? This is the first we've seen of you around here since you set a fire under us on that Atherton case! How have you been?"

He was beaming with cordiality. Manny Beck nodded and mumbled a greeting.

"I'm hearty, thanks," Hicks said, and sat down.

"You look it," Corbett declared enthusiastically. "Driving a taxi seems to agree with you."

· The glint in Hicks's eyes could have been dislike, or merely their reaction to the glare of the reading lamp. "You keeping tabs on my career?"

"No, no," Corbett laughed. "Ha ha. But here we've got a murder on our hands, and here you are on the spot, so naturally we phoned New York to satisfy our curiosity. Driving a taxi! Ha ha. You're a character. Out here on your day off?"

"No. I took on a little job."

"Well, of course, I know you did." Corbett beamed at him.

"I know better than to try any subtlety with you. I'll just come right out and ask you, why were you following this Mrs. Cooper?"

Hicks shook his head. "Now ask me why I was selling turnips without a license."

Corbett laughed. "I'll get around to that later. But I know all about your following her. You came out on the same train that she did."

"It was a public train."

"And you told the taxi man at the station to follow the car she was in."

"Did I? Have you got him here? Get him in here. As I remember it, I happened to overhear her telling her man she was going to Dundee's on Long Hill Road, and I told mine I was going to the same place."

"Now come," Corbett protested genially. "You know darned well you were following her. Weren't you? Yes or no."

"No."

"This is on the record, you know."

"I see it is."

"Would you like to discuss it with me privately?"

Hicks shook his head. "Nothing to discuss."

Manny Beck growled suddenly and not at all genially, "If you weren't tailing her, what were you coming here for?"

"You remember Manny Beck," Corbett said. "He gets impatient because he knows I'm just a good-natured boob."

"He's wrong on two counts," Hicks said. "You're not good-natured and you're not a boob."

"Thank *you!*" Corbett threw back his head and laughed. He turned it off abruptly. "But at that it's a fair question."

"Yeah," Beck growled. "What were you coming here for?"

"On business."

"What kind of business?"

"Mr. Dundee's business. Confidential. You'll have to ask him."

"We have. Now we're asking you."

"I can't tell you without Dundee's permission."

"Hicks is a lawyer," Corbett put in. He asked Hicks playfully, "Or shall I say, *was* a lawyer?"

"Suit yourself."

"Anyway, you know the law. Manny and I are beneath

contempt. Ha ha. You decline to tell us what Dundee sent you out here for?"

"Yes."

"But he did send you?"

"Yes."

"He sent you out here to this house, which he owns, to do something for him?"

"Yes."

"Then how does it happen you didn't even know there was a house here?"

"Didn't I?" Hicks's brows went up. "That's odd."

"Very odd. The taxi man asked you if you wanted to come to the house or the laboratory, and you looked surprised and asked, 'Why, is there a house?'"

"Did I say that?"

"You did. Is it plausible that you would come out here on confidential business for Dundee and not even know there was a house here?"

"No," Hicks said emphatically. "It's inconceivable. So either I'm lying about being here on Dundee's business, which seems pretty farfetched, or else I was kidding the taxi man. That was probably it." Hicks leaned forward. "Look here, let's boil it down. I don't know any of these people, except Dundee. I never saw any of them, including Mrs. Cooper before today. The only thing I could tell you would be about the job I was on, and I won't tell you that unless Dundee tells me to. Except, of course, where I was, and what I did and saw and heard, since I got here at ten minutes to three this afternoon. Naturally you can have that if you want."

"I'll take it for a starter. Go ahead."

Hicks did so. Luckily, there was no need for him to falsify in any particular regarding his movements or to resort to any elaborate inventions. Of his first visit to the laboratory, he omitted the detail of Heather Gladd's tears, and Dundee's reaction on finding him there. His brief conversation with Heather at the bridge had been, he said, about nothing in particular. He made the point that as far as Heather was concerned, her alibi had more than him to rest on, since dictation had come from Brager over the loud-speaker every few minutes, and her typing of it was down in black and white. After being called to the terrace by Cooper's cries, and making sure that Mrs. Cooper was dead and notifying the police, he had stayed at the house until the police car entered the drive and had then gone to the laboratory to tell Dundee about it. Later, when Miss Gladd came to the laboratory, it had been apparent that she scarcely knew what she was doing, and he had started back to the house with her, and had stopped in the woods to give her a chance to pull herself together. She had said she wanted to be alone and he had left her there.

Corbett and Beck had questions. They took him back all over it, tightening it up, while the windows went dead as night took the outdoors. Hicks did not underrate Corbett and Beck. While Beck had nothing special in the way of brains, his capacity for vulgar skepticism was practically unlimited; and for all his infantile pseudo joviality, Corbett was smart, and, in a matter involving peril, might be dangerous. Hicks, committed to lies, and, more privately, to the temporary concealment of a fact which he already suspected might prove to be the central clue in the solution of a brutal murder, left no more holes than he had to. He was caught off balance only once, when Corbett suddenly asked:

"Do you know Mrs. Dundee?"

It was totally unexpected, and the answer was not on his tongue where it should have been. To cover the second's inevitable hesitation, he asked, "Mrs. Dundee? Why?"

"No particular why. Do you know her?"

"Slightly. I know her when I see her."

"Did you see her here today?"

"No."

"You're sure you didn't see her or hear her here today?"

"If I did it was in my sleep, and I wasn't asleep."

He was alert now, fully alert, because he had no notion what could possibly have interested them in Mrs. Dundee. Had Dundee himself carelessly made a slip? If so, and they came on at him now. . . .

They didn't. They dropped her as abruptly and unexpectedly as they had taken her up. Corbett asked a few more questions about Heather Gladd, and was obviously about at the end of the string, when the sound of sudden commotion and raised voices from the other side of a closed door caused all heads to turn in that direction.

The door burst open. The man in a Palm Beach suit and a battered Panama hat came in, cast a glance around, and called over his shoulder to someone in the other room:

"He's not in here!"

Manny Beck growled. "Who's not?"

"The husband. Cooper."

"He's outside. One of the cadets has him."

The man shook his head sadly. "On the contrary," he declared in a tone of melancholy satisfaction. "He's gone. Nobody has him."

"Fer crisake!" Beck bellowed, and bounded from his chair and out of the room. All the others followed him.

Eight

GEORGE COOPER WAS GONE.

At half past eight Hicks sat at the table in the dining room eating ham and eggs. At his right were Brager and Heather Gladd; across the table were the Dundees, father and son. What talking there was came mostly from R. I. Dundee. Hicks listened to him with one ear, his brain being preoccupied with a violent disapproval of the latest turn in events.

Apparently Cooper had taken to the woods. As Hicks had patched it together from various pieces he had gathered, shortly after sundown, on the terrace, Cooper had become ill. When the spasms had become less acute he had asked for whisky, the policeman had suggested coffee, and they had gone to the kitchen. There the policeman had left him huddled on a chair, waiting for Mrs. Powell to prepare the coffee. Another policeman, sent by Lieutenant Storrs, had come to take Mrs. Powell to the library. When the first policeman returned to the kitchen, somewhat later, no one was there. That was all. Cooper had disappeared. Nobody had seen him go. The cars parked outside were all there. The guard stationed on the drive had nothing to report. Now the inquiry was in abeyance while all hands sought the fugitive.

Hicks didn't like any part of it. For one thing, he had

wanted to talk with George Cooper at the first opportunity. He had followed Martha Cooper from the restaurant, and on to Katonah, on account of the remarkable resemblance of her voice to Mrs. Dundee's; he had a hunch about that, and it had become more than a hunch when he learned that Dundee's proof of his wife's treachery was a record of his wife's voice on a sonotel plate. But by the time he had learned that, Martha Cooper was dead, and a new and more terrible suspicion forced itself on him, hunch or no hunch. Then came this jolt. Did Cooper's flight mean that he had murdered his wife just to get her out of the way? It looked like it, and it was highly unsatisfactory.

Hicks glanced around at the faces. The other men had eaten as well as he had, but Heather had swallowed only half a piece of toast, in spite of the urging of Mrs. Powell. Hicks's eyes glittered at her disapprovingly. He didn't understand why she was there, and he resented anything he didn't understand. Since she couldn't eat, why the devil did she stick around in that dismal company? Why didn't she go up to her room and lie down, or pace the floor, or cry, or sit at the window and look out at the dark?

R. I. Dundee was eating apple pie and announcing that he was going to remain for the night. Naturally he could leave whenever he pleased, since by his flight the man Cooper had confessed his guilt, but he was staying, and he wanted Brager and Ross, as soon as they had finished their coffee, to go with him to the laboratory.

Ross put down his coffee cup and said no, he would stay at the house. Dundee said he wanted him at the laboratory. Ross said stiffly that he was sorry, he couldn't go.

"Why not?" Dundee demanded.

The young man stared at his father. "My God," he blurted, "don't you have any feeling about anything? Leave Miss Gladd here alone, with all—the way things are and the way she feels?"

"Nonsense," Dundee said testily. "What good can you do her? Mrs. Powell is here, and those men around, and here's Hicks. Certainly I have feeling. Is there anything any of us can do, Miss Gladd?"

"No," Heather said.

"Of course not." Dundee frowned at her. "I should say, you have my sympathy. My deep sympathy. I'm very sorry this has happened to you here at my place. I hope I don't need to say I'm sorry. I'm clumsy at things like this, but if

56

there is anything we can do, say so. I suppose you'll want to take a day or two off."

Ross made a noise that could have meant indignation.

Hicks asked, "When's the next train to New York?"

They looked at him. "Are you leaving?" Dundee demanded.

Hicks said he was. Brager said there was a train at nine-twenty. Heather suddenly stood up and said:

"I'll drive you down to the station."

"He can phone for a taxi," Ross said. "There's time."

"No, I'll take him," Heather insisted.

So that's it, Hicks thought. That's why she's hanging around down here, she wants a conference with her lawyer. He pushed back his chair and got up.

Ross and Brager were both telling Heather that she shouldn't try to drive a car, she ought to go to bed. Dundee told Hicks he wanted a word with him, and arose and led the way to the kitchen, where Mrs. Powell was washing dishes, and on outdoors. There he peered around into the dark, faced Hicks, and demanded:

"Well?"

"All right," Hicks said. "I told them if they wanted to know what I came here for they'd have to get it from you."

Dundee uttered profanity. "And that man killed his wife and ran away, and now they'll catch him, and that's that. I was a damn fool to tell you anything. But you put it over on me, and I'm not a whiner. I want to handle this thing my way, and if I don't find that plate I want to keep that sonotel operating in Vail's office, and if you tell my wife about it she'll tell Vail. It's worth a thousand dollars to me if you don't tell her. Cash. I'll give it to you tomorrow. Come to my office—"

"No," Hicks said. "I have a previous engagement."

"Nonsense. I'm only asking you to wait—"

"Forget it," Hicks snapped. "No sale. What and when I tell your wife will be decided by secret ballot, with only one voting. Nor were you a damn fool. If I had told them why I was here, it would have been pretty unpleasant. By the way, what did you say to them about your wife?"

"To whom?"

"The police or the district attorney."

"Nothing. Why should I? Look here, if you'll wait—"

"No. Forget it. Somebody must have. They asked me if

I knew Mrs. Dundee, and if I had seen her here today. I said I hadn't, and they asked if I was sure I hadn't. How did they ever know there was a Mrs. Dundee?"

"I don't know." Dundee was incredulous. "They asked if you saw her here today?"

"They did. You didn't mention her at all?"

"Certainly not. And I don't believe—"

He cut it off as the kitchen door opened. Heather Gladd was there an instant in the rectangle of bright light, then she closed the door behind her and moved forward, calling:

"Mr. Hicks?"

"We're talking," Dundee said sharply.

"We're through talking," Hicks said. "I'll miss that train."

"We can make it," Heather said. "It's after nine o'clock, but it's only three miles."

"Then you're taking me?"

"Yes."

Hicks dashed into the house. He found his hat where he had left it in a closet in the hall. In the living room there was no one but the man in a Palm Beach suit and an old Panama hat, which apparently was glued on. He was reading a magazine.

"I'm going to New York," Hicks said.

"Okay." The man surveyed Hicks with gloomy interest. "You're that Alphabet Hicks. Got one of those cards with you? I'd like to have one."

Hicks took one from his wallet and handed it over.

The man looked at it. "L.O.P.U.S.S.A.F. What does that stand for?"

"Lover of Peace Unless Somebody Starts a Fight. I'm in a hurry. Miss Gladd is driving me to a train. All right?"

"Sure. So you really do carry these things. I'll be damned. Crazy as hell. We've got your address. The bellboy on the drive will let you by. If not, yell for me."

He returned to his magazine.

Hicks found Heather Gladd seated behind the driver's wheel of a modest sedan at the edge of the graveled space in front of the garage. Only three of the parked cars remained, and one of those was R. I. Dundee's. The engine was already going, and as soon as Hicks had climbed in beside her and shut the door Heather engaged the gear and the car moved forward. Short of the entrance they were stopped by a policeman, but after a couple of questions and a glance inside the car he nodded them on.

They turned into the public road, and went a mile or so, and no words passed.

Hicks turned his head to look directly at her profile. "There isn't much time to talk," he remarked.

She was silent for another half a mile, then said only, "I don't . . . feel like talking."

"I suppose not, but wasn't there something you wanted to say to me?"

"No." She turned the wheel for a curve. "Except—they didn't ask me much. Just a few questions, and they asked me if I knew anything—if there was any trouble between Martha and George and I told them no. Yes, and I ought to thank you—I don't mean I ought to, I mean I do thank you—for keeping your promise not to tell them. You did keep it, didn't you?"

"Yeah." Hicks was gazing at her profile. "What else did you want to say?"

"Nothing. That's all."

"Then why did you insist on taking me to the station when you could hardly stand up?"

"Oh, I—don't mind. I like to drive."

"Yeah, it's fun." Hicks's tone suddenly became peremptory. "Pull up at the side of the road."

"What?" The car swerved and she jerked it straight again. "What for?"

"We're nearly at the village. Get off the road and stop the car or I'll stop it for you."

She obeyed. The car slowed down, bumped onto the grassy roadside, and stopped.

"What—" she began.

"Leave the engine on," Hicks said curtly. "Where is he?"

"I don't know what you're talking about. We'll miss the train."

"That's all right, more trains tomorrow." In the dim light from the dashboard Hicks could see her tight lips and wide eyes. "I am referring to George Cooper. You know where he is. You wanted an excuse to leave. You're going to phone him or you're going to see him—"

He stopped abruptly, gazing at her. She made no sound. In a moment he said softly, "I'll be doggoned," opened the door on his side, started to get out, suddenly turned back, and commanded her:

"Get out of the car."

She didn't move.

"As a precaution," he said. "You might go on without me."

"Please don't," she faltered. "Oh, please! What does it matter to you? If you—"

He turned off the engine, removed the key and slipped it into his pocket, opened the door and climbed out, walked to the rear of the car, and seized the handle of the door to the luggage compartment. It wouldn't turn. Heather came running and grasped his arm.

"Don't—" she pleaded. She tugged at him.

He shook her off and took the key from his pocket and unlocked the door and flung it open.

"You're too darned smart," Heather said bitterly.

In the darkness not much could be seen of the man's figure stuffed into the compartment like an embryo in a jar except the white blotch that was his face. But Hicks saw his eyes blink and there was a movement.

"You're alive, huh?" Hicks said.

"I didn't tell him," Heather said.

"Come on out," Hicks commanded. "Take it easy—wait a minute—hold it—look out!"

The lights of a car had suddenly appeared around a curve coming from the direction of the village. Hicks reached for the edge of the compartment door and pulled it shut, telling Heather urgently:

"Bend over and vomit!"

She stared at him. His arm shot across her shoulder. "Bend over! Vomit!"

The next moment the lights were on them, and the car was stopping in the road right there, not ten feet away. A voice called:

"Having trouble?"

"Nothing serious," Hicks said.

A man got out and approached, and as he stepped into the light Hicks saw that it was the policeman who had been sitting on the terrace with George Cooper when Hicks returned to the house.

"Oh, it's you," the policeman said. He looked at Heather, though with the performance she was putting on she was not specially pleasant to look at. "What's the matter?"

"Spasmodic ejection." Hicks kept his arm around Heather's shoulders. "She was driving me to a train and she got sick."

"I'm better," Heather gasped.

The policeman went to their car and looked in, front and back, and returned. "Did you just come from the house?"

"Yes."

"You won't catch that train."

"Then I'll get one at White Plains. Do you want to run me down there? Miss Gladd ought to go home and go to bed."

"I'm all right," Heather said. "I will be in a minute."

"They'll take you home and I can take the car."

"No, thanks. No, really."

The policeman was looking at the ground. "You don't seem to have got much result."

"That's the trouble," Hicks said. "She only ate half a piece of toast. You can check that at the house. Ask Mrs. Powell."

"It's no occasion for wisecracks."

"It's no occasion for much of anything, if you ask me."

The policeman looked at him, hesitated, looked at Heather, walked to his car and got in, and the car sped away.

When the sound of the car and the sight of its lights were entirely gone, Heather suddenly began to giggle.

"Stop that!" Hicks said sharply. "Stop it! Get back in the car. I'll drive."

"But you won't—"

"We're getting away from this road. Get in."

After she was in the seat Hicks went to the rear of the car to make sure the latch of the luggage compartment was caught, then climbed in behind the wheel and took the key from his pocket and started the engine. It was less than a mile to the village. He asked Heather the way to Route 22, and she told him the turns through the village, and again they were out on the unlighted highway. Heather asked where he was going, but he didn't reply. A couple of miles south of Katonah he suddenly left the pavement to turn right onto a narrow dirt road which almost immediately began to wind through a wood. A little farther on, at a wider spot, he steered to the roadside, stopped the car, and turned off the engine and the lights.

"It's dark," Heather said in a small voice.

Hicks twisted in the seat to face her, though it was indeed too dark to see much, and demanded, "What kind of a double-barreled idiot are you, anyway?"

"I am not," she said in the same voice.

"No? What were you going to do, put me on the train and then skedaddle with him?"

"No. I wasn't."

"You say. What were you going to do?"

"I don't know. But I couldn't—" She stopped.

"How did you get him into the car?"

"I didn't get him in. He got himself in. When I went back to the house I went to the kitchen door and he was just coming out. He had a big knife in his hand. He was crazy— I mean the way he acted and talked. He said they were going to arrest him for killing Martha, and he didn't do it, and he wouldn't let himself be arrested—he had me by the arm, making me go with him out to where the cars were. He had the knife, and I couldn't call for help because I was afraid he would do something terrible with the knife—not to me, to himself. He opened the luggage compartment of a car— I think he thought it was the one he came out in, but it wasn't, it was one that belonged there—and he crawled inside and told me to drive the car to New York. He was just simply out of his mind. I said the guard on the drive wouldn't let me by, and he said I could if I watched for a chance and he was going to stay there until I did, and he pulled the door down and shut himself in. I opened the door and begged him to give me the knife, but he wouldn't. So I got the key from the dash and locked the door, and kept the key. Then I didn't know what to do. I thought if I told someone—he still had the knife. Then I thought I might get a chance to get him away and get alone with him and talk with him."

She stopped. Hicks emitted a grunt.

Heather said, "I don't think I'm an idiot. What about you?"

"Well, what about me?"

"When that car came and you told me to vomit."

"Yeah," Hicks growled. "That's it. I simply do not like to deliver anybody to a cop. You notice I didn't have time to figure that out, I did it instinctively. I'm mentally or morally defective or both. I don't even believe he's not a murderer. I guess he is."

"He is not."

"You seem sure of that."

"I am sure." Heather had a hand on his arm. "I've known him for years. I know he couldn't do anything like that, not even to anyone, and not to Martha. But even if he could, if something happened to him and he did it, he would never say he didn't do it. I know that for sure. That's what makes me sure, I know he wouldn't deny it, not to me anyway, no matter how crazy he was. If he did it, then he did. But he'd admit it. And he swore to me he didn't. So I know he didn't."

Hicks opened the door on his side. "I'd like to get his opinion on the matter."

Heather held onto his arm. "He has that knife—"

Hicks pulled loose, climbed out, went to the rear of the car, and opened the door of the luggage compartment. It was too dark to see anything until there was movement, when something like a leg came poking out, and then another. Hicks reached and had an elbow. The torso and head emerged, and the man was out, half erect, when suddenly he crumpled into a heap on the ground.

A croak came from him: "Jesus! Oh, Jesus!" It was much nearer prayer than profanity.

"The knife," Heather gasped. "Is he—"

"Give me a chance," Hicks said irritably. He lit a match and examined the man's face and throat and chest, then lit another and stuck his head inside the luggage compartment. When he backed out and straightened up he had something in his hand, and the light of a third match showed him the clean sharp long blade of the knife. He took the blade's tip between thumb and forefinger and sent it sailing away into the woods.

The man was struggling to arise.

"Don't try to stand up," Hicks told him. "Work your legs."

"They won't work," the man croaked.

"Certainly they won't work, they're asleep." Hicks turned to Heather. "Hold the back door of the car open."

She was steadying herself against a fender. "But what are you going—"

"Who do you think you are, the general manager? Open the door!"

She obeyed, opening the door on the left and holding it. Hicks bent over, got an arm under Cooper's shoulders and another under his hips, hefted him bodily, carried him with no great effort apparently to the side of the car, got a foot on the running-board, and deposited him inside on the floor. He pushed in the benumbed legs out of the way, banged the door, got into the front seat, and said to Heather, who was climbing in on her side:

"I want to have a talk with him. That's the only reason I'm doing this. For practical reasons. Tomorrow morning, as soon as he gets some food in his stomach, if he has any sense he'll report to the district attorney at White Plains and go on through with it. Who owns this car?"

"He's out of his head," Heather said. "He doesn't even know who we are."

"I'll tell him later. Who owns this car?"

"The company. R. I. Dundee and Company. We all use it."

"Good. I'm working for the company too. I'll drop you at Bedford Hills and you can hire a car to take you home. Tell them we missed the train and tried to catch it at Bedford Hills and missed it again, and I took the car on to New York. Have you got any money?"

"I have some at home."

Hicks looked over the back of the seat and saw that Cooper was where he had put him, making no attempt to move. "You stay down," he commanded, and started the engine, got the car turned around, and headed back for Route 22.

There was no hitch in the program. Heather had evidently abandoned her aspiration to be general manager, and about the only talking was when Hicks gave her his address in New York, without a telephone number because he had none. At a garage in Bedford Hills he arranged for a car to take her home, two dollars for the six miles, and went on his way. The passenger in the rear made neither sound nor movement. The car was in good condition and the southbound traffic light, and he made good time.

His wrist watch said five minutes past eleven as he rolled to a stop in front of the address on East 29th Street. The windows of the Italian restaurant on the ground floor were only dimly lit. Hicks got out and opened the rear door, took a look at what was there, and asked gruffly:

"Can you walk?"

Without moving Cooper said, "I don't want to walk."

"Nuts." Hicks got him by the shoulder. "Listen, brother. My bed is two flights up. You can either walk to it or be taken to Bellevue, which is only three blocks away, and let them carry you."

Cooper pulled himself to a sitting posture. "I don't want to go to Bellevue."

"Then upsy-daisy. Snap out of it."

"I don't want to go to bed."

"You don't have to. You can sit in a chair. Come on."

Cooper muttered something, but showed an inclination to move, and Hicks got hold of him and helped him out. His legs supported him, and a firm grasp on his arm was all he needed to steer him across the sidewalk, into the entrance, and up the two flights of stairs.

The medium-sized room that Hicks ushered him into was neat and clean and bare-looking. The bed and dresser and table and two chairs were devoid of any pretense at embellishment, and for decoration the walls displayed a picture of Abraham Lincoln, a chart of the human body showing muscles and blood vessels, a drawing of an airplane flight cut from a magazine, all unframed, and a large framed canvas that was a brilliant splash of red and yellow. When asked, as he had been once, where he got the Van Gogh, Hicks replied that someone he had done something for had given it to him.

Hicks closed the door. Cooper looked around, focused his eyes on the bed, and staggered across and fell on it before Hicks could reach him. Hicks stood and glared down at him. He stooped for a closer look, and straightened up again.

"The unspeakable bum," he said in a tone of disgust. "Out. Asleep. And the only bed I've got. I can do one of two things, undress him or toss him out of the window."

The decision, apparently, was for the former, for he started the undressing, beginning with shoes. They were heavy brown oxfords. One was off and deposited on the floor when the sound came of voices and footsteps outside on the stairs. Someone en route for the fourth floor, Hicks thought, going for the other shoe, and had it in his hand when there was a loud knock at his door. He jerked around and called out:

"Who is it?"

The reply came, "ABCDXYZ! Open up!"

Hicks made a face. Bill Pratt of the *Courier*, carrying between ten and fifteen drinks.

"I'm not at home!"

"Oh, yes, you are! You must be, because we saw the light in your window. Don't keep this lady waiting, she's a friend of yours. Let down this barrier."

"What lady?"

"An old, old friend. Here hanging onto me. I'll count ten and bust the door down. One, two . . ."

Hicks put down the shoe, stepped on the table and switched off the light, crossed to the door and opened it just wide enough to slide through, and was in the hall with the door closed behind him and the spring lock caught.

"I was just going out," he explained.

Bill Pratt, tall and loose-jointed, with careless clothes and a carefree face, said indignantly, "Then you can go back in again. We're here on business."

"That's him all right," said the girl.

"Do you deny it?" Pratt demanded. "Do you deny that you promised this girl a year's subscription to the *Movie Gazette* and maybe a trip to Hollywood? Wait! Wait till I tell you. I met her this evening at the Flamingo. She's a fine girl and a swell dancer."

He looked at the girl. "My God, you're a good dancer."

"You met her at the Flamingo," Hicks said.

"I did. Any objection to that?"

"No."

"Okay. She said an inmate of an insane asylum with a card having the name A. Hicks and a string of letters on it told her this morning that if she could identify some photographs she would get a year's subscription to the *Movie Gazette*. Let's go in and sit down."

"In a minute. So what?"

"So of course I knew it was you. I want to know two things. I want to know what kind of a gag it is, and I want enough to make at least a column, and I also want to know when her subscription to the *Movie Gazette* is going to start. She's the best dancer in New York and I want to know when her subscription is going to start, and I also want—"

The girl put in, "You haven't told him about the photograph."

"What photograph?"

"The one I didn't know. I told you about it."

"I forgot that part. Tell it again."

"There was one I didn't know, but I know it now, because she came today to see Mr. Vail. Only I don't know her name."

Hicks's eyes fastened on the girl. "She came to see Vail today? What time?"

"Around noon. Just before I went to lunch."

"How long did she stay?"

"I don't know, but she left before I came back from lunch."

"Why don't you know her name?"

"Because she didn't give it. She said she was expected, and Mr. Vail said to send her in."

"That's why I know it's a story," Pratt said. "Let's go in and sit down. You see, going there with that photograph, you must have known that woman was going—"

"It *is* a story," Hicks admitted. "But I need a drink, and so do you. We all need a drink. Come along."

"He was going to show me your room," the girl protested. "The kind of a place a famous man lives in. He says you're cuckoo."

"Some other time." Hicks herded them to the stairs and got them started down. "We've got to talk this over and we've got your subscription to attend to."

"A drink is a splendid idea," Pratt said positively. "And music for dancing. My God, she's a good dancer."

On the sidewalk Hicks explained that there was no place for dancing in the neighborhood, but plenty of drinks. He took them to Second Avenue and north a block, and into a Bar & Grill. After they had slid into a seat of a booth he said:

"Excuse me a minute. Go ahead and order and make mine the same."

He went through a gap in a partition leading to the front, glanced back to make sure he could not be seen, proceeded to the entrance, and emerged to the street. A block farther north he entered a drugstore, looked up Judith Dundee's number in the phone book, shut himself in a booth, and dialed it. Three minutes later he came out again, took another route back to his address on 29th Street, to avoid passing the Bar & Grill, got into the car he had parked there, and headed uptown.

Nine

THE SLIGHTLY GRANDIOSE LIVING ROOM OF THE DUNDEE apartment on Park Avenue was dimly lit, and quiet, with only faint intrusion of the midnight noises of the city. The upholstery of the divan, and the cushions on it, were a dark rich red, which made an effective background for the gold-colored dressing gown Judith Dundee wore, with mules to match, and no stockings.

Hicks shifted his chair to alter his field of vision. He didn't like bare legs with long skirts.

"I'll keep my eyes open if I can," Mrs. Dundee said. "I don't often take a sleeping pill, but I did tonight. I was in bed when you phoned."

"Sorry," Hicks said gruffly.

"Not at all. Not if you have news for me."

"I've got nothing that's much good. There have been a few little developments." The sharp glint of his eyes contrasted with her lackluster gaze from under heavy lids. "I thought you might be able to furnish some information that would help. Have you heard anything?"

She frowned. "Heard anything? You mean from my husband? No. As for information, I told you everything yesterday—"

"I don't mean yesterday. Today."

"No." Her frown deepened. "I told you my husband refuses to discuss it with me, and anyway I haven't seen him—"

"I have. And a few others. There has been a murder."

"Murder?" Her lids opened wide. "*Murder!*" she repeated incredulously. "Who—" A cushion tumbled to the floor as she leaned to clutch his arm. "Ross? Dick? My son? My husband?" She pulled at him, shook him. "Don't sit there glittering at me—"

"Not your son or husband. A woman named Martha Cooper."

"They're all right?"

"So far as I know. Did you know Martha Cooper?"

"No. What—"

"I'm telling you. Do you know a girl named Heather Gladd who works out at the laboratory at Katonah?"

"No."

"Have you ever been out there?"

"No."

"Mrs. Cooper is Heather Gladd's sister. She went out there today to see her. Some time between two-fifty and four-forty this afternoon, on the house terrace, someone hit her on the head with a brass candlestick and killed her."

Mrs. Dundee stared at him. "How awful! There in the house at Katonah? Where my son lives?" A little shudder ran over her. "Who did it?"

"Not ascertained. Brager and Miss Gladd and I are out because we were all at the laboratory. Whereas Cooper, the husband, and Mrs. Powell and Dundee Senior and Junior were all at the house during that period—"

"Dick was there?"

Hicks nodded. "And still is. Also Ross. Both voluntarily. They're not held by the police—not yet—"

"Nonsense," Mrs. Dundee said sharply. "They don't hit women with candlesticks. But for heaven's sake, what was it? What were you all doing there? How did you get there?"

"Me, by train. I'll tell you all about that if and when. When you've told me a couple of things; for instance how and where you've spent the day."

"Where *I* have spent the day?"

"That's right."

Mrs. Dundee gazed at him, and, sleeping pill or no sleeping pill, her eyes did not lack luster nor did the lids droop. "Really," she said, "I suppose I have no right to complain of your impudence—"

"Save it," Hicks cut her off rudely. "You asked me to do a job for you and I started to work on it. I might have had more sense, even if I did need a new suit. I'm not trying to find out if you have an alibi for the time a murder was committed, I'm merely asking where you were between noon and five o'clock today, which is not in itself an offensive question. The simplest way is just to go ahead and tell me."

"Nevertheless—under the circumstances—it *is* impudent."

"Okay, it's impudent. Where were you? Here? At home?"

"No. I went out a little before noon. Shopping. Later to the Modern Museum."

"Car and chauffeur?"

"No, taxicabs."

"Did you go anywhere except shopping and the museum?"

"Afterwards I went to Rusterman's with some friends—"

"I mean before the museum. Only shopping?"

"Yes."

Hicks got out his wallet, took some bills from it, counted them, and laid them on a cushion of the divan. Then he stood up.

"Very well," he said. "There's what's left of your two hundred. Seventeen dollars. The account is closed. I figure I don't owe you anything, because I am not something you work with strings. Don't sputter. If you hire somebody else, and I think you'd better the way things are going, I advise you to deal off the top, and don't forget to tell him about your visit to Vail's office today. But although you're a liar, you deserve something for your money, which I've spent. Your husband has a sonotel, which is an electric eavesdropper, planted in Vail's office, and the proof he had is a record of a conversation you had there with Vail on Thursday, September fifth. I suppose tomorrow he'll have a record of your conversation today."

Mrs. Dundee was goggling at him in consternation. "Good heavens!" she said, aghast.

"And goodness gracious," Hicks said dryly. "You're in a nice fix now. Happy landing." He turned and was going.

He did not see her leave the divan, but the movement must have been swift, for he had gone only three paces when the grasp of her fingers on his sleeve stopped him; and when he wheeled sharply she held on and was jerked off balance, so that she had to use her other hand to seize support, a fold of his coat; and there she was against him, looking up at him.

"You listen to me," she said harshly. "Maybe you think you're picturesque, but you're not going to quit me like this. My husband hasn't got any record of any conversation I had with Vail in his office. I was never in his office in my life."

"You were there today."

"All right, I was. I was never there before. I went to tell him about this and tell him if he couldn't get along without stealing Dundee formulas at least I wasn't going to be dragged into it."

"That was a good idea." Hicks's yellow-brown eyes slanted down to meet her upturned gaze. "He could explain to your husband just how he got the formulas and that would let you out. Did he give it to you in writing?"

Mrs. Dundee let go of his coat. "I know I made a fool of myself," she acknowledged. "He merely said he has never got any Dundee formulas. And there's nothing very pictur-esque about your sarcasm, either. When you asked me where I had been today, there was no point in admitting that I had been idiot enough to go and appeal to Jimmie Vail."

She stepped to the divan and picked up the seventeen dol-lars, returned and stuffed it into his coat pocket, and demanded, "Is that all that's left of it? Then you'll need more. I'll give you a check." She went back to her seat on the divan and put her hands to her forehead. "I'm getting a headache from that darned pill. Sit down and tell me about that record of a conversation that never took place. Did you see it or hear it?"

Hicks sat down. "You're pretty remarkable," he observed. "You haven't asked how I knew you went to Vail's office today."

"What does it matter? I suppose you bribed somebody. With my money. I want to know about that record. There couldn't be any such record. What does it say?"

"I didn't hear it. Your husband told me about it—"

He broke off as a sound cut in.

"The doorbell," Mrs. Dundee said. She stirred and sank back again. "The maids have gone to bed." She glanced at her wrist. "It's after midnight."

"Shall I go?"

"Please."

Hicks crossed the living room and passed through an arch into the large reception hall, traversed that, and opened the door. He did not swing it hospitably wide, but only enough for the breadth of his own shoulders; and after one glance into the foyer he kept his shoulders there.

Hicks said, "Hello."

The man in the foyer said, "Hello."

Hicks said to the elevator boy, who had waited there in his open door for the bell to be answered, after the custom in apartments with private elevator foyers, "Everything is under control, thank you," and, after a fleeting moment of hesitation, the boy let his door go shut and the hum of the descending car followed.

Hicks, still blocking the door, met the cold gaze of the small gray eyes of the visitor. "Tag?" he inquired.

The man shook his head. "I'm as surprised as you are. Maybe more. *And* interested. I'm here to see Mrs. R. I. Dundee."

"She has a headache. I'll be glad to give her a message."

"I'd like to talk to her."

"At this time of night?"

"This is the only time there is right now."

"Wait a minute."

Hicks closed the door in the man's face, made sure it was locked, returned to the living room, crossed to the divan, and told Mrs. Dundee:

"It's Mr. Manny Beck, chief of the Westchester County detectives."

"What—" Her jaw dropped.

"He was there this afternoon. He's investigating that murder. I don't think he knows anything about your trouble with your husband. He says he didn't follow me here, he came to see you, but I don't know why. You can let him in or not as you please. If you don't he'll be back in the morning, and it might be more picturesque to take him on while I'm here. I came here, by the way, to discuss with you a confidential matter which is none of his business, and of course I have told you about the murder."

Mrs. Dundee was sitting straight, her hands in her lap, the fingers interlaced, tight. "But I know nothing—What can he possibly—"

"Same here. Shall we find out?"

"Yes."

"Good for you." He patted her on the shoulder. "If he springs a surprise, shut your eyes and groan from your headache. I told him you've got one."

He went back to the hall and opened the door and told Manny Beck:

"She really has got a headache, but you can have ten minutes with me present as timekeeper. To relieve your curiosity, she is interested in the job I'm doing for her husband, and I came to report on that. Naturally I told her about the murder."

"Naturally," Beck growled, and crossed the threshold.

If what Beck had was a surprise, it did not appear that he regarded it as one, for he made no effort to build up to it, and the question that revealed it came out quite casually.

After acknowledging the introduction and taking the chair Hicks placed for him, he apologized, if not with urbanity, at least with civility, for intruding at that late hour, and even said he was sorry that Mrs. Dundee had a headache. Then he said he understood that Hicks had told Mrs. Dundee of what had occurred at the house at Katonah that afternoon.

She nodded, and pressed a palm to her forehead.

Beck asked, "Do you know Mr. George Cooper?"

"No."

"Did you know his wife? Martha Cooper?"

"No. I'd never heard their names until Mr. Hicks told me a little while ago."

"Yeah." Beck scowled and then unscowled. "About Hicks telling you. I thought maybe you already knew about it."

"About what?"

"What happened up there. The murder."

"How could I?"

"I thought maybe it happened before you left. What time did you get there?"

Mrs. Dundee's eyes widened. "What are you talking about? Get where?"

"Katonah. That house. This afternoon."

Her eyes stayed wide. "I have never been to that house."

"Before today?"

"This is ridiculous! I wasn't there today."

"You weren't!"

"Certainly not!"

Beck emitted a grunt so skeptical as to be derisive. "Your son Ross phoned you at five minutes to six this afternoon, didn't he?"

Her eyes went shut. "He—" The eyes opened again. "I don't know what time it was that he phoned."

"It was five fifty-five. He phoned from the extension in the upstairs hall. He asked you how and when you got there this afternoon, and what time you left, and you refused to tell him."

"Wait a minute," Hicks put in. "This is a—"

"It's absurd," Mrs. Dundee said scornfully. "I didn't refuse to tell him. I told him he must be dreaming because I hadn't been there."

"And he said," Beck growled, "that he knew you had been because he heard you talking."

"Ah," Hicks said.

"What?"

73

"I said ah."

"Ah what?"

"Nothing. Go ahead. Two minutes left."

"This," Mrs. Dundee said emphatically, "is perfectly absurd. I told my son he couldn't have heard me talking because I wasn't there, and he said he must have been mistaken and told me to forget about it, and rang off."

"Sure," Beck agreed, "because he caught on that he was being overheard. So he hung up. Naturally he don't want his mother mixed up in a murder investigation, and naturally you don't want to be. Therefore, the best way to avoid that is to tell me what time you got there, and what you did, and how long you stayed."

Mrs. Dundee looked at Hicks and said incisively, "This man is a fool."

"No," Hicks contradicted her, "he's a little above the average. He merely has a bum steer. Do you remember, Beck, in the Atherton case I gave you my word that that bicycle you found in the pond had nothing to do with it? I give you my word now that Mrs. Dundee was not out there today. As a favor, to save you trouble."

"Thanks," Beck said in no tone of gratitude. "That settles it. Maybe, you think. People don't go from New York to Katonah and back again on a magic carpet. Have you considered that?"

"Certainly. That's what I meant about saving you trouble. If you won't take my word for it—" Hicks shrugged. "The ten minutes is up. If there's anything else you want to know, make it snappy."

Beck stood up. His little gray eyes bored down at Mrs. Dundee. "If you weren't involved in that business out there, Mrs. Dundee, you're not acting sensible. Believe me. You're not acting sensible." He wheeled and stooped to tap Hicks's knee with a blunt forefinger. "Listen, bub. You made a monkey of me once. That's enough. Once."

He turned and marched off. Hicks followed him out to the door, and stayed there until the elevator arrived. Beck, entering it, turned and held up a stiff finger.

"Once," he growled. "Plenty."

The door slid across.

When Hicks got back to the living room Mrs. Dundee was bent over with her elbows on her knees and the heels of her palms pressed against her eyes. He sat down and folded his arms and regarded her with one side of his mouth screwed up. After a minute he said gruffly:

"I'll beat it and you take another pill and go to bed."

She shook her head. In a moment she raised it. "This is ghastly, simply ghastly." Her voice had the metallic hardness that made it a new voice. "And that woman murdered—there—today—it's simply grotesque!" She made a gesture. "Tell me. That record. Tell me . . ."

When Hicks left, at one o'clock, he had another check in his pocket, but no additional information of any importance. Mrs. Dundee had arrived at Vail's office a little after twelve noon and spent twenty minutes there, receiving for her pains only cool courtesy and a flat denial that he had ever obtained Dundee trade secrets by any means whatever. The phone call from her son around six o'clock had lasted only a minute or so and had been as Beck had reported it. She had tried twice to call him back but the wire had been busy. She insisted that she had never been in Vail's office before that day. She knew quite well what a sonotel was; indeed, one had been installed in her own apartment for purposes of experiment, until after a month she had insisted on its removal, something over a year ago.

When Hicks arose to go she accompanied him to the door, and he drew his finger back from the elevator button to say:

"By the way, that picture you gave me yesterday. That photograph of yourself. Have you been passing them around?"

"Not indiscriminately. Why?"

"I just wondered. I happened to be in Brager's room up there, and I noticed he has one."

"Oh." She frowned. "That could be funny if anything could be funny now. He asked for it and I gave it to him." The frown tried to be a smile but didn't make it. "He has it in view? Then he doesn't adore me any more. A fresh calamity. If he did he would keep it in a secret drawer. Are you by any chance asking if I have bestowed favors on Mr. Brager?"

"Lord, no," Hicks said hastily.

"I assure you I haven't. At my age adorers get to be more of a rarity and things like pictures go much more cheaply."

"You even gave me one," Hicks agreed, and pressed the elevator button.

On the street, he walked around the corner to where he

had parked the car. Driving downtown, he considered taking it to a garage on First Avenue, but decided to save a dollar by leaving it on the street, and spend the dollar on a bed he knew to be vacant on the floor above his own. Not only that, he would transfer George Cooper to the upper floor, if necessary by portage. That mattress was his own property, a good mattress being one of the few items of impedimenta which, in his blueprint of life, a free man might reasonably encumber himself with.

But he didn't lie on it that night.

Leaving the car at the curb, he mounted the two flights, let himself in with his key, switched on the lights, and saw an empty bed. He stared at it a moment, then tramped out and down to the next floor. No George Cooper was in the bathroom. He returned upstairs, stood scowling at the bed, decided that the occasion required the eating of chocolates, crossed to the bureau and opened a drawer—and the scowl became ferocious.

"Good God," he said aloud in accents of consternation, "the damn louse stole my candy!"

He sat on the edge of the bed and considered the situation. It had already been sufficiently cloudy and complex, what with three plausible theories regarding Mrs. Dundee's trouble and at least four regarding the murder, and now it was chaotic. If Cooper was merely a guy with a screw jolted loose by shock and grief, nothing was altered by this latest development besides the candy, but if theory number four on the murder was the true one, it was quite a different matter. There might be a second murder before the night was out.

It might already have happened . . . it might be happening now. . . .

He went out and down the stairs to the street and climbed in the car. The dashboard clock said half past one as he turned north on First Avenue.

Ten

OUT IN THE COUNTRY THE SEPTEMBER NIGHT WAS COOL and the orchestra of crickets and katydids applied itself to its intricate lovely symphony—or its infernal racket, to those who felt that way about it—with an urgency that forecast the imminence of an early frost to chill the musicians into silence.

The windows of the office in the laboratory building had been closed to keep the night air out, so that the cricket concert came only faintly to the ears of the three men who sat there around midnight, but it appeared from the expressions on their faces that they would not have been attentive to it in any case. Herman Brager looked exasperated and peevish, Ross Dundee stubborn and truculent, and R. I. Dundee about ready to explode.

He did explode. He pushed the record-playing machine away, shoved aside stacks of sonograph plates, and pounded the desk with his fist.

"It's a damned farce! I've spent twenty years of my life building this into one of the soundest and most successful businesses in the country, and this is what I've come to! You don't like it, do you? My God, neither do I! I'll repeat it and keep on repeating it, my own wife selling me out, and one of you helping her do it! Shut up! And stealing the evidence I got of it! It wouldn't surprise me if you were both in on it! Not a bit! Not a bit! By God, I'll clean it all out, this place and the factory and the office, the whole works, and start over again!"

He sat trembling.

"I can resign," Brager said in a strained voice. "That is all I can do with dignity. I can resign. I resign."

"So can I," Ross said. His face was white; his eyes focused on his father. "I guess Mother was right, I shouldn't have gone to work for you. We should both have known better. We might have known something impossible would happen. But I told you this afternoon—even when you lose your temper you shouldn't say things that are absolutely crazy."

Dundee got up and walked to a window and stood there with his back to them.

"Everybody loses his temper once too often," Brager said. "I don't dare lose my temper. I haven't lost my temper for thirty years. All I can do and keep my self-respect—I can resign."

There was a long silence but for the outdoor orchestra, which no one heard. Finally Dundee turned around and faced them.

"Facts are facts," he said harshly.

Brager shook his head. "Not in science," he declared. "A fact is a phenomenon observed or recorded by an imperfect instrument."

"Bosh! A sonotel may not be perfect, but it doesn't lie. As you do, or my son does, or both of you. I heard that record, and I heard my wife's voice. That is a fact."

Brager's lips tightened. "I will not lose my temper. I will repeat, I know nothing of that record. Your son may lie about it, I don't know. A boy will do many things for his mother. But try to be reasonable about it, Dick. I am not in his position, am I? Why should I do such a thing?"

"I don't know, but I can guess. I once heard you talking to my wife."

"I have often talked with your wife."

"I know you have. This time you didn't know I was there. I listened because it was amusing. It was amusing then. Nor did I resent it. I never have resented it because other men have found my wife attractive and desirable, why the devil should I? But if you ask me why you should lie for her, or even why you should conspire with her to sell me out, I say I can guess why. I tell you straight, Herman—where are you going?"

It was not Brager who had moved, but Ross. He was on his way to the door. With his hand on the knob he turned:

"I'm leaving."

"You're staying here till we settle this."

"No. I'm leaving. I was going to go without saying anything." Ross's jaw quivered. He clamped it shut and went on through his teeth: "I didn't say it this afternoon, but I'll say it now. You're my father, and I've known you all my life, and I think you're trying to get rid of Mother, and I think that record is a fake and you did it. I didn't want to say it!"

He was out and the door was closing behind him. Dundee started for the door, but Brager, surprisingly quick, intercepted him and caught his arm.

"Let him go, Dick," Brager said. "Let the boy go and cool off."

Ross did literally cool off, physically if not mentally. The air outside was chilly under the stars, and in the black darkness of the woods, where he halted on the bridge over the brook, he shivered his reaction to it. He stood there as if he were listening to the brook but actually didn't hear it. He was thinking about his father and mother. All his life he had been emotionally aligned with his mother, he was aware of that, and regarded it as proper and natural, but that only made it the more imperative to keep his faculties free and his reason clear in a situation like this. Though it was hard to see how any further consideration of the facts could help any. In the past few days he had done about all the considering he was capable of. Besides, his mind wouldn't stick to it; it kept flying off.

She loved that brook. He heard the brook again.

She was probably lying on her bed with her eyes open, or sitting on a chair or walking up and down her room, thinking of her dead sister.

He went on through the woods and crossed the lawn to the house, and found that she was doing none of those things. She was sitting on the side terrace, in a chair not ten feet away from the diagram marking the location where her sister's body had lain. The white chalk-lines were plainly visible in the starlight.

Ross swerved from the path to the door and went over to her. She turned her head to him as he approached, turned it away again, and said nothing.

"I want to talk to you," he said.

She made no answer.

He moved a chair so that it was at right angles to hers, and sat on it. In the dim light of the stars her face, in profile, could have been any face to most eyes, but he was seeing it.

"Are any of those fellows around?" he asked.

"I think not." She stirred and was quiet again. "Not in the house. Their cars are all gone."

"I suppose they're all out looking for him. I don't know how to feel about that, because I don't know how you feel. I want to feel the way you do about it. Of course, if he did that—to your sister—"

"He didn't."

Ross stared in astonishment. "But he must have!" he exclaimed. He added, at once, hastily, "I'm sorry. Only I didn't think there was any doubt about it. There was no one else—who else was here?"

"You were here. And your father and Mrs. Powell."

He continued to stare. "For God's sake. That's the first stupid thing I ever heard you say. Me? My father?"

"I'm often stupid." She moved in her chair. "You asked who else was here and I told you. You were upstairs when Mrs. Powell went shopping to the village, and she was gone over an hour. Anyone could have walked in from the road."

"But good heavens. . . ." Ross sounded dazed.

"I don't want to talk about it," Heather said. "I can't think about it. My head just whirls around."

"I'm sorry I said you were stupid. I have a bad habit—"

"That's all right. I am stupid. As you remarked once before."

"I didn't."

"It doesn't matter. But you did."

"I did not. That isn't fair. It was a general observation regarding laymen who discuss scientific technique."

"It doesn't matter. I forgot it long ago."

Ross opened his mouth, and abruptly closed it again. That inconsequential action, the opening and closing of his mouth, marked the end of an era for him and the beginning of a new one. It was a crucial victory of matter over mind, the matter consisting of a particle of flesh and bone weighing a hundred and nineteen pounds and distinguished from other particles not by its chemical formula but by the wholly unscientific appellation "Heather Gladd." The young male mind sells logic dearly, and he had sold. The point his mouth had opened to make was unimpeachable: she mentioned something he had once said, distorting it, and then immediately declared that she had forgotten it long ago. But his mouth had closed again.

Not that he was sitting there analyzing it and saying farewell to an epoch; he was not thinking in terms of epochs.

"I always do get off on the wrong foot with you," he began after a silence. "I did the very first day—not the first day

80

I saw you—but you know—that day. When I asked you to go to the movies."

"You commanded me to go to the movies."

"Good lord! Command! Me command you! I know exactly what I said, the exact words. I said, 'Get the car out while I change my clothes and we'll go to the movies.' Isn't that right?"

"Something like that. It doesn't matter. That's approximately it."

"And you said you didn't care to go, and I went with Brager and Mrs. Powell, and three minutes after we left you took the station wagon and went by yourself, merely because you resented the way—"

"I didn't resent it. I merely preferred to go alone."

"Well, you didn't like it. Did you?"

"Certainly not." Heather was looking at him. "But I'm not as touchy as all that. It was just that it was obvious that being Mr. Dundee, Junior, you regarded me as being at your disposal as the fancy struck you, and it didn't strike me that way."

"What! You don't mean that!"

"Of course I do. It was obvious. For heaven's sake don't think I'm complaining, it hasn't bothered me any, and I'm quite aware that a conceited kid like you often doesn't know what he's doing anyway."

"Conceited! My God!"

"You don't even know you're conceited? You're the type. Perfect. The boss's son. All the best firms have them. Sometimes I've thought there must be a book of rules for it and you were following them."

"Of all the—" Ross was stunned.

The crickets and katydids were tapering off.

"Listen," Ross said earnestly. "This is ridiculous. You must be kidding me. I may be a little conceited about my work—but no, I'm not even conceited about that, I just know I'm pretty good at it. If you think I'm conceited about girls—why listen, I've hardly ever looked at a girl. The fellows at school used to ride me because they thought I was girl-shy, but I wasn't. Once about four years ago I gave a lot of consideration to it, why girls didn't seem to impress me any one way or the other, and I decided that it was only because I was more interested in other things. Oh, I danced once in a while, and so on, but you know, all that kissing around and stuff, I tried it a few times, but I never really

got into it. I decided I probably had a mother-fixation, but
a fellow, the only one I ever discussed it with, said he
didn't think so because if I had I would be more emotional
about it. He used some other word, but he meant emotional.
Anyway, I never had the feeling that I had to kiss a girl,
the way some fellows seem to feel that they've got to kiss
a girl or bust—I never felt like that until that day in the
office I leaned over and kissed you on the cheek. Then I
knew it wasn't—"

He stopped abruptly.

"Good lord," he said in a tone of stupefaction, "you
thought I was being conceited!"

Heather didn't say anything.

"I certainly can stick my thumb in my eye," Ross declared. "The way you acted that day I kissed you, at first,
I admit it made me sore, because a kiss on the cheek is
not anything involving moral turpitude, but if you thought I
did it because I was conceited and expected you to like it—
it wasn't that at all, I did it because it came on me and
I couldn't help it. Anyway, I never did it again, and I could
never get started talking to you. You wouldn't let me. You
never gave me a chance. So I got what I thought was a pretty
clever idea. But I see now, you probably thought I was only
being conceited, it was just a conceited idea."

He stopped.

Heather asked, "What idea?"

"Those records."

"What records?"

"Don't do that," he implored. "Please don't. I don't blame
you, I have no right to ask you, I know I haven't, but
that's what I wanted to talk to you about. Otherwise I
wouldn't—"

"Oh! That's what you've been talking about."

"I didn't say I have been, I said I wanted to. Another
one got in by mistake, a record I've simply got to have."

"Have you looked in the filing cases?"

"It's not there. It's unmarked. It would be with the ones
you've got. If you played it—"

"You seem," Heather interrupted, "to be under the delu-
sion that I have a precious hidden treasure of unmarked sonograph plates. I don't know how—"

"I didn't say they're precious. I don't say they're any
treasure. But you must have done something with them.
Darn it, you couldn't eat them! I'm asking you—please! Don't

you realize how embarrassing and humiliating this is for me? I can't very well tell you—"

"Someone's coming. Your father and Mr. Brager."

They could not be seen on account of the intervening shrubbery, but the sound of their voices was quite close. Heather arose abruptly, said good night, and disappeared into the house. Ross, to escape an exchange of words with his father, tiptoed quickly to the far end of the terrace and was in an angle of the shrubbery by the time the footsteps of the two men reached the flagstones. He heard the door open and close behind them. In a quarter of an hour he went inside, listened a minute at the foot of the stairs and heard no sound from above, and ascended to his room. When he wound his watch before getting into bed it said five minutes after one.

The indefatigable orchestra was still at it an hour and forty minutes later when a car with its lights dimmed went creeping along the road in front of the house, passing the entrance without turning in. A quarter of a mile farther on it stopped, backed into a lane to turn around, and retraced its route, passing the entrance again. A hundred yards beyond, it swerved onto the roadside and stopped.

The driver turned off the lights and the engine, climbed out, and walked back to the entrance. There was no glimmer of light from the house, vaguely discernible through the trees.

"Nuts," Hicks muttered. "A peaceful rustic scene."

He started up the curving driveway, half expecting momentarily to be challenged by a police guard, but he reached the house and circled it to the hedge of shrubbery bordering the side terrace without being halted. There he stood on the grass and frowned at himself. What was he going to do now? Go back to the car and drive home and go to bed? Get a flashlight and search the place for a corpse? Rouse everyone and tell them he had come to see if they were all alive?

"This is me," he muttered at the darkness. "Life size. Why in the name of God—"

He wheeled sharply and stopped breathing. A door had creaked and he recognized the creak, having caused it himself some eight hours earlier when he had entered the kitchen and scared Mrs. Powell out of her wits. The creak came again. Silently and swiftly on the grass, avoiding the flagged walk, he stepped to the rear corner of the house and, shielded by the foliage of a vine, was peering through the interstices of the leaves when he hastily drew back flat against the wall and stood rigid.

The figure passed so close to him that there was no doubt of its identity; it was Heather Gladd, in a long dark coat. She walked rapidly, but not at all furtively, with no backward glances, straight across the lawn to the entrance of the path in the woods.

Hicks waited until the woods had swallowed her and then followed. If from cover she turned for a look to the rear he would of course have been seen on the open lawn in the starlight, but there was no sign that she had; and once in the woods himself, he saw the beam of a flashlight forward on the path. It bobbed along thirty yards ahead of him, and he let it increase its distance, sure now that she was bound for the laboratory, and concentrating on the effort not to betray his presence by a misstep in the pitch darkness of the woods.

Suddenly he halted, for the light had stopped bobbing and had changed its direction. He stepped from the path for the protection of a tree trunk, thinking she had heard him and was turning for an inspection of the rear, but the beam swept only to a right angle and began bobbing again. Apparently she had left the path, about where the bridge was. Hicks went forward with more speed and less caution, for he could hear the brook plainly and knew it must be a tumult in her ears. Almost with too little caution; he reached the bridge sooner than he expected, caught a toe on it, and nearly fell.

He left the path for the protection of a tree trunk and watched a strange performance not twenty paces away. There at the edge of the brook she had placed the flashlight on a rock and removed her coat. The beam of the light was aimed down at the rushing water, not at her, but he could see that she was removing her shoes or slippers and rolling up the legs of her pajamas, and he wondered idiotically if the upshot was going to be that he had driven fifty miles in the dead of night to sneak up on a pretty long-legged girl and watch her go wading.

Then he saw that she had brought something with her. He could not tell what it was; he could see only that it was something fairly large which she picked up from the flat rock where she had also placed the flashlight. With it in one hand, and the light in the other, she stepped gingerly into the brook, waded in a few feet, and stooped over until she was bent double. Her back was to him and he couldn't see what she was doing with her hands. At length she straightened up and waded back to the bank, and one of her hands was empty. She put the light down on the rock and started unrolling her pajama legs.

Hicks knew his location wouldn't do. The tree wasn't big enough, and on her return to the path the beam of light would be directly at him. The best course was to cross the bridge. He moved cautiously, and was about to step on the bridge when suddenly he whirled around.

It could not have been a sound that alarmed him, above the commotion the brook was making, but something did, for he whirled completely around before the blow fell. He saw something moving, right there at him, and then he went down.

Eleven

A BLOW ON THE SIDE OF THE HEAD WITH A TICK CLUB could, certainly, kill a man; at the least it might be expected to crack his skull. But to an owl on a limb the nocturnal tableau there in the somber woods, in the instant following Hicks's cropper, would have seemed much closer to burlesque than to tragedy. There was no outcry, even from the girl in thin summer pajamas who stood on a rock manipulating a flashlight. Its quivering beam spotted first a man who from his position might have been saying his prayers, and then another man with his features contorted in an expression of desperate resolve, gripping in his uplifted hand the shattered remnant of a rotted piece of sapling. And as though not to spoil it for the owl by giving it a gravity it did not deserve, the girl called sharply:

"George! Behave yourself!"

Hicks, on his feet again, was momentarily stunned not by the puny blow which had caught him off balance but by surprise. If, as he went down, he had found leisure to guess at the identity of his assailant, certainly the last on the list would have been George Cooper.

Cooper's uplifted hand slowly came down and the remnant of his club dropped from his fingers. The light swung away from him back to Hicks.

"Have you gone crazy too?" Heather demanded shrilly.

"I'm not crazy," Cooper said in the tone of a scolded boy denying that his hands were dirty. The tone suddenly changed: "You! You keep away from her!"

Hicks, stepping over stony uneven ground in the dark, paid no attention to him. Heather, in her pajamas, was a pillar of white. Reaching it, Hicks demanded gruffly:

"Let me have that light."

"I'll keep the light," she said determinedly. "I'd like to know—"

"So would I," Hicks declared. "What's more, I'm going to." He snatched the light from her fingers and walked into the brook.

That is, he got one foot in, before she grabbed him. It was not precisely an attack; she didn't hit or kick or scratch; but she got his coat with both hands and pulled so violently that, with his insecure footing, they nearly went over in a heap.

"Let go," Hicks commanded. "I'm going to see what you were up to."

"You are not!" She held on, tugging at him. "Give me— if you dare—"

Something hard and heavy came through the air and hit Hicks on the shoulder and staggered him. Swinging the beam of light, he saw Cooper, not ten feet away, straightening up with a second large rock clutched in his hand. Hurling Heather from him and leaping sidewise with one effort of all his muscles, he got the light on Cooper again just as he was letting the rock go. This time the missile caught him squarely in the chest and knocked the breath out of him. He faltered an instant, recovered, bounded forward, and landed on Cooper's jaw just as he was coming up with another rock. The rock dropped to the ground with a soggy thud; Cooper, merely sinking in a heap, made no sound.

Hicks whirled with the light to Heather. She stood with

one hand clutching her pajamas where they had been torn from her shoulder, unblinking against the light, her lips parted, like a wild thing in the woods.

"You hurt him," she said harshly. "How much did you hurt him?"

"That's a darned shame," Hicks said sarcastically. He felt himself and took a deep breath and decided his ribs were intact. "He'll survive. I might have got killed being romantic. I could have held you in my arms close to me and let the next one hit you." He went and got her coat and held it behind her. "Put this on before you start sneezing."

She let her arms go in and he pulled the coat around her and then flashed the light on her feet and saw that they were shod.

"Give me that light," she demanded.

"When I get through with it. I'm going to see what it was you put in the brook. And don't try any—"

"I didn't put anything in the brook."

"You had something in your hand. And you didn't throw it in, you rolled up your pajamas and waded in. The most sensible thing you can do—"

"Listen." She had his sleeve, was close to him, her face lifted to his. "Please listen! Will you listen to me?"

"Not all night."

"What that was—what I put in the brook—it's absolutely silly! It has nothing to do with anything!" She shook his arm. "You must believe me! It's just simply absolutely nothing!"

"Okay, I'll wade in and see if I can find nothing. I've already got one shoe full of water. And if you undertake anything like rock throwing, I'll tear your pajamas into strings and tie you up, which is meant literally."

"You're a fine romantic, you are—"

Hicks pulled loose and stepped into the brook. A stone turned under his foot beneath the water. When he had recovered his balance he glanced over his shoulder at Heather, but apparently she intended no assault from the rear, so he went on. The water, nearly up to his knees, felt ice cold as it sloshed around his calves. Facing upstream, he got the light at the proper angle to make the bottom visible, and began the search. Bottom, consisting of brown rocks of various shapes and sizes, was all he saw. After some minutes he took bearings again from the big flat rock on the bank where she had previously left the flashlight, moved a few feet downstream and a little to the right, bent closer to the water for another try, and saw a rock under the water of a different shape and color from any other. He peered at it. It was a rock—no, it was not a rock. He plunged his hand under the surface to feel it, and knew immediately, from its smoothness and circular edge, what it was—or rather, what they were; and in their middle, holding them down, was a heavy rock. He removed the rock, grasped the circular edge firmly, and came up with it.

An exclamation came from Heather.

Hicks waded back to the bank.

"You see?" Heather said through her teeth. "I told you it was nothing. You see?"

"I wouldn't say that a dozen sonograph plates are simply absolutely nothing," Hicks said dryly.

"It's not a dozen, it's eight," Heather took a step. "Listen, Mr. Hicks. You were nice to me. I thought you liked me. Don't you like me?"

"Sure, I'm crazy about you."

"Don't be like that. Please don't. Give them to me. Or put them back where they were. Just put them back. Don't you trust me? Do you think I'm a liar? I swear to you—"

"Save it," Hicks said curtly. "We're all going to catch pneumonia. Here's the program. It's a nice night for a concert—wait a minute."

He put the light on Cooper, who was sitting on the ground staring blankly around.

"You, Cooper!" Hicks said. "George Cooper! Recognize the name?"

"Go to hell," Cooper muttered. "Who are you?"

"He's all right," Hicks asserted. "Here's the program. I'll get him to the laboratory. I can manage without the light. You take it and go to the house and get the key to the office and bring it over. Then you can go back and go to bed."

"What are you going to do?"

"Have a concert. Listen to these plates."

"You are not!"

"I am."

"I won't get the key to the office."

"Then I'll wake Brager and get it from him." Hicks patted her on the shoulder. "Use your head, dearie. You say you God knows why, but that's what you want. Maybe after I want these plates under a rock at the bottom of the brook,

88

listen to them I'll put them back there. Maybe I won't, but maybe I will. One thing sure, I'm not going to turn loose any of them before I hear what's on them. As much as I like you. And you ought to put on some warm stockings. Take this light and go get the key."

She took the light. "I'll tell you one thing," she said fiercely. "*I* don't like *you*. What about George? Why did you bring him back here? When you promised you wouldn't?"

"I didn't promise I wouldn't. But I didn't. He got away from me."

"You're lying!"

"All right, I'm lying. Which I am not. Ask him, but not now. Go get that key."

She went. For a minute he watched the light bobbing along the path, then, stepping with care in the pitch dark, he moved toward the dim white blob that was Cooper's face.

"What did you do with that candy?" he demanded.

"By God." Cooper's voice was a hoarse rumble. "So that's who you are."

"What did you do with it?"

"I ate it."

"All of it?"

"Yes."

"I don't believe it. You'd be as sick as a dog."

"I am as sick as a dog."

"Good. Get up. Can you stand up?"

"I don't know." Cooper made no movement. "Who are you, anyway?"

"My name is Hicks."

"Hicks?" A pause. "Are you the one that pulled me away from her and pushed me in the house?"

"No."

"What was his name?"

"I don't know. Come on, get up. Here, grab my hand."

"I'll get up in a minute." Cooper groaned. "I don't know what's the matter with me. Sometimes my head is as clear as a bell. Now it's like—I don't know. I wish to God I was dead. I thought I was dead. Did you ever think you were dead?"

"Often," Hicks said.

"Often? I did once. I thought I was dead, and then there I was on a bed and I felt hungry. I never felt hungry like that before. I got up and looked around and found a box of candy in a drawer and sat down and ate it, and my head was as clear as a bell. I remembered everything. Everything! I drank too much. After Martha left me there in the restaurant, I began to drink. The reason I did that, I was getting up my nerve to go out there and have it out with Martha and Heather. I mean out here. We're out here now. Aren't we?"

"Sure we are," Hicks said.

"Sure we are. Certainly we're out here. Actually I was drunk when I borrowed that car and drove out here. That was the trouble, I was as tight as an owl, because that was why I lost my way and the first thing I knew I was in Croton, and I had to ask how to get here. Now I remember that again. And when I got here Martha was dead. If I had got here earlier she wouldn't have been dead, and that's what I mean about being drunk and being too early—"

He stopped abruptly.

"Okay," Hicks said. "I get you."

"The hell you do. After I ate that candy my head was as clear as a bell. I remembered everything. I even remembered you taking me up those stairs. It was you that took me up those stairs, wasn't it?"

"Yes."

"I thought it was. I decided it was you that killed Martha, and you left me there in that room and went back to kill Heather. I was dead sure of that—you went back to kill Heather. So I went out and got a taxi and had him drive me up there. I mean up here. I keep forgetting we're here. I was there on the terrace where Martha was, only she wasn't there any more. I heard you coming along on the grass and I could see you through the shrubbery—and then you went to the corner of the house and then Heather came out and you followed her—"

A fit of coughing stopped him.

"Get up off that wet ground," Cooper complained.

"Not by a long shot. To save my soul, I can't remember what I did with that knife. It was a long knife I got there in the kitchen—"

Hicks stepped around behind him and got him under the armpits and heaved. Once upright, his legs seemed inclined to function, and all Hicks had to do was to steer him by an elbow over the treacherous footing back to the path, and across the bridge. There he balked.

"Where are we going?"

"To Heather's office."

"Where's Heather?"

"She's coming. She'll be there."

Hicks prodded him on. On the narrow path in the black night, they proceeded in single file, slowly, Hicks in the rear making frequent grabs for Cooper when he stumbled. Emerging from the woods, the meadow was under starlight, and it was easier going. At the front entrance of the laboratory building, Hicks sat on a concrete step and took off his shoes and socks. He was wringing all the water he could from the bottoms of his trouser legs when the beam of the flashlight came out of the woods, and in another minute Heather was there. She put the light on Cooper, propped against the steps, and then on Hicks.

"Give me the key," Hicks said. "You can take the light back with you."

"I'm not going back."

Manifestly, by her tone, she meant it; and she had the door unlocked and was inside, and had turned the lights on, by the time Hicks had picked up his shoes and socks. He entered at Cooper's heels. Cooper flopped on a chair and rested his elbows on his knees, and fastened his eyes on Heather with unblinking intensity. After one keen look at him Heather ignored him. She had changed to a brown woolen dress. Hicks, barefoot, draped his socks over the back of a chair, took out his handkerchief, and started to wipe the sonograph plates. Heather went to a cupboard and came with a roll of paper towels and reached for one of the plates. Hicks intercepted her. "No, thanks," he said meaningly.

She opened her mouth to retort, choked it off, and went and sat down. Cooper shifted in his chair.

"Quit looking at me like that!" she burst out at him. "Quit it! I can't stand it!"

"I'm sorry," Cooper said hoarsely but politely. "I'm trying to remember something."

"It's a—" Heather caught her breath with a little quivering gasp. "It's a nightmare," she said.

"Right," Hicks agreed succinctly. He was drying the plates with pieces of the paper towel. Finishing that, he took them to the desk where the record-playing machine was, seated himself, pulled the machine closer, placed one of the plates on the turntable, and looked for a switch.

"Inside front right corner," Heather said.

"Thanks." He found it and pushed it, and the disc turned. The arm swung over automatically and lowered the needle, and in a moment a voice came:

"Heather Gladd! Heather! I love you, Heather. I could say that a million times, just keep on saying it all the rest of my life. I love you, Heather! I wonder if I will ever look at you and say it right to you? Of course I will, if you will ever give me a chance. I'm such an awful boob, the way I acted that first week I met you, so that you didn't like me, and now you have got your mind made up not to like me. . . ."

It was Ross Dundee's voice. Hicks stared at the whirling disc.

"By God," Cooper said in a tone of stupefaction.

"Shut it off!" Heather blurted. "Aren't you proud of yourself? Shut it off!"

". . . but I swear to you I didn't know what was happening to me, because it had never happened before. I suppose you have destroyed the first one of these plates I made, but if you haven't, I wish I had it back, because even then I didn't know what was happening, not completely, and I tried to be witty and amusing. Now I know it's literally a matter of life and death, because there can be no life for me without you. I love you, I love you so! That hot night Tuesday, you left your door open, I could stand there in the hall and hear you breathing. . . ."

Hicks flipped the switch.

"Leave it on," Cooper said. "I want to hear all of it."

Heather was on her feet, coming to the desk. "Don't you dare put on another one! Don't you dare!"

Hicks put a protecting hand over the stack of plates. "I admit," he said dryly, "that this is a considerable surprise. Why in the name of heaven you should sneak out at two A.M. to baptize a bunch of plastic love letters in a brook—"

"It's none of your business why! Don't you dare do another one!"

"If they bore you," Hicks said imperturbably, "go outdoors. Or go back and go to bed. I'll compromise. I'll run through them first, doing only a sentence of two. Go back and sit down. You know darned well I can tie you up if I want to."

She took another step forward, hesitated, marched back to her chair, and sat breathing through her nose. Hicks started another plate.

"I love you, Heather. In my room last night I wrote down what I would say on this plate, but when I read it this morning it was silly and insipid, so I tore it up. I never will be able. . . ."

"That's a sentence," Heather snapped.

Hicks removed the plate, put another one on, and started the machine.

"I dreamed about you last night, Heather. You were picking flowers in a meadow, not our meadow, and I begged you to give me one. . . ."

Hicks took it off and started another.

"Good lord, let me sit down and gasp a while! I know I'm late, but I had an awful time getting here. I never saw such traffic. . . ."

As Heather started from her chair with a cry of incredulous amazement, Hicks stopped the machine. Cooper was bolt upright, as if suddenly straightened and held rigid by a current of electricity, his jaw hanging.

"Martha!" Heather cried. "That's Martha!"

"Is it?" Hicks asked quietly. "And how come? In among your love letters?"

"I don't know!" She was at the desk. "I don't—let me see it! Let me—"

"No, no." Hicks held her off. "You're putting on a good show, but—"

"I'm not putting on a show! It's a trick! You had it—you put it—"

"Shut up," Hicks said curtly. "And don't be silly. You said there were eight plates. Here they are, and this is one of them. You had them. You knew darned well what was on them. You've listened to them. And now you pretend—"

"I've never listened to that one! I've never heard that! I tell you it's Martha! My sister!"

"You were hiding it in the brook with the others."

"I wasn't! I didn't know it was—there was one I hadn't—I only got it—"

Heather stopped. She gazed at Hicks, and he saw the change in her eyes.

"Oh," she gasped.

There was a chair beside her and she dropped onto it.

"I—" She gulped. "I never heard that before. I don't know what it is. I don't know how it got there. I wish you—I want to hear it—all of it—"

Hicks's eyes—the eyes which Judith Dundee had called the cleverest she had ever seen—were going straight through her. For a long moment she met them unfalteringly.

"So you don't know how it got there," Hicks said softly.

"No. I don't."

"You just admitted that you knew there was one of them you hadn't listened to. How did that one get there?"

"I—it—" Her teeth caught her lip.

"You're not doing so well," Hicks said sympathetically. "Certainly you know how it got there. I saw you beginning to wonder how Ross Dundee ever got hold of a record of your sister's voice, and I admit that would take some wondering. Let me try a little guessing. How did Ross get these plates to you? Slip them under your door?"

Heather didn't answer.

"I'm going to find out. Shall I ask him?"

"Don't you—dare—"

"Then open up, and wide. Did you find them under your pillow?"

"No. In the racks. At the office. In among the others."

"You mean you would find one of them in with the regular plates that you were to type from?"

"Yes."

"You wouldn't know what was on it until you began to run it off, would you?"

"At first I didn't, the first time or two. But they were unmarked, and if I came to one that wasn't marked I would put it aside and later I would—I was just curious—when no one was there—"

"Certainly. And this one you say you never listened to?"

"It was the last one. I just got it—it was in the rack—"

"What day? This week?"

94

"Wednesday." She hesitated. "No. Tuesday. Because Monday evening George came, and it was the next day, and I didn't feel like—I didn't want to hear it—so I took it and put it with the others—"

"Where? In your room?"

"Yes. I had to put them somewhere. They're indestructible. I couldn't just throw them away."

"Of course not. But that raises a point. The plates have been in your room all the time. The brook has been here all the time. Why did you suddenly get the idea of immersion at half past two in the morning? *This* morning?"

"Because I did."

"Why?"

"Because I—I just happened to."

Hicks shook his head. "It's an important point. I may have to ask Ross Dundee if he can throw any light on it."

"You will not," Heather said fiercely. "You promised you wouldn't if I told you about it."

"I promised nothing. But anyway, you aren't telling me. Maybe I can help. Did Ross tell you that he wanted one of the unmarked plates back? And you pretended you didn't have them because you didn't want to admit you had kept them? And apparently he wanted that plate so badly that you figured out a way of getting it to him? Namely. Put them in the brook and then tell him that was where you had been getting rid of them, and he could go and get them. That way he wouldn't know you had been saving them up. Something like that?"

"You knew—" Heather was gaping at him. "He must have told you—you knew that plate was there—"

"No. I didn't. Once a year my head works. Did Ross explain why he was so anxious to get one of the plates back?"

"No."

"Did he ask if you had listened to it?"

"No. I didn't—I wasn't admitting that I had listened to any of them."

"Did he tell you what was on it?"

"No. And I don't understand—Martha! That's Martha's voice! And you knew about it too—you don't need to pretend you didn't—"

Heather stood up, her jaw set with determination. "I'll tell you one thing," she said. "I'm going to find out about this. I don't expect you to tell me anything—you think I've just barely got enough brains to take dictation and run a typewriter—but Ross Dundee will tell me, and he'll tell me now!"

She started for the door. The barefooted Hicks got ahead of her.

"Get out of my way!"

"In a minute," Hicks said soothingly. "The idea with brains is to use what you've got. You mean you're going to get Ross out of bed and make him explain where he got that record of your sister's voice?"

"I certainly am!"

"I offer two objections. First, you'll have to tell him how you suddenly found out about it in the middle of the night, which will be a little embarrassing, since you have hitherto refused to admit that you were saving his love letters. Second, there is better than an even chance that you'll be committing suicide."

Heather goggled at him. "Committing—what?"

"Suicide. That you'll die shortly." Hicks, facing her, took hold of her elbows. "Listen, dearie. I am not hell on wheels, but I can add and subtract. It is true I had some knowledge of that sonograph plate, but I didn't know where it was, and my knowledge was incomplete in other respects, and still is. There's only one person who knows all about it, and that's the man who murdered your sister."

Heather stared, and he saw the horror in her stare.

"No," Hicks said. "I'm not saying it's Ross Dundee. I don't know who it is. You were right that it's not George Cooper. And I'm right when I tell you that if you let out a word about that sonograph plate, your chances of living out the week are slim. That's all I can tell you now, but I'm telling you that. And the same goes for Cooper."

Heather said, "You'll have to tell me more than that."

"I will when I can. I can't now."

"You have to. I have to know how Ross Dundee got it. And why he wants it."

"You will." Hicks released her elbows. "In the meantime, you are not to mention it. To anyone. This is bad."

"Bad," Heather said. "My God, bad!"

"Very bad," Hicks conceded. He went to the chair where he had hung his wet socks, sat down, and started pulling one of them on. "Cooper, too. I wish to heaven they had him at White Plains. I'll have to take him back to town with me. I need some sleep. So do you. I had better take all the plates, too. If Ross asks about it again, stick to it that you don't know anything about them. Will you do that?"

"I—guess so."

"No guessing." Hicks paused in his tussle with the second sock to look at her. "Promise?"

She met his eyes.

"I promise," she said.

_{▬▬▬▬▬▬▬▬▬▬▬▬▬▬▬▬▬▬▬▬▬▬▬▬▬▬▬▬▬▬▬▬▬▬▬}

Twelve

_{▬▬▬▬▬▬▬▬▬▬▬▬▬▬▬▬▬▬▬▬▬▬▬▬▬▬▬▬▬▬▬▬▬▬▬}

ROSARIO GARCI, WHO OPERATED THE RESTAURANT ON the ground floor of 804 East 29th Street and owned the building, such as it was, weighed a hundred and ninety-two pounds, was five feet six, had a face as round as a dinner plate, and was called Rosy by his friends and most of his customers. At one o'clock Friday afternoon he looked up from his doughboard in his kitchen when a form darkened the doorway leading to the front of the premises.

"Ah, Mr. Heecks! Did she work?"

"Pretty good." Hicks relieved himself of his burden, a bulky wooden box-shaped phonograph, by depositing it on a table. "She needs oil."

"I warn you she's a pip."

"She's all of that. Much obliged. I'm going out. That fellow upstairs will probably sleep all day, Rosy. We didn't get to bed until six o'clock. If he wakes up, feed him. If you could run up once in a while—"

"Sure. Work off some fat." Rosy cast his eyes swiftly upward. "Maria, for the love of Christ, if you catch me eating! When Franky comes home from school he can sit on the stairs and listen."

"That will be fine. But don't disturb him."

"Never in God's world," Rosy said solemnly.

Hicks went to the sidewalk and got in the car that was the property of R. I. Dundee and Company, and started uptown.

While eating the cutlets and spaghetti and salad that he had asked Rosy to send up when he went down to borrow the phonograph, he had listened to the sonotel plate a dozen times, and at the end would have had to toss a coin to decide whether the voice was Judith Dundee's or Martha Cooper's.

As he listened, he could have sworn it was Judith Dundee, but that had to be discounted because he had heard Martha Cooper speak not more than a hundred words altogether. And Heather and George had both, immediately and unhesitatingly, taken it for Martha.

The text was not illuminating. The other voice of the conversation was unmistakably Vail's, and most of his words came through clearly, but a great part of the female voice was in so low a tone as to be nearly inaudible. Plainly, though, she expressed the hope that Vail would be pleased with what she had brought him, and he replied that he would be if it turned out to be anything like carbotene. And twice Vail spoke of "Dick," which of course would be Dundee; and at the end he spoke of money, and said he would see her again when he had looked over what she had brought.

And he called her Judith. Wasn't that conclusive? No, Hicks told himself stubbornly. Remembering that other voice, so amazingly like Judith Dundee's by one of nature's freaks, now never to be heard again, nothing was conclusive.

Up the West Side Highway, over the Henry Hudson Bridge, on the wide parkways, Hicks rejected all conclusions.

At White Plains he found a parking space for the car and walked two blocks to the Westchester County courthouse. In the anteroom of the district attorney's office a dozen people were waiting on chairs, precisely the people to be found any day of the year in a district attorney's anteroom, and after sending in his name Hicks became one of them. He sat for a quarter of an hour, idly watching comings and goings, with his mind off on other errands, when suddenly he bounced up to intercept a man on his way out.

He got the man's elbow.

"Mr. Brager, if you have a couple of minutes to spare—"

"I haven't," Brager snapped. His eyes were popping with fury. "Do you realize that this world is full of fools? Of course you don't! You're one of them!"

He scurried off, was gone.

"Genius," Hicks muttered. "He had better be."

"A. Hicks!" a voice sounded from his rear, in a tone to be heard nowhere on earth but in a courthouse. Hicks turned, saw that the gate was being held open for him, and passed within.

At the end of a corridor he was ushered into a spacious, even pleasant room, which he had visited on several occasions some eighteen months previously. Three men were there. A youth with a supercilious nose sat at a table with a notebook. Manny Beck, not arising, squinted his little gray eyes and emitted a grunt that could have been meant for greeting. The district attorney, Ralph Corbett, got up to extend a hand across his desk, his pudgy face beaming with cordiality.

"This is an honor!" he declared. "Really! An honor! Sit down!"

Hicks took a seat, crossed his legs, and gazed at Corbett's baby mouth with a glint in his eye.

"That was quite a coincidence last night," Corbett said.

"Which one?"

"Beck running into you at Mrs. Dundee's. I had a good laugh when he told me about it. You saying yesterday that you knew her slightly! And there you were at midnight having a tête-à-tête, and her in negligee! Really! If that's how it is when you know them slightly, what must it be like when you really get acquainted? Ha ha."

"Then it's something," Hicks said unsmilingly.

"I'll bet it is. Beck told me what you said you were there for. Also that you gave him your word that Mrs. Dundee wasn't at Katonah yesterday. Maybe you came to tell us that you've changed your mind about that?"

"No. I came to make a deal."

Manny Beck growled and shifted in his chair.

"A deal?" Corbett asked.

"Yes."

"On behalf of?"

"Myself."

"Shoot. What have you got?"

"A hunch. I'm not sure I've got anything. But what would you give for Cooper?"

Beck growled in a different key.

"Cooper? The husband? About a dime," Corbett said.

"Make it a bent nickel," Beck snarled.

"What's the matter?" Hicks asked in surprise. "Am I too late? Have you already got him?"

"No." Corbett tilted his chair back and clasped his hands behind his head. "I'll tell you, Hicks. As I said yesterday, I know better than to try any subtlety with you. You know as well as I do that Cooper didn't kill his wife. The way I know, we've checked him in New York at a quarter to three, borrowing a car, and in Croton at four o'clock, asking the way here, and at ten minutes past five the doctor said that she had been dead over an hour. That's the way I know. Now just to even up, tell me how you know."

"You mean how I knew?"

"Sure."

"That Cooper didn't do it?"

"Sure."

"If I had known that, would I be apt to come all the way up here to try to trade him in?"

Beck uttered a word which the stenographer certainly did not record.

"You sure would," Corbett chuckled. "Knowing you as I do. That's exactly the point. If you really want to make a deal, if you really want something nice, like a year's lease on the sunny side of Main Street for instance, why don't you offer something interesting? How about trading in the murderer?"

"Glad to. Write his name and address on a piece of paper—"

"Horse around," Beck said disgustedly. "You know damn well what he came for. He wanted to find out what we've got. He wanted to know if we still had Cooper down for it. Okay. Now he knows. Anything else, Hicks? How about a timetable? Here."

Beck shuffled among papers on the desk and found one. "Here's the timetable. Like to have a copy? '2:45, Martha Cooper arrives at house. 2:50, you arrive. 2:58, you meet Ross Dundee at the bridge over the brook. 3:05, you arrive at the laboratory. 3:02, Ross arrives at the house. 3:15, Mrs. Powell goes to the village to shop. 3:50, R. I. Dundee arrives at the house.' And so on. Want a copy?"

"No, thanks. Those things just mix me up."

"Me too." Corbett looked reprovingly at Beck. "I don't think it calls for sarcasm, Manny. We have no reason to suppose that Hicks is actually an accomplice. He is merely obstructing justice. All we are sure of is that he knows a lot more about those people than we do, he almost certainly knows why that woman was killed, and he probably knows who killed her."

Corbett addressed himself to Hicks with great affability. "Naturally, as soon as we checked Cooper definitely out, which we finished with this morning, we checked everybody else in. Take for instance that triple alibi, you and the girl and Brager."

"Take it?" Hicks smiled. "I'm devoted to it. I cherish it. Speaking of triples, those three things you are sure I know give you a percentage of zero. I don't know any of them."

Beck grunted derisively. Corbett laughed, ha ha, and then tightened his baby mouth.

"Absolutely straight," Hicks asserted. "Of course I know things about Dundee's business, since I am on a confidential job for him, but I'm groping in the dark for any connection between him, or any of them, and Martha Cooper. That's what I came up here for. I might be able to help a little before this is over, and I thought it would be a good idea for you to pass me anything you may dig up about Martha Cooper."

"Jesus!" Beck snorted. "Gall? Match it! Try and match it!"

"You notice," Corbett observed, "that I am not trying to put you through anything."

"Yeah. Much obliged."

"Not at all. I don't believe in wasting energy. But I'll make a remark. You are not a member of the bar. If things should warm up, you will not be able to plead privileged communication. And I shall be inclined to do my duty as the prosecuting officer of this county. My full duty. So I had better ask you one question for the record. Do you possess any information about the murder of Martha Cooper, regarding opportunity, motive, identity of the murderer, that you have not given me?"

"Yes," Hicks said.

Corbett looked startled. "Yes? You do?"

"Sure." Hicks got up and took his hat from the desk. "I know that if her voice had been soprano instead of contralto—" he was on his way out and turned at the door— "she wouldn't have got killed."

Beck told Corbett, "I'd give a year's pay to break his goddam alibi."

Hicks had intended, after finishing at the courthouse, to go on to Katonah, for, among other things, assurance that Heather was keeping the promise she had made him; but now that Cooper was out of it he wanted to get rid of him without delay, and before doing that he needed a talk with him. Heather had stated that her sister had not known Brager or Vail or either of the Dundees, or anyone connected with the Dundee firm or Republic Products; but that, Hicks decided now, would not do. That was the hole to explore, and the best way to start the exploration was with George Cooper.

It lacked a few minutes of four by the dashboard clock when he stopped the car in front of the address on 29th Street. Before going upstairs he dived into the restaurant, and found the proprietor in the kitchen.

"Okay, Rosy? Feed him yet?"

"By all means okay," Rosy declared. "He has been served like a king, in his room. He can drink coffee, that man. And there is another man up there."

"What! With him? You let—"

"No, no. Not with him. A man to see you. I invite him to sit in my restaurant, not a bad place, not a dirty place, but he insists he will wait upstairs. If he expects me to carry a chair—"

Rosy stopped because his audience was gone. Hicks went to the stair entrance and mounted the two flights. A guess was in his mind as to the identity of the visitor, but it proved to be wrong. It was not Ross Dundee. The man waiting in the upper hall in front of the door to Hicks's room was larger and older and fleshier than Ross Dundee, and as Hicks reached the landing he recognized him. It was James Vail, the head of the Republic Products Corporation.

Thirteen

"WAITING FOR ME?" HICKS ASKED.

Vail said yes.

Hicks stopped in front of him and surveyed him with a swift inclusive glance. The Vail corporeal substance presented no feature that appealed to him; it lacked all semblance of grace; and he was stirred to active and irritated dislike by the broad insensitive nose, the cold shrewd eyes, and the thin selfish mouth. His fingers twitched with a desire to pick the visitor up without further ado and toss him downstairs; controlling that, he unlocked the door of his room and invited him to enter, let him have the comfortable chair, and turned the other chair around to face him.

"I tried to phone you," Vail said, "but you don't seem to have one."

"No. If I had a phone people might call me up. Also it costs too much."

Vail's thin lips twisted with what was presumably intended as a smile. "I was asking my friend, Inspector Crouch of the police, about you this morning, and learned that you're a very interesting character."

"I don't suppose," Hicks remarked, "that you came down here just to tell me that?"

"Oh, no. I came to ask the purpose of your call at my office yesterday."

"To try to find out whether Mrs. Dundee had ever been there to see you, and if so when and how often. Is that all?"

"I see." Vail leaned back in the chair and stuck his thumbs in his vest pockets. "Then she didn't send you. You're working for Dundee."

Hicks didn't speak.

"Aren't you?"

"Try another one," Hicks suggested. "Ask me who darns my socks."

Vail frowned. "All I'm trying to do," he said evenly, "is to establish a basis. We may be able to discuss things to our mutual advantage, but before we can do so we shall have to establish a basis. I am prepared to be quite frank. For instance, does this interest you? Mrs. Dundee did call at my office yesterday noon."

"Not much."

"That doesn't interest you?"

"Not much." Hicks gestured impatiently. "Forget the basis and start with the mutual advantage. What have I got that you want?"

"You have intelligence. According to my friend the inspector, an extremely acute intelligence."

"You can't have that. I'm planning to keep it."

"I don't want it. I manage well enough with my own. I merely want you to use your intelligence." Vail removed his thumbs from his pockets and leaned forward with his palms on his knees. "And persuade Dick Dundee to use his, if he has any left, which seems dubious. I put the facts squarely to you. Over two years ago Dundee took a hostile attitude toward me, but it was a long time before I learned why, that he suspected me of getting his formulas. I tried to tell him his suspicion was absurd, but he wouldn't listen. The fact is, of course, that coincidences continuously occur in all fields of scientific research, and that is especially true of a field as specialized as ours. Dundee ought to know that; he does know it. Somehow he got this idiotic idea in his head. But I didn't know until yesterday that it had become an obsession with him. From what his wife told me, he has acquired the fantastic notion that she has been selling his secret formulas to me. That's ridiculous. Simply ridiculous."

Hicks scratched the side of his nose and offered no comment.

"Well?" Vail inquired.

"I didn't say anything."

"I am telling you that Dundee's suspicion that I have bought his formulas from his wife is ridiculous. Where did he get it? What evidence can he have?"

"Search me."

"There is no evidence. There can be none."

"Then he hasn't got any."

"And it was in an effort to get some that you came to my office yesterday. Isn't that correct?"

"Nuts," Hicks said disgustedly. "You're not that clumsy.

Maybe we do need a basis. Cut out the act that you came here to try to pump me. That's kindergarten stuff. Possibly you're leading up to something reasonable, I don't know, but I do know why you came. Because you're good and scared."

The substitute for a smile twisted Vail's lips. "Scared? My dear sir. Of Dick Dundee? Of you?"

"I don't know who of, but I know what about. Murder."

Vail's brows went up. "Murder?" He made a noise evidently intended to signify mirth. "Do you mean I am afraid of being murdered? By Dundee?"

"No. The murder has already been committed."

"Not on me. I am quite intact."

"Martha Cooper isn't."

"Martha Cooper? What—" Vail stopped. He wet his lips. "Oh! That's the name of the woman who was killed by her husband up at Dundee's place near Katonah. Isn't it? Martha Cooper? I saw it in the morning paper. May I ask where you got the strange idea that there is anything in that to concern me?"

"It just occurred to me," Hicks declared, "sitting here looking at you. I thought I'd try it out. Something has certainly happened to change you since yesterday. Then you ordered me out. Now you go to all the trouble of asking your friends the police about me, and digging up my address, and traveling down here in the slums—do you suppose it's another coincidence in scientific research?"

Hicks smiled at him.

"I begin," Vail said acidly, "to question Inspector Crouch's opinion of your intelligence."

"You're wise. Crouch exaggerates."

"And I regret it." Vail leaned back and stuck his thumbs in his pockets again. "Because I assure you it wasn't fright that brought me here. I sent you off yesterday in a fit of temper. I shouldn't have done so. Dundee's absurd suspicions have annoyed me, and he has refused to discuss the matter, and you offered an opportunity for discussion and I should have seized it. That's why I came to see you. But wish your ridiculous remark about murder—"

"Forget it." Hicks waved it away. "I get spells like that."

"I would advise you to control them. Under the circumstances it may be useless to mention the proposal I intended to make. . . ."

"Suit yourself."

"But it can do no harm. I propose that you call on the

105

director of our research department, Dr. Rollins. He will open the records for you. He will demonstrate that all of our new introductions for the past two years, including carbotene—I mention that because I understand Dundee has charged that that formula was stolen from him—they have all been developed independently in our laboratories. You will be permitted to investigate fully, and I am sure you will be satisfied that my contention is justified. And that you will be able to satisfy Dundee also, if he hasn't entirely lost his reason."

"That might work if I—"

"Just a moment." Vail was slowly rubbing his palms together. "I want to be completely fair about this. I am aware that it would not be to your advantage to accept this proposal. The investigation you are making for Dundee might go on for months, and of course he is paying you well, whereas if you do what I suggest the matter can be closed up in a few days. I have no right to ask you to make that sacrifice. If and when it is closed, I am willing to make up the difference to you personally. The most satisfactory arrangement would be to agree in advance on a flat sum. Say a cash payment of ten thousand dollars?"

Hicks appeared to be considering. "In twenty-dollar bills?"

"Any way you like." Vail wet his lips. "The arrangement would of course be confidential."

"I warned you that Crouch exaggerates."

Vail brushed that aside. "And the sooner it is done the better. Mrs. Dundee's call on me yesterday was disturbing. Very. Say tomorrow morning at the factory? I'll take you out there myself and instruct Dr. Rollins to—"

The door swung open and George Cooper entered. He came in three paces, was there before Hicks could move. glanced from one to the other, and fastened his gaze on Hicks.

"Where's my hat?" he demanded.

Hicks, on his feet, realized with one glance that this was a different George Cooper. This Cooper was in his senses, completely in command of himself. His eyes, bloodshot and swollen as they were, were steady and fully perceptive.

"You haven't got any hat," Hicks told him. "If you'll wait for me downstairs in the restaurant—I'll be down in a couple of minutes—"

"I'll get along without a hat," Cooper interrupted. His

tone was not friendly. "Also I'll get along without you, but I want that phonograph record and I want it now."

"What phonograph record?"

"My wife's voice. It begins, 'Good lord, let me sit down and gasp a while! I know I'm late but I had an awful time getting here I never saw such traffic.' That's how it begins—"

"You're dreaming," Hicks said curtly.

"Oh, no. I'm through dreaming."

"Then you're batty. It is conceivable that I might have swiped your hat. But where and how and why did I swipe a phonograph record of your wife's voice?"

"You're lying," Cooper said, but not with conviction.

"Not at present." Hicks crossed to him and took his arm. "Listen, brother. You're hearing things. I would advise you—"

"I don't need any advice." Cooper pulled his arm loose. "And I'll tell you something, I know what happened, don't think I don't. I haven't got it straightened out, but I'm going to. I'm going up there and I'm going to straighten it out." He was frowning in concentration. "If it's the last thing I do on earth, and maybe it will be."

He turned and was gone. Hicks stepped to the threshold and saw his head descend out of sight, down the stairs, then closed the door and went back to his chair. He looked at Vail, and saw that Vail's lids were so narrowed as to make his eyes tiny colorless beads, the eyes of a wary and malevolent pig.

Hicks asked softly, "You know him, do you?"

Vail's head moved just perceptibly for a negative shake. "No. But I recognized him. From his picture in the paper."

"Oh. Of course."

"Is it customary for a murderer to drop in and ask you for his hat?"

Hicks smiled. "It is a bit rococo, isn't it? The poor guy's brain is curdled. Looking for a phonograph record of his wife's voice! Can you beat that?"

"I am a little curdled myself. He is a fugitive from the law. You made no effort to detain him."

"Neither did you." Hicks was smiling at him. "But take it from me, his trade-in value is away down. It isn't worth the effort. Not in the same class with the offer you were making when he popped in. I wish I could accept that. I sure do."

"I trust you have the good sense to accept it."

"I haven't." Hicks continued to smile. "If you knew me

107

better you would be going. It takes a while for an idea to work its way into my chest. When that happens, say in another half a minute, with the idea that you had the gall to try to bid me in, belly, guts and all, for a measly ten thousand bucks, I shall start operating on you." The smile had gone and Hicks's eyes were glittering. "If you knew me better you would know that."

"My offer was merely—"

Hicks stood up.

"—a business proposal—"

Hicks moved.

To do Vail justice, his departure was more of a withdrawal in order than a flight. He moved with expedition, but not precipitately, in getting his hat, opening the door, and passing through.

Hicks shut the door again, crossed to a window and stuck his head out, and looked up and down the street. There was no sign of Cooper. In a moment Vail appeared on the sidewalk below and strode off in the direction of Second Avenue. There was determination and purpose in his stride.

"Healthy and happy," Hicks muttered. "Not a mark on him. I sure am developing a remarkable self-control."

He left the window, went to the bureau and opened the bottom drawer, and from underneath a pile of pajamas took out the sonograph plates and counted them. Eight. Near the center of the one on top was a deep scratch in the form of a V which he had put there himself with his new pocket knife. Getting his hat from a hook on the wall, he went down to the restaurant, asked Rosario for paper and string, and made a package.

"He went out," Rosario said. "You know?"

"Yeah, I know. How much do I owe you?"

"You owe nothing. He paid."

"The dickens he did."

"And here is eighty cents change he didn't take."

"Keep it."

Rosario dropped the silver into his pocket, glanced around to make sure that the room was empty, and whispered hoarsely, "I saw his picture in the paper."

"Okay, he probably won't get far." Hicks got the string tied, took another look at the disc he had kept out to make sure it was the one with the V on it, and handed the package to Rosario. "Here, will you keep this in a safe place for me?"

"Sure."

"You are a great man, Rosy. You don't ask questions. A great man."

"Great enough," Rosario agreed. "Except too fat. God above, if you catch me eating!"

Hicks left him. At the curb he climbed into the company car. At the corner of Second Avenue he halted at a newsstand for an evening paper and slipped the sonograph plate in its folds. At 31st Street he stopped in front of a drugstore, entered and found the phone booth, and called the Dundee number at Katonah. Heather Gladd's voice answered.

"This is Hicks. How are you?"

"Oh—I'm all right."

"Where are you, at the house?"

"No, at the office. I'm trying to clean up some work. I wasn't—I couldn't just sit any more. Where did you—"

"Are there any cops around?"

"I think not. Two of them left about an hour ago—"

"Well, here's some exercise for you. Mental. One of them may be listening in at the house, or they may even have the wire tapped. If so, they don't need to know your private affairs. You will probably have a visitor in an hour or so, the gentleman who was present at the reading of your love letters. He is no longer in a fog. He intends to straighten things out, which he is not competent to do, and among other things he will want to know about the one that was not a love letter. I have told him he is dreaming. You will tell him the same. You will discuss nothing with anyone whatever. Have you kept your promise?"

A silence.

"Have you?"

"Yes. But I want those—"

"Don't use any words that a third-rate intelligence would understand. You're in danger. Your life is in danger. I'll be up there later, or I may phone you. You shouldn't be around in the open. You could come to New York—"

"Nonsense. Nobody has any reason to do anything to me." Heather's voice was scornful. "But if he comes—the police—"

"Forget it. He's out of it."

"How do you know—"

"I know everything. Up to a certain point. You be a good girl and hold everything until you hear from me, and drink plenty of water and keep your feet warm."

Hicks rang off, and dialed another number. The second conversation was much briefer. He asked to speak to Mrs. Dundee, and after a wait her voice was in his ear.

"This is Hicks. I'm coming to see you. I'll be there in fifteen minutes."

"I don't know . . ." She hesitated. "My husband is here—"

"Good! Keep him! Fifteen minutes."

Fourteen

IT COULD NOT HAVE BEEN CALLED A HAPPY FAMILY SCENE.

A man habitually careless in apparel and grooming may yet be quite personable, and often is, but when one who is ordinarily well combed and brushed and closely shaven, and impeccably dressed, becomes temporarily unkempt, the effect is deplorable. R. I. Dundee, seated on a Louis Quinze chair in his wife's dressing room, presented the appearance, if not exactly of a bum, of a man who had been bumming. By contrast, his wife, even with visible puffs under her eyes and a sag to her shoulders, was dainty and fresh and congruous in the daintily furnished and decorated room.

She was standing when Hicks was ushered in, and shook hands with him. Dundee stayed in his chair and offered no hand. Hicks, invited, took a seat when Mrs. Dundee did, covering his lap with a newspaper folded only twice—not a common way to carry a newspaper.

"You were here last night," Dundee said irritably.

Hicks nodded. "I'm working for your wife."

"Damn little work you seem to be doing for anyone." Dundee's tone was a sneer. "For her or me or anyone. I came here to try to get her out of this mess and keep her out. She has betrayed me, she has half ruined my business that I've spent my life building up, but she still bears my

name, she is my wife, and I don't intend to have her involved in that idiotic murder!"

"I'm not trying to involve her," Hicks declared mildly.

"You might as well be!" A fleck of moisture came from
between Dundee's lips, sailing into the air. "Excuse me," he
said bitterly. "I even spit when I talk! You advised her to
tell that detective she wasn't there yesterday! You told her
to deny it!"

"You're insane, Dick," his wife said quietly. "I denied it
because it wasn't true. I mean it literally, you're insane."

"You're damn right I'm insane!" His chin trembled.
"You're damn right I am!"

"Even so," Hicks put in, "you might help us to clear up
a point. Calm down a little. What makes you so sure your
wife was there yesterday?"

"I've told her!"

"Tell me."

"It's perfectly absurd," Mrs. Dundee said. "The same
thing that man said last night. Ross heard me talking. Of
course he didn't."

Hicks's eyes stayed on Dundee. "The chief trouble with
you," he stated, "is that your blood goes to your head too
easy. You need a valve fixed. It makes you assume that everyone but you is a fool. I'm not a fool. About that murder,
they're trying to involve your wife because they've learned
that Cooper, the husband, didn't do it, and they think
they've caught your wife in a lie."

"He was here again this morning," Mrs. Dundee said.
"And he'll keep on coming. Whereas the only ones who
have lied to them, to my knowledge, are you and me."
Hicks was looking at Dundee. "What if I decide to protect
myself by telling the truth? Wouldn't that be nice? I want
to know where Ross was when he heard his mother's voice."

Dundee was scowling, with his lips compressed. He
opened them enough to say, "He was on the terrace."

"What time was it?"

"About three o'clock. When he got to the house. Just
after he met you by the bridge."

"Where did the voice come from?"

"Through the open window. From inside the living
room."

"Didn't he go in?"

"No. He went around to the rear and up the back stairs
to his room. He didn't want to meet his mother just then.

He knew I was coming out to have a talk with him, and he wanted to talk with me first. He thought she had come with me. Later, out of his window, when he saw me drive in, he thought she had come with you. He called to me from the window and I went up to his room, and we had a talk, but he didn't tell me his mother was there. After I left to go to the laboratory he went downstairs to see her, and she wasn't there. Of course she did go with you, and when she saw me drive in she left."

"You say. Did Ross go to the terrace?"

"No. The house was empty. Mrs. Powell had gone to the village. He called his mother and got no answer."

"What was it he heard her saying through the living room window?"

"She said, 'Then I'll wait here for you.'"

"Just that?"

"Just that. Then he heard her hanging up. The phone. He thought she might be coming to the terrace, so he hurried off." Dundee was glaring at Hicks. "Later, after the dead woman was found, he got worried, and the damn fool phoned here to ask his mother about her being there, and discovered he was being overheard. Then when that detective came here you and she made it worse by denying that she was there. You should have admitted that she went out there with you and came back alone. You can't lie about things like that when a murder is being investigated. Maybe she couldn't be expected to have better sense, but by heaven, you could!"

"Then you and Ross are both convinced she was there?"

"Certainly we are!"

"On account of that one short sentence he heard through a window?"

"He knows his mother's voice, doesn't he?"

"I suppose he thinks he does." The glint was in Hicks's eyes. "And rather than asume he was mistaken, which is not beyond possibility, you prefer to think that your wife is lying about it—not to mention me?"

"She has been lying to me for God knows how long," Dundee said bitterly. "Living a lie!"

"You can't reason with him," Judith Dundee said wearily. "It's no use. Either he's mad, absolutely mad, or something has happened that I wouldn't have believed—he wants to finish with me—"

Husband and wife stared at each other, as only a husband and a wife can stare when, after a quarter of a century of the little explosions that punctuate married life, a bomb has utterly destroyed all bonds of communication and understanding.

Hicks said, "Let's drop that for the moment. I want to try something more interesting and possibly more helpful. Have you got a phonograph here?"

The stares went to him.

"What?" Judith asked in astonishment.

"A phonograph. I've got a record I want you to hear." Hicks slipped the plate out of the newspaper. "If you—"

"What is that?" Dundee was on his feet, reaching, demanding. "Let me see that!"

Hicks held him off. Judith was on her feet too. "Is that—" She stopped, went to a large console against the wall which had been designed and decorated to match the furniture, and opened a lid. "This radio has a record player. Here . . ."

She turned dials. "This is the volume, this is tone control." She made way for Hicks. He fixed the plate in position, turning the switch, saw that the pick-up arm was automatic, and stood there, leaning on a corner of the cabinet. A voice came from the loud-speaker:

"Good lord, let me sit down and gasp a while!
I know I'm late, but I had . . ."

"By God!" Dundee blurted. "That's it! Where—"

"Shut up," Hicks commanded him sharply. "Your wife wants to hear it."

Judith Dundee stood motionless three paces off from the cabinet, facing it, looking at the loud-speaker grill. Hicks watched her face. At the beginning it was intensely interested and faintly contemptuous, but at the first sound of Jimmie Vail's voice she started with amazement and gaped incredulously. Then she was rigid again, her chin uptilted, her lips apart, and stood without moving a muscle right to the end. The automatic switch clicked and the disc stopped turning.

The effect on Dundee was pronounced. He had sat down and gazed as if hypnotized at the back of his wife's head. Now he said, not with heat, not in triumph, but in a tone of gloomy and harsh finality:

"There it is. There it is, my dear." He looked at Hicks and demanded, "Where did you get it? From Brager? From

113

my son?" He looked at his wife again. "There's nothing you can say. Of course. What have you got to say?"

She said nothing. Hicks addressed her:

"That's the evidence I was telling you about last night. From a sonotel planted in Vail's office. That's what you hired me to do, get the proof your husband said he had. Done. Huh?"

Judith Dundee moved. In no haste, deliberately, she returned to her chair, sat, and folded her hands in her lap. With no glance at her husband, she looked at Hicks, and there was a tremor, the tremor of controlled passion, under the metallic hardness of her voice.

"Yes, you did it," she said. "But you're not done. I have quite a little property of my own. You can have it—any or all of it. Whatever it takes, whatever you want, when you find out how that contemptible trick was played, and who did it, and why."

"Good God!" Dundee was gawking at her. "Trick! You mean you're trying to deny it?" He pointed a trembling finger at the radio. "Did you hear it? Good God, didn't you hear it?"

He left his chair and stood in front of her. "I know you, Judith," he said, trying to keep his voice steady. "I know you've got iron inside of you. I didn't ever think you would do a thing like this, but you did. Now you won't admit it, I know you won't, but I wanted to show you that I know. Not that I suspect, I *know*." He pointed a finger at the radio again. "There it is!" He shook the finger at his wife. "And I'm warning you about that other thing, your being up there yesterday. As your husband, I warn you! In that you're not dealing with me, you're dealing with the police. With murder! Do you want to be suspected of murder? Do you want this whole dirty business shouted about in a courtroom and printed in the papers? Will you, for God's sake, will you come to your senses and tell the truth, so we can decide what to do?"

"You are either crazy, Dick," his wife said in the same hard voice, "or I have lived with you for twenty-five years without even getting acquainted with you. I'm not proud of that."

"Look here," Hicks said. "Both of you. You're only making it worse. When I said listening to that thing might be helpful I meant it. I'm going to run it through again, and I want—"

An inarticulate noise came from Dundee's throat, and he turned and tramped from the room.

Hicks gazed after him, then moved away from the radio and sat down. Mrs. Dundee pressed her palms to her eyes.

After a silence they heard, from a distance, a door closing.

Judith looked at her hands, dropped them again onto her lap, gazed at Hicks's face a moment, and said, "I don't like your eyes. I thought I did, but I don't."

"You're tough, all right," Hicks said admiringly. "Do you want to hear that thing again?"

"No. What good would that do?"

"Is it your voice?"

"No."

"What!" His brows lifted. "It isn't? At that, it may not sound like it to you. People are often astonished at a recording of their own voice."

"It may sound like my voice," Judith said. "I don't know. But I know it isn't me. It isn't simply because it couldn't be! I never had any such conversation with Jimmie Vail, and another thing, there are some phrases that I never say. It isn't me." Her hand made a fist and hit her knee. "It's a despicable trick! It—"

She got up and started for the radio, but Hicks was on his feet and there ahead of her, blocking the way.

"Don't be absurd," she said scornfully. "I merely want to look at it. Anyway. it's mine. I paid you to get it for me."

Hicks removed the plate from the turntable. "You can look at it," he conceded, "but I'm delaying delivery." He held it before her eyes. "Not that I have any use for it at present, but I think it's going to be needed as evidence to convict someone of murder."

She stared at him. "Nonsense," she said shortly. "Just because that woman was killed at that place—it was her husband—"

"No. It wasn't her husband."

"But it was! The papers—and he ran away—"

"The papers print what they know, which isn't much. I know more than they do, but not enough. Maybe I know who killed her, but I'm not—"

"If you think it was my son or my husband, you're an idiot."

"I'm not an idiot." Hicks smiled at her, tucking the plate under his arm. "Nor do you think I am, or you wouldn't be offering me all your worldly goods to find out who cooked this up." He tapped the edge of the plate with his finger. "What I'm telling you, when I do find out, you're going to get more than your money's worth. You're going to be a witness at a murder trial. The only way to avoid that would be to throw this thing in the garbage can, and leave the perpetrator of it undisclosed and unpunished. Is that your idea of a happy solution?"

Mrs. Dundee, meeting his eyes, said without hesitation, "No. I think perhaps you are being too clever. I don't believe the murder of that woman, a stranger to all of us, had any connection with—this other."

"But even if it had, I go ahead?"

"Yes."

"That's fine." Hicks patted her on the shoulder. "Of course I was going to anyway."

"Don't you think I knew it?" Judith demanded scornfully. "Neither am I an idiot."

Fifteen

WHEN HE LEFT THE DUNDEE APARTMENT AT A QUARTER to six, Hicks was bound for Katonah. With a double purpose; he meant to get Heather Gladd away from there, and he wanted certain information from her or Mrs. Powell or both of them.

If he had started for Katonah immediately, and driven recklessly, a life might have been saved; but he did neither. First he stopped at a haberdasher's and procured a cardboard box and tissue paper for packaging the sonograph plate; next he drove to Grand Central and checked the package in the parcel room; and then he went to Joyce's on 41st Street and ate baked oysters and arranged his mind.

By that time it was too late. At the moment, twenty-five

minutes past six, that Hicks was spearing his second oyster, Heather Gladd was sitting in the kitchen of the house at Katonah, finishing a lamb chop and drinking tea, and trying to pretend to listen to Mrs. Powell. The usual dinner hour was seven, but Heather, not wishing to join any gathering, however small, at the table, was anticipating it. The sun, she thanked heaven, was getting low; the day would soon be over; perhaps she would be able to sleep tonight. . . .

The door from the dining room swung open and Ross Dundee was there. Heather glanced at him, and sipped her tea; the hand that held the cup was quite steady and she frowned at it. Ross looked at her uncertainly, stood hesitant, and blurted:

"You've been dodging me."

"Leave her alone!" Mrs. Powell snapped.

"I wasn't aware," Heather said, "that I was dodging anybody."

"But you—" Ross stopped himself. "There I go. Damn it, I never do say anything right! I mean to you. What I meant, I only wanted to ask you—" He stopped again, cocked an ear to listen, and strode across the room to peer through a window screen at a car that was coming along the drive.

"My father," he said. "Fine. You dodge me and I dodge him." Three swift paces took him to the door and he had gone.

"It's terrible," Mrs. Powell asserted disapprovingly. "A son and father like that! No wonder things happen!"

Heather had no comment. She went to the garbage pail with her plate and disposed of the scraps, put the plate in the sink, and returned to her chair.

"You look terrible," Mrs. Powell said. "You look like a cabbage plant that needs watering. Go up and go to bed."

"I'm going to." Heather sighed. "It's hot up there."

A voice came bellowing from within the house: "Ross! Ross!"

Mrs. Powell started for the door to the dining room, checked herself at the sound of footsteps, and the door came swinging in, bringing R. I. Dundee with it. He glanced from one to the other and demanded:

"Where's my son?"

"He's not in here," Mrs. Powell declared.

"I see he isn't. I'm not blind. Is he at the laboratory?"

"I don't think so. I guess he's outdoors."

"Is Brager back from White Plains?"

"Yes, he got back about an hour ago. I think he's over at the laboratory."

"Has anyone else been here?"

"You mean police." Mrs. Powell's tone plainly implied that if he meant police he ought to be straightforward enough to say police. "Not since you left." She turned at a sound behind her—the back door opening with a complaining squeak—and announced as if she had accomplished something:

"Here's Mr. Brager."

Brager, entering, looked around at them, ending with Dundee. "Oh, you're back," he said. He seemed more pop-eyed, and hence more bewildered, than usual. "Just get back?"

Dundee nodded. "Is Ross at the laboratory?"

"No."

"What took you so long at White Plains?"

"Fools." Brager was wiping sweat from his face with his handkerchief. "Fools!" he repeated. "Nothing but foolishness. I shall tell about it later." He looked at Heather. "Miss Gladd, that transcript is all wrong. There are sections missing. You will please come and look at it."

"Leave her alone!" Mrs. Powell snapped. "She's going to bed."

Brager glared at her, but Heather stopped the argument before it got started by arising and saying that it would only take a few minutes and she would rather go and get it done. Brager opened the door and they went out. Mrs. Powell, muttering, got a pan from a drawer and deposited it on the table with a savage bang. Dundee stood and scowled at her a moment and then disappeared by way of the dining room.

Brager and Heather skirted the corner of the house, crossed the lawn, and entered the woods at the path. She was swinging along in front and he with his short legs was trotting to keep up. Her weary and harassed consciousness, grateful for the excuse, was concerned with the problem of the transcript. Had she skipped a whole plate? But she always checked them back. . . .

Her mind slid off that wretched little hummock, back into the morass of reality, when, nearing the bridge over the brook, the grotesque events of the night were recalled. She broke her stride as she glanced aside at the scene of that nocturnal farce, then went on, crossing the bridge and turning with the path. . . .

"Miss Gladd! Stop a minute!"

She halted and turned. Brager was right there, close enough to touch her.

"That was a lie," he said. "About the transcript. That wasn't what I came after you for."

Suddenly and preposterously Heather began to tremble. She felt it in the muscles of her legs, around her knees. She had not, at least not consciously, been alarmed by Hicks's warning of a possible danger to her person; certainly she had not been frightened; and if she had entertained any thought of peril the source last to be suspected would have been the popeyed flustery Brager. Yet now, suddenly and inexplicably, there in the depth of the woods alone with him, her knees were shaking and she wanted to scream. She nearly did scream. She wanted to back away from him and couldn't. But she knew, she saw, that there was nothing threatening or sinister in the expression of his face, his comical round face.

She made her knees rigid. "This is ridiculous!" she said sharply.

Brager nodded. "Everything is ridiculous," he agreed. "I have all my life been ridiculous, except in my work. Now I cannot work. All this—" He made an odd little gesture. "This disturbance. It is impossible! The trouble is, I tell you frankly, I am sentimental. I always have been, but I suppress it. Science and work cannot be sentimental. But I cannot work. So I become sentimental, and therefore a fool. Cooper is there and wants to see you. Your sister's husband. But I think I should be with you."

Heather's eyes were wide. "Where is he?" She looked around as though expecting to find him behind a tree.

"No, no. In the office. I told him I would bring you. He is unhappy. I have never seen a man so unhappy, and he is not guilty. He is absolutely not guilty!"

"He's waiting in the office?"

"Yes."

"I'll go on alone, Mr. Brager. You go back."

Brager shook his head. "No," he said stubbornly, "enough things have happened here already."

Heather looked at him, decided it was useless to argue the matter, turned and resumed her course along the path. The senseless momentary panic that had seized her was entirely

119

gone. As for George, she had no desire to see George, but there was something she wanted to say, a question she wanted to ask him. . . .

The late afternoon sun was full in her eyes as she crossed the meadow, with Brager at her heel, until they were in the shadow of the oak trees and the laboratory building. She ran up the steps and opened the door to the office and entered. A breeze from an open window had scattered sheets of paper over the floor from her desk basket. She noticed that before she saw that there was no one in the room. No George was visible. She turned to Brager inquiringly. His eyes were bulging in astonishment.

"He's not here," Heather said.

"He was here," Brager said complainingly. "In that chair!" He pointed. "I wonder if he—" He trotted to the door leading to the laboratory and disappeared within. Heather jumped when one of the sheets of paper, caught in an eddy from the window, flapped against her ankle. She gathered up the sheets, returned them to the basket, and put a weight on them.

Brager came back. "Not there!" he said angrily. "Not anywhere!" He faced Heather as if she had subjected him to a personal affront. "I tell you this is finally too much! Where is he?"

Heather was going to laugh. She knew she was going to, and she knew she must not. All day she had not cried, and now she was going to laugh, because the sight of Brager being mad at her on account of George not being there was irresistibly funny. She set her teeth on her lip.

"It is outrageous!" Brager insisted. "Outrageous! It is at last too much! He sat in that chair and said he must speak to you! Did I telephone? No! I would not telephone because I thought someone might hear! I leave him here and I go after you! Because I thought he was unhappy! Because—"

He stopped because the air exploded. Cracking, shattering the air, came the sound of a gunshot.

Sixteen

THE TWO THOUGHTS—IF SUCH CEREBRAL LIGHTNING FLASHES can be called thoughts—that came to Heather as she stood frozen for a fraction of a second, were, first, that she had been shot, and, second, that Brager had shot her. Both betrayed the state of her nerves. The first was not repugnant to reason, since people have been known to remain upright after being pierced by a bullet; but the second was manifestly absurd. Brager was frozen as stiff as she was. She looked down at herself. . . .

"That was a gun," Brager said. "Outside."

"Yes," she agreed.

"Shooting a pheasant again." Brager crossed to a window and peered through the screen; then he crossed back, to the door, and went out. After a moment's hesitation Heather followed. Brager had disappeared around the corner of the building; she descended the steps and walked to the corner. Rounding it, and seeing Brager, she stopped, and stopped breathing. Then, without breathing, she ran the ten paces to him, to where he was bending over the figure of a man lying on the ground close to the wall of the building. As she got there Brager straightened up. She saw the face of the man on the ground, and breathed, a convulsive gasp.

"Be quiet!" Brager said harshly. "I think I hear him."

He was peering into the woods, which on that side were only a dozen yards from the building. Heather could hear nothing. She was staring at George Cooper's face, wanting to look away but unable to. It was the most horribly repulsive thing she had ever seen, with the lips twisted into the grimace of an imbecile, and two flies, a small one and a large one, perched on the edge of a hole in the right temple only an inch away from the corner of the eye. It was the flies that made it unbearable. She clenched her teeth and stooped to chase them away, but by the time she was upright again one of them, the small one, was back.

121

"Here," Brager said. He took off his coat and spread it over the grimacing face. "Can you stay here?"

She asked inanely, "Where are you going?"

"Inside to telephone." He was trembling, and from his voice it was rage. "That is all I can do. I am not a brave man. I am not a resourceful man. This happens here by the wall of my laboratory, under my nose, I hear it, and all I can do is go inside to telephone. That is what men do nowadays when terrible things happen. They go inside to telephone. Bah!"

He went. When he came out again, minutes later, Heather was standing backed against the wall, her clenched fists at her sides, her eyes shut.

So when, around eight o'clock, Alphabet Hicks arrived, too late, the place was considerably more inhabited than he expected to find it. In the pleasant twilight, cars of sightseers and reporters were lined up on the grassy roadside in front, and at the entrance of the driveway a cluster of them, men and women and boys, were gathered around a tall and handsome state policeman on guard there. Hicks, seeing that from down the road, backed his car into the entrance of a pasture lane and got out and walked. His jaw was set and his chest was tight. He was thinking, "If he got that girl I'm a worm. No better than a worm. I should have taken her away. . . ."

He asked the policeman at the entrance, "What's going on?"

The policeman eyed him and demanded, "Who wants to know?"

"I do. The name is Hicks. If it's a secret you can whisper in my ear." There were titters. Hicks glanced around, picked a promising face, and asked it, "Between you and me, what's up?"

"Murder," the face said. "A man murdered."

"What man?"

"A fellow named Cooper. The husband of that woman that was killed here yesterday."

"Thanks." Hicks started up the drive.

The policeman let out a squawk, and, when Hicks disregarded it and kept going, dived after him. But no real difficulty developed, because Hicks saw a man coming down the drive, stopped in his tracks, ignored the policeman who grabbed his arm, and beckoned to the approaching man, whose Palm Beach suit and battered Panama hat had surely not been removed, nor the hat even shifted, since the day before.

The man's face did not light up with recognition as he caught sight of Hicks, but he said morosely, "Hello there."

"Hello," Hicks said. "Is this Adonis holding my arm your superior or your inferior?"

"Nobody knows. It's a case of brawn and brains. If you're a lover of peace, what the hell are you showing up here for?"

"Business. I came on an errand."

"You know we've had another casualty?"

"I just heard about it."

The man shook his head reproachfully. "It's beyond me. Okay, come on, I'll take you in to Corbett. Have you got another one of those cards? My sister wants one."

Hicks got out a card as they crossed the lawn, and handed it over. On the front terrace, which was deserted, the man asked him to wait and started inside, but Hicks stopped him:

"If you don't mind, what happened to Cooper?"

"Killed. Homicide."

"I know. Drowned, suffocated, strangled, stabbed—"

"Shot."

"Here?"

"Over at the laboratory."

"Anybody charged?"

"I don't know. That's all I know. Nobody ever tells me anything. I get it on the radio when I go home."

The man opened the door and disappeared. In a few minutes he emerged again and told Hicks, "Come on in. It looks like you're welcome."

District Attorney Corbett was installed again in the large and pleasant living room, at the big table with the reading lamp. Standing across the table from him was R. I. Dundee, and at one end of it a stenographer was seated. At the other end Manny Beck slouched in a chair. A policeman was just inside the door, and a man in plain clothes was in the background. When Hicks entered Corbett was speaking to Dundee in a tone of exasperation. That alone answered several questions for Hicks, knowing as he did that Corbett rarely addressed anyone old enough to vote in tones of exasperation, particularly a man of position and property like Dundee. Corbett was saying:

"Certainly you're not under arrest. Certainly not! No one is under arrest! But under the circumstances I have a right to insist on your co-operation as a responsible citizen and ask you not to leave here without permission. It is a fact that neither you nor your son can furnish corroboration of your whereabouts at the time Cooper was killed. I didn't say you are suspected of murder. And your remark about persecution of your wife is utterly unwarranted. Utterly!"

"We'll see," Dundee sputtered angrily. "I'll stay here till my lawyer comes. I want to use the phone again."

"Certainly. This one?"

"I'll go upstairs."

"One more question before you go. About Hicks. You said you sent him here yesterday on confidential business. Did you send him here today on the same business?"

"Hicks?" Dundee turned and saw him. "No!" he blurted, and tramped out.

Hicks went to a chair near the table, sat down, and observed, "When he's mad he's mad."

Corbett made no reply. He offered no hand and was obviously in no condition to make a pretense of geniality. He looked at Hicks as if he had never seen him before, chewed at his lip, and said nothing.

Manny Beck snarled savagely, "Where have you been?"

"My goodness," Hicks protested, "I seem to have come to the wrong place."

"Where've you been?"

"Born in Missouri. Boyhood on a farm. Harvard. Graduated law school 1932—Where have I been when?"

"Since you left the courthouse this afternoon."

"New York."

"Where in New York?"

"Now listen. Name a time and I'll name a place."

"Six thirty."

"Joyce's restaurant on 41st Street, eating baked oysters. The waiter and the hatcheck girl will sign it. I left there a little before seven and drove straight here."

Beck grunted and glared. Corbett's baby mouth looked as if he intended to whistle, but instead he spoke:

"You missed out with your trio on the alibi today. Only two of you made it."

"Two is better than one," Hicks said sententiously. "Provided they jibe."

"They jibe all right. Your two pals. Have you discussed it with them?"

"As I told you, I just got here."

"I thought you might have had a phone call at that restaurant, say a little after six thirty. Maybe the waiter would sign that too. I thought perhaps you left just after getting a phone call."

"Nope. No phone call."

"What did you come out here for?"

"I was under the impression I came on Dundee's business, but he says not. So I guess I'm investigating a murder. I'm finding out who killed Martha Cooper."

Manny Beck grunted. Corbett said sarcastically, "That's kind of you."

"Not at all. I'm interested."

"A few hours ago you were trying to trade in her husband."

"Yes, I know. Of course that's out, now that you've got him in custody. He can't very well slip away again if he's dead."

"Who told you he's dead?"

"A gentleman out front informed me. I'll be glad to discuss it with you if you'll tell me the details. All I know is that it happened at the laboratory, and he was shot. So naturally you have the advantage of me."

"That's a goddam shame!" Beck rasped. "I swear to God, Ralph—"

"Be quiet," Corbett admonished him. "Look here, Hicks. At the moment I have no way of tightening any screws on you. Being a very smart man, you know that. You also know that while I am not as smart as you are, I am not half-witted. Let me ask you a question. Do you know what happened here about two hours ago?"

"No."

"No one phoned you about it?"

"No."

"For the present I'll accept that. About a quarter to six Brager was in the office at the laboratory building when the door opened and Cooper walked in. This is what Brager says. Cooper sat down and started to talk. He was rambling, incoherent. He talked about his wife, and his life being ruined, and he didn't kill her but he was going to find out who did, that was all he wanted to live for. He went on and on. When Brager went to the telephone Cooper wouldn't let him use it. Finally Cooper started on the subject of his sister-in-law, Heather Gladd. He thought Heather knew something about her sister's death that she would tell him if he got a chance to talk with her, and that was what he had come for. He was so earnest about it that Brager believed him and took pity on him. So Brager says."

Hicks nodded. "I wouldn't quote you on it."

"Right. Brager went to the house and found Heather in the kitchen with Mrs. Powell and Dundee. Corroborated. He got her away by a pretext, and on the way to the laboratory told her about Cooper wanting to see her. When they got there Cooper wasn't in the office where Brager had left him. Brager looked in the laboratory. No Cooper. He returned to the office and they were discussing the situation when there was the sound of a shot. Right in their ears. That's the way Heather put it. Windows were open. Brager went to the window and then outdoors, and Heather followed him. Cooper was lying on the west side of the building, two feet from the wall, dead. Brager thought he heard someone moving in the woods, but saw no one, and the sound stopped. He went in the office and phoned. They both stayed right there until the police arrived. Bullet hole in Cooper's right temple. No powder burns. No weapon found."

Hicks was frowning. "Does Miss Gladd confirm all that?"

Corbett nodded. "To a T. She is a charming girl. A very beautiful girl."

"Are you talking to me?"

"Well." Corbett looked at Manny Beck and back at Hicks again. A little sound which could have been called a chuckle escaped from him. "God knows I don't blame you for having good eyes and a warm heart. Remember you haven't confided in me. For instance, you may or may not know that Cooper was madly in love with the younger sister before he married—and when he married—the older one."

"I wasn't acquainted with them."

"Neither was I. But naturally we've been checking up. You know how these things are. A lot of ideas come to you, most of them foolish, but you keep trying. First we were interested in Cooper, then when he was out, one idea we got was about Heather. Cooper came out here to see her Monday evening. In a jealous scrap with her sister, you know? In a rage, temper? She could easily have swung that candlestick."

"I get it." Hicks smiled at him. "I alibied her because she has a pretty face and nice legs. I sure go cheap. What about Brager?"

"There is reason to believe that he is by no means immune to female charms. And she has been living right here in the house with him for over a year."

Uh-huh, Hicks thought, you've been looking under blotters too. He said, "Of course I ought to be indignant, but I'll save it. What about Cooper, then? I'll bet she shot him. Sure she did, and Brager's got her alibied for that too. That puts him one up on me."

"Horsing around," Manny Beck growled. "You sure can take it, Ralph."

Hicks gestured in irritation. "I'll tell you, Corbett. In plain words. You're funny and you're slick and you're dirty. You don't any more believe that junk than I do."

Corbett chuckled. "Time for me to be indignant. I said it was just an idea. For instance, what if Cooper knew she had killed her sister, and she had to shut him up? You don't like it?"

"I wouldn't even say that. I don't even not like it." Hicks stood up. "So with your permission—"

"Wait a minute. Sit down."

Hicks sat down.

Corbett rested his elbows on the table, rubbed his palms together, and cocked his head on one side. The expression on his face was apparently intended to be judicial. Manny Beck, with his eyes closed, was slowly shaking his head right and left, as if to indicate that the immediate external world, both of sight and of sound, was too painful to be borne.

"I'll put it to you this way," Corbett said. "There is no question about your being in possession of information about these people directly or indirectly relevant to these murders. Of course you are. I want it. The people of the State of New York want it, through me. How are they going to get it? By coercing or threatening you? No. Not you. For two reasons among others: you're bullheaded, and you don't like me. Forget about me. You're dealing with the people of the State of New York. You know more about it than I do, but it's quite possible that if you had come clean yesterday or this afternoon, Cooper would still be alive. I appeal to you. There's a murderer loose. The chances are twenty to one that we'll get him. Or her. I appeal to you. You ought to help us. If you do, we'll get him quicker, that's all and I give you my word here and now that we'll do everything possible to protect the interests and private secrets of any innocent person. We'll stretch that point as far as it will go."

Manny Beck groaned.

"Pretty good speech," Hicks said.

"Well?"

Hicks shook his head. "No. You and the people of the State of New York have too much in common. I wouldn't trust either of you to tell up from down. They kicked me out of my profession because I didn't keep my mouth shut when I saw a rotten stinking piece of injustice being perpetrated in one of their courts, and now you say they want me to get chummy with you and tell you everything I know about a bunch of people who are having trouble. They can go right on wanting. Nowadays I make my own decisions regarding what I tell and don't tell, and especially whom I tell and don't tell. You say you're going to catch this murderer. I don't think you are. I don't believe you're ever going to get a smell of him. I think I'm going to catch him."

Corbett cleared his throat.

"Didn't I tell you?" Beck straightened up in his chair. "The only thing in God's world that would get under this guy's hide is three hours in the basement."

Hicks smiled at him. "You'd enjoy that, wouldn't you?"

"I would indeed, son. I would indeed."

Corbett said, "You may regret this. I'll try to arrange that you do. Meanwhile, stay on the premises."

"What am I charged with?"

"Nothing. But don't leave."

"I'll make my own decision about that too."

"You will? Then it's like this. If you try to duck you'll be arrested as a material witness. I can back that on the strength of your offer to deliver Cooper this afternoon. You may even have known where he was, and his movements since he skipped last night are certainly a vital part of this investigation."

"Oh, I'm willing to tell you that." Hicks stood up. "I took him home with me and gave him a good bed and a good meal. Then he came up here to get killed. Also he stole my candy."

"Ha, ha," Corbett said.

"You're as funny as a funeral," Beck growled.

"When I do tell you something," Hicks complained, going out, "you don't believe it."

Seventeen

AT THE MOMENT OF MIDDLE TWILIGHT WHEN HICKS WAS backing his car into the pasture lane, Heather Gladd was up in her room, seated by a window, looking out but not seeing anything. She had gone there as soon as her interview with the district attorney had ended.

She was thinking about herself. Until yesterday she had never seen a dead person except in a coffin. Then her sister —who had been the only person alive whom she had deeply loved—so suddenly and unexpectedly and shockingly. Then George, with the two flies at that hole in his head. What she was thinking about herself was that she was a completely different person from what she had been two days ago. Then her attitude toward the emotional tangle in which George and Martha and she were involved had been unbelievably puerile and infantile, in spite of the tears she had shed. She had been exasperated and petulant, that was all, as at some petty annoyance like finding that all her stockings had runs in them. And she would have gone on like that, she admitted grimly, possibly forever, a frivolous shallow simpleton, if death had not come to teach her. She had literally not known that there was anything in the world as ugly and final as death, and that things that happen between people could bring it. The first thing about death, when it came close to you like this, was that it made you feel dead yourself. She had not cried since she had found Martha dead. That was because she was dead herself. Yet she had acted sometimes as if she were alive—for instance, with Ross Dundee about

129

those sonograph plates. Why hadn't she simply gone and got them and given them to him? What difference did it make now? And why had she acted. . . .

That knock was at her door.

She got up and crossed the room and opened it.

"Oh," she said.

"May I come in?" Ross Dundee asked.

"Why—why, yes." Heather stood aside. "I thought maybe they were sending for me." She started to close the door, decided not to, changed her mind, and closed it.

Ross stood. She stood. Their eyes met. "They may not send for you again," he said lamely. "I hope not."

"It doesn't matter. Only I can't tell them any more than I've already told them."

"You were sitting down. Sit down."

She hesitated, then returned to the chair by the window. He went and stood in front of her. Silence.

She looked up at him. "Did you want to ask me something?"

"Well, I . . . wanted to tell you something. To say something. This is the first time I've ever been in this room."

"Is it?"

"Yes. I started to come in several times when you weren't here, but I never came farther than a step in. I had an odd feeling about it." He dismissed it with a gesture. "But that wouldn't interest you. I don't imagine anything anybody named Dundee could possibly say would interest you."

"I have nothing against anybody named Dundee."

"You ought to have," Ross said bitterly. "You have every reason to. You'll always remember this place, and us, with— I don't know what. Hate, I suppose. I know that and there's nothing I can do about it. I admit I didn't believe you when you said Cooper didn't kill your sister. I thought he had. Now I don't know what to believe. It's impossible that anyone here could have killed them, no one had any reason to, so I suppose the only thing to believe is that someone came when she was here, and went in the house and got the candlestick and killed her, and came back today when he was here and killed him. I realize how crazy that is, but it's the only thing I can believe, because if that wasn't it my father must have done it. You didn't and Brager didn't and I didn't and Mrs. Powell didn't. You say that fellow Hicks was with you at the laboratory yesterday, so he didn't."

He stopped. In a moment he went on, "One thing you

130

said yesterday. About my father and me being here when your sister was killed. I said it was stupid, but it wasn't. What do you know about us? How do you know we're not homicidal maniacs? It was me that was stupid, not you. Of course I know I'm just a plain ordinary dub, but you don't."

"You don't think you're a dub at all," Heather declared, meeting his eyes. "You think you're pretty hot stuff."

"I do not!"

Heather made a gesture.

"All right," Ross said savagely. "You've had me wrong from the start, and now nothing will ever change you. I realize that. But today I realized that it was actually possible that you suspected me of killing your sister! Why shouldn't you? How do you know I didn't?"

"I never said—"

"I know you never said it, but you hinted at it. And now Cooper too. At the time he was killed I was down at the old orchard. I didn't even hear the shot. I know nothing, absolutely nothing, of who killed him or your sister, or why, or anything. Do you believe that?"

"No."

"But you must! You must believe it!"

"It isn't a question of must. What I believe and don't believe—"

"But you have simply got to!" Ross came a step closer. "I can stand your not liking me, and your not caring a damn about how I feel about you, about how I love you, I can stand that because I can't help myself, but you're not going away from here thinking that I had anything to do, anything at all, with the terrible things that happened here! You are not! You have no right to think a thing like that about me!"

"On the contrary," Heather asserted, "I have."

"You have?"

"I not only have a right, I have a reason."

"Reason?" He stared at her. "You have a reason—"

"Certainly I have," Heather said firmly. "You never knew my sister, did you?"

"I did not."

"You never met her or knew anything about her?"

"How could I? She was in France. You told me about her. I only met you—"

"Then where did you get that sonograph plate with her voice on it? And why—"

131

"Where did I get *what*?"

"That plate with Martha's voice on it. And why were you so anxious and determined to get it back?"

Ross was gaping at her incredulously. "Are you saying—are you trying to tell me—"

A knock, a series of sharp taps, sounded in their ears—not at the door, but on the wall against which the dresser stood. It was followed at once by a voice sharp with anger:

"Damn you, what do you mean by that?"

Then another voice, quick footsteps, a door opening, and, as Heather got to her feet, the door of her room swung open and Brager was there; and entering immediately behind him was a man in the uniform of the state police. The policeman was saying in an unfriendly tone:

"Okay, it's your wall and you tapped on it. If you people aren't careful there's going to be some tapping around here on something besides a wall."

"What's the idea?" Ross demanded.

Brager's eyes popped at him, popping with indignation. "He expects me to keep still!" he sputtered. "He comes to my room! He hears voices at my open window, coming from your open window, and he stands there to listen, and he expects me to keep still! I know policemen do those things, all right, they do, but that is no reason to think I am a swine! To expect me to keep quiet while he listens to you and you are not aware of it! I knocked on the wall!"

He glared defiantly at the policeman.

"Thank you, Mr. Brager," Ross said. "He's quite welcome to anything he heard." He scowled at the policeman. "We'll shut the window and try to keep our voices low enough not to disturb you—"

"I'll save you the trouble," the policeman said dryly. "If the lady will please come downstairs. If you'll just come with me, Miss Gladd?"

"She's been there," Ross asserted truculently. "They've already talked with her."

"I know, but things come up. Will you come, please, Miss Gladd? Under the circumstances?"

Heather went to the door and passed through, with the policeman at her heels. She was filled with mortification, and was furious both with herself and with Ross Dundee. They had acted like children, talking like that, in that house at that time, by an open window without even taking the precaution to lower their voices. Not that she had anything to conceal from anyone, now that George was dead . . . but yes, she had . . . she had given Hicks a promise and said she would keep it. . . .

They were approaching the door to the living room when it opened and Hicks emerged. His eyes darted at her, at her escort, and back to her.

"Hello," he said. "Straighten your shoulders."

She took the hand he offered and the clasp of his fingers was good for her. "I didn't know you were here. I was— George—"

"I know. They've been telling me about it. I'd like to hear it from you. We'll go outdoors."

"I'm being taken in there. To the district attorney."

"Yes? I'll go along."

But that didn't work. Hicks did enter with them, but he was immediately put out, Corbett being in no mood to waste any words on the matter. After the door had been closed again, and Heather had been seated, the policeman stood at a corner of the table and reported succinctly what had just happened and the substance of what he had overheard. Manny Beck had apparently left by another door, for he was no longer there. Corbett listened with his baby mouth puckered as though preparing to whistle.

He shook his head at Heather in disapproval. "You see," he said regretfully. "You should have learned that we discover the things you try to conceal from us. That Cooper was in love with you. We learned that, didn't we? And other things. And now young Dundee is in love with you." Corbett wet his lips. "Has he asked you to marry him?"

"Don't be disgusting," Heather said, and compressed her mouth.

"There is nothing disgusting about marriage, my dear. Nor even about love." Corbett wet his lips again. "Not necessarily. This is interesting. Very. You told me only an hour ago that you had no idea of why your sister and her husband were killed, nor any reason to suspect anyone. Now it seems that you do in fact suspect Ross Dundee. Why?"

"I didn't say I suspected him."

"What she said," the policeman put in, "was that she didn't believe him when he said he didn't know anything about it."

"I'll handle this," Corbett said sharply. "Why didn't you believe him, Miss Gladd?"

"Because I don't know what to believe. He was there, that's all."

"Do you think he's a liar?"

"No."

"Do you—uh—return his love?"

"No."

"What specific reason did you have for telling him to his face that you didn't believe him?"

"I had no specific reason. Just what I said."

"My dear young lady." Corbett was reproachful. "This will never do. You heard the officer say that you told Ross Dundee that you had a reason, and he asked what it was, and you said it was a sonograph plate of your sister's voice. That is something else you have been concealing from us, and obviously something important. Have you got the sonograph plate?"

"No."

"Where is it?"

"I don't know."

"What's on it? What does your sister's voice say?"

"I don't know." Heather swallowed. "I know nothing whatever about it. It is a private matter. I don't intend to talk about it or answer any questions about it."

"That's a strange attitude for you to take, Miss Gladd."

"I see nothing strange about it."

"I do." Corbett gazed at her. "It's more than strange. We are investigating the murder of your sister, whom you say you were fond of. But instead of helping us you hinder us. You deliberately and defiantly withhold information. You say it is a private matter! If the dead could speak I would like to ask your sister you were so fond of whether she agrees that it is a private matter."

"I won't—" Heather's chin was quivering. She made it stop. "I won't listen to things like that." She stood up. "You can't make me listen to things like that. I won't listen to you and I won't talk to you."

She started for the door. A policeman moved to get in her path, and, making no attempt to detour, she stopped. For a brief second it was a tableau, a drama in suspense; then, just as Corbett piped, "Let her go, officer," the door burst open and Ross Dundee marched in, with an angry and expostulating individual coming for him from behind. In the confusion Heather slipped around them and through to the hall.

She had formed a resolution, impulsively but unalterably, and the immediate necessity was to communicate it to Alphabet Hicks, not so much to enlist his help as merely to communicate it. He was not in the hall. She went to a door at the end of it and entered the dining room, found it empty, and passed through to the kitchen. Mrs. Powell was there, pouring a cup of coffee for a man in a Palm Beach suit and a battered Panama hat.

Heather asked, "Have you seen Mr. Hicks?"

"No," Mrs. Powell said, "and I don't want to."

"He's all right," the man said tolerantly, "except he's batty. Why, do you want him?"

"Yes."

"He went upstairs to see Dundee. Last door on the right."

That would be Ross's room. Heather took the back stairs. Her resolution quickened her step, and, on the upper floor, even caused her to omit the common amenity of knocking on the door of another's room before entering. She turned the knob and went in, disregarded Dundee, who stopped pacing the floor to glare at her, confronted Hicks, who was straddling a chair, and told him:

"I can't stay here. I can't! I'm going to leave."

"It would have been a good thing for all of us," Dundee said harshly, "If you had reached that decision a week ago. Perhaps if you hadn't been here—"

"Shut up," Hicks said rudely. He got up to approach Heather. "Don't mind him, he's having a fit. Did the district attorney tell you you can leave?"

"No, but I'm going to. I can't—"

"Okay, we'll see. At least we'll leave this room." Hicks spoke to Dundee: "For God's sake calm down a little. Put cold compresses on your head. Comb your hair."

He motioned Heather ahead and followed her out. Across the hall and down a dozen paces was the door to her room. When they were inside and the door was closed, Heather said:

"I can't talk even in my own room. That's why he was taking me to the district attorney. I was in here talking and Mr. Brager and a man were in his room and heard us, and Mr. Brager tapped on the wall to warn us—"

"Then talk low. Keep your voice down." Hicks went and shut the window and came back. "Who were you talking with?"

"Ross Dundee. I was here and he came—"

135

"To ask about the sonograph plate?"

"No. At least—he didn't. But I did. I asked him where he got a plate with my sister's voice on it."

"Which is what I told you—"

"I know you did. It came out before I knew it."

"Keep your voice down. This should interest you. Cooper was murdered because he mentioned that plate. Maybe you realize now that I wasn't talking through my hat. A man has got himself into a hole that he can't get out of, but before he quits trying he'll kill you and me too if he can manage it."

They were standing, facing each other. Heather's head was tilted so that her eyes, on a level with his chin, were looking straight into his. Her voice came out a whisper:

"What man?"

Hicks shook his head. "Maybe I know. Maybe I don't. I came out here to increase my knowledge and ran into this. Was there ever a sonotel installed in this house?"

"Yes. There's one now, in the wall of the living room."

"That would amuse Corbett. He'd like that, doing his questioning in a room wired for sound. When was it installed?"

"It was there when I came, over a year ago. It was used for experimenting. About two months ago it was taken out and a new one was put in, a new model."

"Who installed it?"

"I don't know about the old one. Ross Dundee installed the new one."

"Keep your voice down," Hicks admonished her. "Today. About Cooper. You were at the laboratory with Brager when it happened?"

"Yes. He came and said George was there—no, he told me that when we were in the woods—"

"Tell me what happened at the laboratory."

She told him. He took it in, asked a few questions, nodded as if satisfied, and said:

"Okay. That'll do for now. We can cover some other points on our way to New York. The best—"

"To New York?"

"Certainly. You say you want to get away from here, which I can understand, and I have something to do somewhere else. So we might as well go together. The car you lent me is backed into the entrance of a pasture lane up the

136

road about four hundred yards toward Katonah. Do you
know where that is?"

"Yes. The other side of the old orchard."

"There's a house a short distance beyond."

"Yes. Darby's."

"We'd better not try to leave here together. They won't
be keeping close watch on you, and if you're any good you
can make it. You know the ground. Circle around through
the orchard and pasture. Are you afraid to try that?"

"Afraid? Of course not!"

"Good for you. I'll join you as soon as I can. I have a little
errand to do here before I leave, and it'll be harder for me
to get away. They'll miss me. Be patient and take a nap in
the back seat. Change to a dark dress and don't try taking
any luggage. In case of a slip-up—wait a minute."

Hicks frowned. "I've got the key to the car. Is there another one around?"

"Yes, in a drawer in the dining room."

"Can you get it?"

"Of course."

"You're a wonder. When you grow up and get big like
me you'll be President." Hicks sat down and untied a shoe-
lace and removed the shoe. He put the shoe on his lap and
got his wallet and a memo book from a pocket. From the
wallet he extracted a baggage check and glanced at it, then
wrote something on a page of the memo book, tore it out,
handed it to Heather, slipped the baggage check into the
shoe, and put the shoe back on.

"There," he said, "keep that in a safe place. Your shoe
will do. It's the number of the check for something I left in
the parcel room at Grand Central. In case anything regret-
table happens to me, here's what you do. Get Dundee's
wife, Mrs. R. I. Dundee, and go with her to Inspector Vetch
of the New York police, and both of you tell him everything you know. Everything. Don't hold out on him. Give
him the number of that check and tell him to get it. Vetch
is a good guy, once you get used to his mannerisms. You'll
like him."

"But what—" Heather was gazing at him. "Why do you
think anything—"

"I don't. But this individual we're after has apparently got
a screw loose. Getting Cooper like that in broad daylight!
He's so scared there's no telling what he'll try next, so just
to fool him we make these little arrangements. By the way,

I should warn you, when you meet Mrs. Dundee you're going to get a shock. Be prepared for it."

"A shock? Why a shock?"

Hicks patted her on the shoulder. "You'll understand when you meet her. Go ahead and change your dress—or wear that long dark coat you had on last night—"

"I'm not going to meet her," Heather said, "unless you—unless something—"

"Right. So the chances are you'll never have the pleasure. I'll explain further on our way to town. Probably—"

The door swung open and R. I. Dundee barged in.

"Irving's here. My lawyer," he snapped.

"Coming," Hicks said. He smiled at Heather. "See you later."

He followed Dundee out.

Eighteen

HEATHER HAD SCORNFULLY REPUDIATED HICKS'S SUGGES-tion that she might be afraid.

She would certainly have denied that it was fear that made her heart beat faster when she entered the kitchen and found that Mrs. Powell was still there, washing up, and a state policeman in uniform was standing by the corner cupboard, drinking coffee. Mrs. Powell glanced at her, saw the long dark coat, and asked:

"Going out?"

"Just for a breath of air," Heather said.

From the corner of her eye she saw that the policeman was looking at her, and, though he said nothing, she was convinced that if she started for the door he would stop her. She hesitated, became acutely aware that she was acting un-naturally, and turned and made for the door to the dining room, where she had just come from after getting the extra car key. She stood there a moment, berating herself as a coward and a ninny, and then went on through to the side hall. Without a glance at a man on a chair by the door to the living room, she opened the outer door and was on the terrace, and felt her heart start thumping again at the sight of another state policeman standing in a ray of light from a window. That made her mad. She addressed him without regard for the fact that she was interrupting something he was saying to Ross Dundee:

"If anyone wants me you can call," she said. "I'll be around within hearing."

"Very well, Miss Gladd," he replied, in a tone not only acquiescent but positively sympathetic.

Lord, I'm a simple-minded fool, she thought as she rounded the shrubbery and stepped onto the lawn.

She had decided on her route: straight back to the vegetable garden, around to the rear of the garage, on through the birches to the upper corner of the orchard. In the vicinity of the house there was enough light to go by, but farther on she found that clouds were obscuring the stars and it was so completely black that she barked her shin on a wheelbarrow someone had left at the corner of the vegetable garden. She went more cautiously, skirting the berry patch and threading her way through the slender birches.

She was in the orchard, towards the middle of it, when, stopping by a tree to decide whether to bear more to the left she heard a noise behind her. Her head whirled around and her heart stopped.

An apple falling, she thought.

She could see no movement, nothing whatever.

This is one on you, my fine brave girl, she thought. You're scared stiff. An apple falling.

She went on, bearing to the left, walked faster, tripped on something and recovered her balance without falling. Still she went faster, walking straight into a low-hanging limb. Had someone enlarged the darned orchard? No, at last, here was the stone fence. She climbed over, deciding that she wasn't so scared after all since she was carefully avoiding the poison ivy, and started across the meadow. Soon she came to the lane and turned right on it; and, stopping for a look to the rear, saw something moving.

A cow. No. There were never any cows in here; they mooed. It continued to move; it was coming closer! now she could hear it. Her legs were running, she was running.

No, she wasn't, she was standing still. She made her legs stop running. . . .

A voice said, "It's me. Ross Dundee."

She was stunned, speechless with rage.

"If you call this around within hearing," the voice said, from a face now near enough to be a blotch in the darkness.

"You—you—" Heather choked with fury.

"I'm sorry if I frightened you. I didn't—"

"I'm not an utter coward," she said contemptuously. "Will you let me alone? Will you stop following me around?"

"Yes. I will." The face was near enough now so that it was a face. "I'll stop following you around when you're back inside the house. But I want to know where you got the fantastic idea that I had a sonograph plate of your sister's voice."

"I'm not going back. I'm never going inside that house again."

"You're not?"

"No."

"You're leaving like this? At night? Walking? Without your things? Running away? No. You're not. By God, if I have to carry you—"

"You try carrying me! You try! I'm walking to the road. I'm walking there now. You touch me!"

She turned and walked, not precipitately, with sufficient care on the ridge between the ruts of the lane. Without looking back she followed the lane to the bars in the fence gap, straddled the lower bar to get through, bumped into the rear of the car that was parked there, went around to the front door, and climbed in behind the steering wheel. As she banged the door shut the opposite one opened, and Ross Dundee was there beside her.

She felt suddenly, overwhelmingly, that if she wasn't terribly careful and terribly strong she would cry. She might anyway. She wanted to order him to get out, in a tone of calm and concentrated disdain, but she didn't dare to try to speak. In a moment she would. . . .

He said, incredibly, "This car happens to be the property of R. I. Dundee and Company."

That fixed her. There was no longer any necessity for crying.

"I suppose," she said, in precisely the tone which only a moment before had seemed out of the question, "I can't get rid of you without telling you what I am going to do.

Mr. Hicks drove this car here. Since he is working for your father, I presume he is using the car with his permission. I am going to wait here for him and we are going to drive to New York."

"You and Hicks?"

"Yes."

"You don't know him! What do you know about him? Listen, for God's sake—"

"I'm not going to listen. About that sonograph plate, I shouldn't have asked you. I don't understand about it and I don't expect you to tell me. I don't understand anything about all this awful horrible business. If I stayed in that house another night, sitting there and lying there not understanding anything, I'd go crazy. I think Mr. Hicks understands it, or he's going to. I don't think that dreadful district attorney would ever find out anything. Whether anybody finds out anything or not, I can't stay there and I'm not going to, and I won't talk about it. Now you can go back to the house and tell the police, and they can come and get me. I'll be right here."

Heather was looking, not at Ross, but straight ahead through the windshield into the darkness. He was gazing at her profile. He told it:

"That's a fine, noble, generous thing to say. Me telling the police. You have no right to say a thing like that, even to me."

"You can tell them if you want to."

"Thanks. I don't want to. Anyway, I can't, because I won't be seeing them. I'll be going to New York with you and Hicks."

"You will not!"

"I will. But I'll settle that with Hicks. You said you won't talk about all this awful business, and I don't expect you to, but I've got to ask you one question and I hope you'll answer it. About that sonograph plate. Do you mean the one that was in with those other unmarked plates?"

"Yes."

"Then you did keep those plates."

"No, I didn't. I kept only one. I kept that one because it was my sister's voice and I didn't understand how you got it."

"It wasn't your sister's voice."

"It was!"

"It wasn't. It was my mother's voice. Where is it?"

A car came around a curve and was there on the road, its lights full on them, dazzling in their faces. It roared on by and was gone.

"They saw us," Heather said. "Whoever it was. That's the kind of a nitwit I am. This is ridiculous. I'm not going to talk about that plate or anything else."

She opened the door and got out, opened the rear door and climbed in, and lay down on the back seat. It required an acrobatic disposal of her long legs, and even so was not an eminently comfortable position, but it served the double purpose of concealing her from the beams of another car's lights and of isolating her from her unwelcome companion. She heard the sound of movement in the front seat but didn't open her eyes. If he said anything, no matter what, she wouldn't reply; but he didn't say anything. She shut her eyes tight, but that only made them sting, so she opened them and stared at the dark. After a while she closed them again. She wished Hicks would come. Not that his coming, or anything else, would ever make things clear again and bring life back. Nothing would ever do that. Only she couldn't go on forever having nightmares . . . not sleeping . . . not sleeping . . . .

Whenever the lights of a car showed in either direction, Ross ducked out of sight. Frequently, at brief intervals, he looked over the back of the seat into the tonneau. From the sound of the breathing, surely she was asleep, but that was hard to believe. He wanted her to be asleep. If she was asleep, he was there guarding and protecting her, which exactly fitted his idea of the matter to begin with. He sat as quietly as possible, not to awaken her. He wanted to turn on the dash light to see what time it was, but refrained from clicking the switch. Not that he was impatient; it would suit him all right if Hicks never came.

Footsteps on the grassy roadside. He cocked his head; from the right—no, the left. Hicks from that direction? Then he saw it wasn't Hicks, from the size of the moving perpendicular blob, just as a squeaky voice came out of the darkness:

"That you, Miss Gladd?"

Ross spoke in a low voice: "Tim? It's Ross."

But there was movement in the back seat, and Heather had the door open by the time the boy got there, and was asking, "What is it? Who is it?"

"It's Tim Darby, Miss Gladd. I've got a message for you.

Gee, it's exciting. Only he said you'd be alone. Only of course Ross is all right."

"A message?"

"Yeah, on the telephone. He said you'd be here in the car. Here, Mom wrote it down. It says you're to meet him. . . ."

Heather took the slip of paper, turned on the ceiling light, and peered at the penciled scrawl:

> *"Don't drive past Dundee entrance. Go around by Route 11 to Crescent Road. Am in a car parked half mile beyond Crescent Farm. License JV 28. ABC."*

"Thank you, Tim," Heather said, hardly aware that Ross's fingers, reaching over from the front seat, were removing the paper from hers. "Thank you very much."

"You're welcome, Miss Gladd. Gee, it's exciting. We're not going to squeal. Mom says she won't. I'll wait here till you're gone. If the cops come I won't tell 'em where you went, no matter what they do. No matter if they torture me."

"Attaboy, Tim," Ross said. "We know we can count on you. It might be better if you'd go right back home and lay low. Then the cops won't know anything about it. When did the message come?"

"Just now. Just a minute ago."

Heather was back in the front seat, behind the steering wheel. She got a key from her coat pocket, inserted and turned it, and pushed the starter button. The engine roared and subsided. She turned her head to Ross:

"Give me that paper and get out. If you have the slightest remnant of manners . . . I can't put you out. Will you get out?"

"Certainly not. You don't even know who that message is from. Do you think it's from Hicks?"

"Of course it is. It's signed ABC. His name is Alphabet Hicks."

"How did he get over to Crescent Road in a car? If he's loose in a car, why didn't he drive here?"

"I don't know. Because it's so close to the house. Will you get out?"

"I should say not. How did he know Darbys live there? How did he know to phone Darbys?"

"Because I told him their name."

143

"When?"

"This evening. Before I left the house. Will you—"

"You said you were waiting for him here. Was this phone message prearranged?"

Heather pulled the gear lever to low. "I'm not going to sit here and argue," she declared fiercely. "I'm going to remind you of something that I certainly didn't think I would ever be forced to mention. You said you loved me. You know all the things you said. If you love me so darned much, prove it. Get out of this car!"

"That would be a fine way to prove it. A fine way!"

"You won't?"

"No!"

Heather switched on the driving lights, let the clutch in, and rolled onto the road, turning left toward Katonah.

It was not a sociable ride, since not a word was spoken. From the Dundee entrance to Crescent Farm on Crescent Road it was only three miles by the direct route, but going around by Route 11 doubled the distance. Ordinarily Heather was a good driver, neither a crawler nor a crowder, but now she stammered and staggered along, slithering to the perimeter on curves, jerking the gas in, and when she met a car a little short of the turn onto Route 11 she went so wide she nearly slid into the ditch. She twisted her neck for a swift glance at her companion, but he didn't even grunt. Two miles farther on came another right turn onto Crescent Road, which was little more than a lane as modern roads go. After a long rise over a hill and a gradual descent beyond, it wound through a wood, was in open country again for a stretch as it passed Crescent Farm, and then dipped into another wood, becoming so narrow that the branches of the trees made an overhead canopy for it. . . .

Heather stamped on the brake so energetically that the car shivered in protest and dug its rubber into the dirt, then shifted to low and cautiously sidled over onto the bumpy roadside. Barely twenty feet ahead, also off the road, stood a large black sedan. Its lights were off, but Heather's lights were bright on the license plate, JV 28. She pushed a knob on the dash, and everything was pitch dark, but Ross reached over and pulled the knob out again.

"Let there be light," he muttered. "You wait here."

He climbed out and started for the other car, from which there had been no sign of life, and Heather opened her door and slipped out and followed him. She was at his

144

elbow as he glanced through the window and saw that the driver's seat was empty; and so was the rear. As his head turned to her for a comment, she seized his arm convulsively, and, seeing her stare, he wheeled around. A man who had been concealed at the front of the car, presumably crouching there at the bumper, was now erect; and in the glare of the lights of their car his narrowed eyes, above his broad nose and thin mouth, were amazing like the eyes of a wary malevolent pig. A pistol in his hand was leveled straight at them.

Nineteen

HICKS STOOD IN THE UPPER HALL FROWNING AT SPACE.

The conference with Dundee and his lawyer in Ross Dundee's room, where he had just left them, had made no inroads upon the world's available supply of cordiality. Dundee had been splenetic, the lawyer croaky and coldly suspicious, and Hicks himself somewhat trying. The result had been conspicuously negative. Hicks would have walked out on them much sooner, only he wanted to allow plenty of time for Heather to get out of the house and to the car before moving to join her.

Now it was desirable to make sure that she had left the house, and inadvisable to make any inquiries. He went to the door of her room and entered, glanced around, went out again, and proceeded downstairs. Strolling about, he found that most of the rooms below were populated, but exclusively by males. Having covered all the rest of the territory, he asked a man outside the side door to the living room:

"Who's in there?"

"There are several people in there."

"I mean of us victims. Brager?"

"No. He's upstairs. Mrs. Powell is with the district attorney."

"When he's through with her I'd like to speak to him. I'll be out on the terrace."

Hicks moved toward the outer door, but because he moved with no particular haste and the other man did, he didn't reach it. The man was there facing him, his back to the door, in an attitude that was unmistakable.

"You can wait right here," the man said. "There's a chair."

"I prefer the terrace. I can manage, thanks. I've been opening doors alone all my life."

The man shook his head. "Orders. You're not to leave the house."

"Whose orders?"

"Chief Beck's."

"A general order? Or does it apply only to me?"

"You I guess. That's the way I got it."

"And if I assert my constitutional right to locomotion in any desired direction?"

"If you mean go outdoors, you don't. You get taken for a charge."

"I see." Hicks pursed his lips and stood a moment. "As you were."

He turned and went back through the dining room to the kitchen. The man in the Palm Beach suit and battered Panama hat was seated by the table reading a magazine. Without speaking to him Hicks headed for the back door and was halfway there when the man spoke:

"Hold it, son. Not an exit."

Hicks stopped. "Meaning?"

"You stay in the house."

"Seriously?"

"Yeah."

"For a nickel I'd test it."

The man shook his head gloomily. "It wouldn't do you any good. There's a bellboy out there. This time they brought everything but the bearded lady. Listen, I hate to bother you so often, but I've got a kid in high school—"

Hicks got out his wallet and extracted a card and handed it over.

"How would you like," Hicks asked, "to have a job slicing skunk cabbage? I think I can get you one."

"That is not a friendly remark," the man declared sadly.

"The hell it isn't. It's positively indulgent. Compared with taking orders from Manny Beck, slicing skunk cabbage would be paradise."

The man arose and stepped over to Hicks and shook hands, and went back and sat down again, without saying anything, either with his tongue or with his face.

Hicks left, mounted the back stairs, went to Heather's room, and sat down.

It was now, of course, not only necessary to leave the house, it was imperative. The two other outside doors he had not tried would unquestionably be guarded, and besides, they could be reached only through the living room. There were plenty of windows, but if troopers were stationed without, that was not feasible. Doubtless he could rush it, but in the hue and cry he might and he might not be able to get to the car in time to get away with Heather. He could go across the hall and poke Dundee's lawyer in the snoot, which would be a satisfaction and a pleasure, and force him to change clothes, but there was no way of changing faces.

A stratagem was needed.

He sat for ten minutes, muttered, "It'll have to do, I haven't got all night," arose and went downstairs to the side hall, confronted the man there and asked:

"Where's Miss Gladd? She's not upstairs. I want to see her if I've still got the right of free speech."

"She went outdoors."

Hicks looked startled. "She went where?"

"Outdoors."

"When?"

"Oh, an hour ago."

"Yeah. She said to call her if she was wanted. Do you want me to call her?"

"If you please."

The man went to the open window and spoke through it to the terrace:

"Al, call Miss Gladd. She's wanted."

There was a bellow outside: "Miss Gladd!" A pause. "Miss Gladd!" After a long pause the bellow swelled in volume. "Miss *Gladd!*"

Another wait, and the bellow was down to a rumble. "She don't answer. Shall I keep it up?"

"After a minute. She probably—hey!"

But Hicks was through the door and inside the living

room, and across to the table, his eyes blazing down angrily at Corbett's pudgy face.

"Haven't you," he demanded furiously, "had enough corpses around here? You and your damn army?"

"What—"

"What what what! They ought to put it on your tombstone! What! That super-simp ordering me arrested if I try to leave the house, and letting that girl out alone unprotected! Now find her! Try and find her! When you do, remember you mustn't move the body until the police arrive!"

"What girl?" Corbett's face had lost some color. "What the devil are you talking about?"

The man from the hall said, "Miss Gladd went outdoors, sir. About an hour ago, maybe a little more. There were no orders to confine anyone but Hicks. She said she'd be around close and to call her if she was wanted. Hicks said he wanted to see her and Al called her."

"Was that the yelling I heard just now?"

"Yes, sir."

"Did she answer?"

"No, sir."

"Find her," Hicks said witheringly, "and maybe you'll understand why she didn't answer. You ought to be up to that."

Corbett stood up. "Why are you so certain she has been attacked?"

"I'm not certain. I didn't do it. I've been in the house. But there have been two people killed here in two days, and one was her sister and the other her brother-in-law, and out she goes to wander around alone in the dark, and is that dumb? Will you kindly give me permission to borrow a flashlight and go out through a door? Or lock me in a closet and go yourself?"

"Shut your trap!" Manny Beck barked, striding across to the door to the hall. As he opened it the bellow came through from the terrace, "Miss Gla-a-a-dd!" Others followed him, including the district attorney. Mrs. Powell elbowed her way through them, muttering unintelligibly, and disappeared into the dining room. A man entered from the terrace and told Beck:

"She don't answer. Do you want me—"

"Phone to White Plains for a basket," Hicks said savagely.

"This is a hell of a note," Beck snarled.

Corbett said curtly, "Get everybody here. Get Lieutenant

Baker. Damn it, call them in here! If something has happened to that girl, with the whole damn barracks and the whole damn county . . ."

Men moved, including Hicks, but he did not join the general stream toward the terrace. Having noticed that the card collector, attracted by the commotion, had shuffled morosely in, Hicks went to the dining room and through to the kitchen. However, it was not empty. Mrs. Powell sat on the edge of a chair putting on rubbers. On the table beside her was a flashlight.

"You going out, Mrs. Powell?"

"I am," she said resolutely. "This is the biggest set of tomfools—"

"What are the rubbers for?"

"They're for dew."

"It's cloudy." Hicks was directly behind her, and, since she was bent over tugging at a rubber, she was quite unaware that he was acquiring the flashlight. "There isn't any dew." Four steps took him to the door, it opened with its creak, and he was outside.

He swung the beam of the light to right and left and picked up no one. Shouted commands from around the corner of the house made it evident that all forces were converging upon the side terrace to be organized into a searching party. Without even bothering to deploy to the rear of the garage, he struck off to the right, made his way through the collection of cars parked on the graveled space, found a gap in the hedge, and a little farther on ran smack into a patch of briars. He got around it without using the light, found himself among white birches which had not been trimmed to head height, and in another two minutes emerged from that into what he took to be an orchard, since round things that he stepped on proved to be apples. The shouts from the direction of the house were now much fainter, barely audible. He bore right, going at a good pace, with a hand guarding his face after he got a twig in the eye, and when he stumbled onto the stone fence which bordered the road he turned left and followed the fence. In a hundred paces suddenly there was no fence, and his hands found the bars that were the gate to the lane. He slipped through, went cautiously not to bump into the car . . .

But there was no car.

He stepped down the little incline to the road and back up again. This was a let-down. Could this be the wrong lane? From up the road he could hear voices raised; since they were at the Dundee house, the distance seemed about right. He proceeded to settle the point by switching on the light and flashing it around—yes, there was the curve, there was the bush at the right—and there, perched on the stone fence, was a man—no, a boy, gazing into the light.

"Hello," Hicks said, turning the light off and approaching the fence. "I didn't know you were there. What's your name?"

"My name's Tim Darby. Are you a dick?"

"I am not," Hicks said emphatically. He was close enough to the boy to see that he had eyes and a mouth. "My name's Al Hicks. How long have you been here? I mean sitting here."

"Oh, I've been here for a considerable time. You're not a cop, because you haven't got a uniform."

"No, I'm just a man. The reason I asked, I left my car here and now it's gone. Somebody must have stolen it, and I thought maybe you saw them. Did you see a car here?"

"Sure I saw a car here. I live right down the road."

"Did you see it go away?"

"Well, I—" That was as far as Tim got.

"You see," Hicks explained, "if I knew what time it was taken it might help. I wouldn't expect you to squeal on anyone. All I want is to get my car back."

"You're a liar," the boy said. "It's not your car, it's one of Dundee's cars. The Cadillac sixty-one. I've rode in it with Miss Gladd often and Ross too. And you're a double liar because your name's not Hicks!"

"Why isn't my name Hicks?"

"Because it isn't! You're not so smart. Because he couldn't—" Tim stopped abruptly.

"You're wrong, Tim," Hicks asserted. "I'm no more a liar than I am a dick or a cop. When I said it was my car I merely meant I was driving it. That's a manner of speaking. You know that. I drove that car here from New York this evening. Now about the name. I'm astonished that you call me a double liar when I say my name is Hicks, because you look pretty intelligent. This evening around eight o'clock you were with a bunch of people around a cop up at the Dundee entrance. Weren't you?"

"Yes, I was."

"Sure you were. I saw you. Didn't a man go up to that cop and say his name was Hicks?"

"Yes, he did."

"Wasn't that man me?"

"How can I tell? I can't see you."

"I *beg* your pardon." Hicks turned on the light and aimed it at his own face. "What about it? Am I that man?"

"Yes, you are."

"Well, do you think I was lying to the cop too, when I told him my name? Why would I do that?"

"I don't know." Tim sounded stubborn. "But—"

"But what?"

"I've got my reasons."

"I know you have. I knew you had reasons when you were so positive I was lying about my name. And I'll bet I know what they are."

"I'll bet you don't!"

"I'll bet I do. You're a friend of Miss Gladd, aren't you? Since you go riding with her?"

"I sure am."

"Okay, so am I. I'll bet she took that car, which of course she had a right to do. I'll bet she stopped at your house and asked you to come and stay here, and gave you a message for a man named Hicks when he showed up, and told you to be mighty careful not to give the message to anybody else. And that was your idea of being mighty careful, telling me I was a liar when I said my name was Hicks. Now you know my name is Hicks, so you can give me the message. Huh?"

"But you *sent* the message!" the boy blurted. "It was signed ABC, but she told Ross it was from Alphabet Hicks!"

On account of the dark, there was no necessity for Hicks to control his gape of surprise. It delayed his reply a second, however.

"You say," he demanded, "she told Ross that?"

"Sure she did! When she was telling him to get out of the car. She didn't want him to go with her."

"Tim, look here." Hicks put his hand on the boy's shoulder. "I'm not a liar, and I'm a friend of Miss Gladd's. Get that straight. Okay?"

"Okay. But—"

"No buts. Miss Gladd is in danger. I didn't send her any message. If she got a message signed ABC it was a fake. It was from someone who wants to hurt her, maybe kill her. How did she get the message? Who brought it to her?"

The boy had slid off the fence. "But gee, I don't—"

"Who brought it to her?"

151

"I did."

"Where did you get it?"

"Mom took it on the phone. He—you telephoned—"

"I did not telephone. It was a fake. What did he say?"

"He said she was to drive to Crescent Road and he was in a car parked half a mile beyond Crescent Farm. License JV 28."

"JV?"

"Yes. And Ross said—"

"Where was Ross?"

"He was sitting here in the car with her."

"How did you know she was here?"

"He said on the phone. He said she'd be here in the car and she was, only he didn't say anything about Ross, only Ross is all right. He said he didn't think it was from you."

"He was right. Did Ross go with her?"

"Sure. He wouldn't get out. He's nuts about her."

"How long ago did they leave?"

"Well, I must have sat—"

"About how long?"

"I guess it must have been about ten minutes before you came. Maybe fifteen."

"Where is Crescent Farm?"

"Over on Crescent Road. If you go straight on past Dundee's, you take the first right, about a mile and a half, and on through Post's Corners about two miles. There's a lot of barns and a big white chicken house, on the right."

"Is there a car at your house?"

"Yeah, but it's not there, my dad works nights. Only Aunt Sadie's car's there, she came over on account of the excitement. Listen, if this is a plot you don't need to worry Miss Gladd will get hurt, because Ross is with her and he'll fight like a tiger. He's strong. Once—"

"That's fine, but I'll go and see. Where's Aunt Sadie's car?"

"Over in the yard."

"Come along and show me."

"Sure."

As they went down the road Hicks explained:

"No matter how strong Ross is, Miss Gladd might get hurt. So I want to get there as quick as I can. Would Aunt Sadie let me use her car if I asked her? What's she like?"

"She's a pain in the neck. Boy, is she stingy! The only

152

way to do, we'll just get in the car and go. Gee, it's an emergency, isn't it?"

"It sure is. But you can't go, Tim. I'd love to have you, but it's against the law. You're a minor and I could be arrested and put in jail for kidnapping you. It's a crazy law, but that's it. We turn in here? Are they on the porch?"

"Naw, they're inside. Gee, I want to go!"

"I know you do and I want you to, but that's the law. Anyway, you'll have to explain who took the car and why, or if they hear it leaving they'll report it stolen. That'll take a lot of nerve. Have you got enough nerve to do that?"

"Sure I have. But—"

It took persuasion to get Tim to agree to stay behind, but, being by nature a reasonable man, he finally consented. He would wait until the car was safely out of the yard and on its way, and would then apprise his womenfolk of the situation.

Luckily the key was in the dash. Hicks got the engine started with as little noise as possible, told Tim he was proud of him and Miss Gladd would be too, eased the car softly down the drive to the road, and turned right.

That, the short way to Crescent Road, took him past the Dundee entrance, but he went right on by at a good clip without meeting any attempt at interference. Evidently Aunt Sadie took good care of her property, for the car, a small sedan, without any pretensions to grandeur, nevertheless ran like a dream. In three minutes he came to the first right, which he took, and in another three minutes a cluster of outbuildings, the largest one square and white, told him that he was passing Crescent Farm; so he slowed down.

He crept along, entering a wood, but saw no car. A mile. Two miles. Three miles. The wood was far behind. At a widening of the road he turned around and started back, keeping a sharp eye to either side; but in another five minutes he was back at the cluster of outbuildings and had certainly had no glimpse of a car, neither a JV 28 nor a Dundee Cadillac. In a smaller building, apart from the others, with trees around it, there was a light and a radio going, and he drove into the lane, got out, and walked across the yard to a door.

"Is this Crescent Farm?" he asked a man in overalls who came and peered through the screen at him.

"This is it, yes, sir. Mr. Humphrey's place is up the road. I'm Walt Taylor, the farmer. You looking for Mr. Humphrey?"

"No, I'm looking for a friend of mine. I thought maybe he stopped to use your phone. Has anybody asked to use your phone the past hour or so?"

The man shook his head. "Nope."

"I was expecting to find him parked down the road. Half a mile beyond Crescent Farm, he said. If you—"

"A big black sedan?"

"That's right. License JV 28."

"I didn't notice the license, but a big black sedan was parked there around five o'clock when I went by to get a load of hay, and it was still there an hour later when I came back with the load."

"It must have been him. What did he look like?"

"Didn't see him. Neither time. Just the car. I kept an eye out, because I figured maybe he was after pheasant, but I didn't hear any shot up to dark."

"Did you hear one after dark?"

"Nope. Not that I was expecting one. It's kind of hard to shoot pheasant when you can't see 'em."

"Have you noticed a car going by in the last half hour? Either direction?"

"No, I've been listening to the radio."

Hicks thanked him and left, went back to Aunt Sadie's car, and headed east. Arriving at the four corners, he pulled up at the side of the road, and sat scowling at the clock on the dash. His fingers, with no command from higher up, took a pack of cigarettes from his pocket and extracted one. Minutes later he was still sitting motionless, still scowling, and the cigarette had not been lit.

Twenty

THE DISPOSAL OF FORCES, AT THE INSTANT ROSS AND Heather caught sight of the man aiming the pistol at them, was like this:

The man stood at the front of the car, against the front bumper. Heather stood by the left running board, at the point where it joined the front fender; and Ross was directly behind her. The man with the pistol was saying:

"What do you want?"

Ross didn't hear him. That is, he didn't recognize the words as words, because he was in no condition to do so. It is possible, when a man aiming a gun at you is only five feet away and the space is clear, to leap for him; but it is foolhardy to try that when he is barricaded by the fender and hood of a large automobile. Certainly a coward wouldn't try it, or a prudent man, or one with any experience to speak of in situations of that kind. Therefore Ross proved that he belonged to none of those categories when he did in fact leap.

It was more a vault than a leap, for as he went up and forward his hand on Heather's shoulder forced her down and back, and he went scooting over the hood with a velocity suggesting a projectile hurled by an explosive rather than a man propelled only by muscle. It was so instantaneous and meteoric that the man with the gun had time for no movement, except the squeezing of the trigger, and that he failed to do. The impact toppled him over. Ross, tumbling by him and on him, grabbing with both hands wildly, got the gun with his right, wrenched it loose, and slammed it against the man's head. The man's knees jerked up and straightened out again, and he lay still.

The engagement had lasted perhaps five seconds.

Heather was there, saying something, but Ross was still not recognizing words. He scrambled to his feet, panting, looked at the gun in his hand, glistening in the glare from the headlights of the other car, started to tremble all over, and said in a loud voice:

"Holy smoke! I hit him with this!"

"He didn't shoot," Heather said. "He didn't, did he?"

"Shoot?" Ross stared at her. "Oh. No, he didn't shoot."

"I thought—I thought he was going to shoot."

"So did I."

"You certainly—went after him."

"I certainly did." Ross looked at the figure on the ground, still motionless. "I guess I hit him pretty hard. I never did anything like that before." He went down on one knee beside the figure. "Here, hold this, will you?"

155

Heather took the gun from him, and stood gazing down at him. In a moment he said:

"I can't feel any heartbeat."

Heather's teeth left her lip to let her say, "Feel his pulse."

Ross's hand went to the man's wrist. After a long silence he said uncertainly, "It feels pretty good to me. Will you see what you think?"

Heather didn't want to. If this was to be death again . . . a blow on the head had killed Martha . . . but she knew she had to. She had to because he had asked her to, and after the way he had jumped over the car straight at that gun . . . She squatted beside him, took the wrist he released to her, and felt for the spot. She couldn't find it; and it took her half a minute to realize that her own heart was beating so violently that it was out of the question to feel another pulse.

"It's all right," she lied.

"Good."

"It really is."

"Good. Let me see again."

She relinquished the wrist to him, arose, took two steps, and sat down on the bumper. In a moment Ross got up and came and sat beside her.

"My knees are wobbly," he said. "Gosh. Now I don't know what to do. I can't just leave him here. I expect he'll come to pretty soon, and then what am I going to do? Maybe I ought to take him to a hospital. Or maybe I ought to take him to the house and turn him over to that fathead district attorney. Darned if I know what to do."

Heather giggled; and, as Ross looked at her in surprise, she giggled again. She knew she was doing it, and was furious; but in spite of the desperate effort she made, she felt it coming once more, up to her throat; it was irresistible; and then suddenly Ross's arms were tight around her, and the last giggle never got out because his lips were against hers, allowing it no avenue of escape, and it was no longer even in her throat, there were no more giggles in her. . . .

She pulled away, pushed him away, and said indignantly:

"I couldn't help it, it was funny. I don't exactly mean it was funny, but your worrying like that about what to do, after you were so brave. I admit you were brave, but you being brave and me being hysterical is no reason for you to do that."

"You mean kissing you?"

"Yes."

"That wasn't why I kissed you. Of course I always want to kiss you, there's never any time I don't, but the reason now was I was having a thought about you and I didn't like it. And I guess I've got to ask you about it, and I don't want to but I've got to."

"A thought about me?"

"Yes. You and Vail."

"Vail?"

"Yes." Their eyes were meeting. "How long have you known him?"

"I never have known him. I don't know him at all. I suppose you mean the Republic Products Vail, but I don't know any Vail. But I want to know why you ask that, because Mr. Hicks asked me the same thing. He asked if I or my sister knew him."

"And you don't?"

"I've never seen him."

"You've seen him now. That's him there."

"That? That—"

"That's Jimmie Vail, head of Republic Products. And I may be dense, but at least I can ask questions, even if I don't know how to get the answers to them. What's Vail doing here? With a gun ready for whoever shows up? And that sonograph plate. Why do you say it was your sister's voice? And why did my mother—but you don't know anything about that. And why did Hicks send you a message to come here to meet Vail? You think Hicks is your friend. Does that look like it?"

"He didn't send me that message."

"No? Who did?"

"I don't know." Heather's heart was quieting down and she was beginning to feel that she had a mind again, though its contents were more of a bewildering jumble than ever. "I don't know anything about anything. But if Vail was here hiding behind the car, waiting with a gun, he might have—"

She stopped abruptly, staring at the thing in her hand. A shiver ran over her. "It may have been this—he shot George with—" Her fingers went loose and the gun dropped to the ground.

Ross stooped and got it and slipped it into his pocket.

"They can tell that. You were saying, Vail might have what?"

"He might have sent me that message himself."

"By short wave?"

"He could have phoned from anywhere. From Crescent Farm."

"And how did he know you were sitting there in the car waiting for Hicks?"

"I don't know." Heather frowned. "It's all crazy. Utterly crazy! And so am I. Anyhow, I was wrong. I mean when I told you to get out of the car and let me come alone and you wouldn't. I mean I ought to be decent about it, and just tell you—I'm glad you came. It's just decent to say that."

"Aw, that's all right. Forget it. But that message—"

Ross stopped himself, at a groan from the figure on the ground, and a movement. They both stood up. Another groan came, considerably louder, and more movement, and as Ross took a step James Vail got himself lifted to an elbow, and then, with his other hand braced on the ground, was sitting. He sat and blinked, with the light right into his face, and groaned again.

Ross said, "Maybe you'd better take it easy."

"Who are you?" Vail croaked.

"I'm Ross Dundee."

"What? Who?"

"Ross Dundee."

"Dick Dundee's boy?"

"Yes."

"How the hell did you get here?"

"I drove here in a car with Miss Gladd. Heather Gladd. She came as soon as she got your message."

"What message?"

"The message you sent her on the phone."

"I sent no message to anyone."

Heather put in sharply, "He was playing possum. He's been lying there listening to us. The way he talks. His head's clear."

"Why the hell shouldn't my head be clear?" Vail demanded. "What happened?"

"Because I hit you," Ross said. "When we came you popped up from in front of your car and pointed a gun at Miss Gladd. I jumped you and took your gun and hit you with it, and you passed out. At least we thought you did. If

158

you didn't, you don't need this explanation, but you're welcome anyhow."

Vail's only reply was a grunt. He shifted his weight to his right hand, propped on the ground, and put his left to his head and felt of it, above the ear. He moved his head from right to left, grunted, forward and back, grunted again, then got onto his hands and knees, pushed himself up, and was on his feet. He felt of his head again, pivoted it slowly to one side and the other, took a trial step, and another. . . .

"Better hold it," Ross said crisply. "I've got your gun. If you get near the edge of the light I'll start shooting at your legs, and I'm not much of a shot."

"You're a jackass." Vail turned to face him. "You're as big an idiot as your father. That message. I didn't send it. What did it say?"

"Don't tell him," Heather said. "Don't tell him anything. Make him tell you things."

"Make him tell me what?" Ross kept his eyes on Vail and his hand in his pocket. "Anyway he's a dirty liar and we couldn't believe anything he said. We won't get anywhere chewing the rag with him. We've got to take him somewhere. We've got to do something with him. I think we've got to go back to the house with him, I don't know what else to do. And the police can take this gun and test it, and if it's the one Cooper was shot with it won't do him any good to try to lie—"

"What's that?" Vail demanded. "Who was shot?"

"Cooper."

"Cooper shot?"

"Yes. If you think—"

"Where? When?"

"Don't tell him," Heather insisted. "Don't tell him anything. The thing to do would be to take him to Hicks, only we don't know where Hicks is."

"We certainly don't," Ross agreed. "Wherever he sent that message from—"

"He never sent that message! If he had he would have been here! If anything had happened—oh!" Heather stopped short.

"I forgot," she said. "I know what I'm going to do. What he told me." Her tone was resolute. "I'm going to see Mrs. Dundee."

"Mrs. Dundee? You mean my mother?"

"Yes."

Ross was gaping at her. "Hicks told you to go to see my mother?"

"Yes, and I'm going to. I won't go back to that house again, anyway. If you want to take him there you can, but I'm not. You can take him in his car."

Vail took a step toward them.

"Hold it," Ross said warningly, as if he meant it.

"I have no intention," Vail said contemptuously, "of inviting bullets in my legs. You children are fantastic. Absolutely fantastic. Discussing what you're going to do with me. I can assure you, the decision involves considerations that you know nothing about. If we go to the police, they'll want an explanation of my presence in this neighborhood at this time, and they'll get it, and it won't be me who will suffer for it. If I'm brought into this, and forced to tell the police what I know, for my own protection, I can't be blamed for what happens to the Dundee family and business."

"Don't believe him," Heather said. "He's putting on an act."

"Are you suggesting," Ross asked sarcastically, "that I hand you back your gun with a God bless you and just forget this little encounter?"

"Not at all. I don't care what you do with the gun, except that it's my property and I want it returned some time. What I suggest is that we go with Miss Gladd to see your mother. It is she who needs and deserves an explanation, and who should decide what is going to be done."

"You mean—" Ross stared at him. "You have the gall to say that you want to explain to my mother?"

"I say that, my boy. It can be left to your mother whether it is an exhibition of gall."

"Take him up," Heather said.

"He's stalling," Ross declared. "He doesn't want to go to the police."

"You're an imbecile," Vail asserted.

Ross regarded him. "Okay," he said finally. His hand came out of his pocket with the gun in it. "You and I will go in your car and you'll drive. Miss Gladd will follow us in the other car. If you try any monkey business. . . ."

"I'll stay right behind," Heather said. "But you'll have to be careful. No matter what he does, you can't shoot him while he's driving. If you shoot him while he's driving, the car might—"

"You don't necessarily," Ross said indignantly, "have to consider me an imbecile just because he called me one. And you'd better try to drive a little better than you did on the way here."

Twenty-one

MARGIE HART HAD DETERMINED, COME WHAT MIGHT, TO hold fast. First, there was loyalty. She had worked for Mrs. Dundee for over twenty years, and was quite convinced that should she die or quit, Mrs. Dundee would be utterly helpless, starving and clothed in rags, within a matter of weeks or even days. Second, there was her pay, which, thanks to an uninterrupted series of annual raises, was now stupendous. Third, there was her curiosity. The scenes recently overheard by her between Mr. and Mrs., the murder, actual murder, at that place in Katonah which she had never seen, the visits and questionings by real detectives in that very apartment—it was an earthquake, a cosmic spasm, a nightmare. Anything could happen. The whole shooting match might be arrested and thrown into jail. She herself might be drawn into the pitiless glare of a murder trial. It was a horrible and fascinating prospect.

But she wasn't sleeping well, partly because she knew Mrs. wasn't, and partly because of the feeling she had that the next development would be that Mr. would come in the night, letting himself in with his key, and kill Mrs. She derided herself for having the feeling, since it was completely unjustified and unreasonable, but she had it; and because she did, she heard, in her half sleep, the front door of the apartment open and close at twenty minutes past midnight. For a second she was rigid under the sheet, unable to move; here it was, here he was, he had come to do it; her heart stopped beating; then she was out and up, clicking the light, grabbing her dressing gown, flying from the room, down the service hall, through the kitchen, dining room, living room, into the reception hall. . . .

"Well!" she cried indignantly.

"Hello, Margie. Is Mother up?"

"This is unseemly," Margie said, showing how flustered she was, for she had not used that phrase to Ross since the far-off days when she had taken him to Central Park. She glared at Ross, at the young woman behind him whom she didn't know, at the man beside him whom she did know . . . but Mr. James Vail wasn't welcome at this apartment any more. . . .

"Your mother's in bed," she said shortly.

"I've got to see her. Tell her I'm here. Will you, please?"

Margie turned and marched out. Ross ushered the other two into the living room, turned on lights, gave them seats, seated himself, and then got up again to help Heather when she started to rid herself of the long dark coat. Though the coat certainly had no aspirations to elegance, he handled it as if it had been chinchilla as he draped it over the back of a chair. A voice from the doorway turned him:

"Ross, my child? You devil of a child!"

He crossed to meet his mother, took her hands, put his hands on her shoulders, looked at her face, and kissed her on the cheek.

"I always forget how big you are," she said. She squeezed his arm and released it. "I was expecting you. That is, I was expecting Miss Gladd, with you probably escorting her. I suppose this is Miss—what—what's the matter?"

Approaching Heather, she halted to stare. Heather was herself staring, her mouth open, her eyes wide with stupefaction and incredulity—the frozen gaze that a ghost might expect to be met with, but not a comely matron in a yellow house gown from Hattie Carnegie. Ross, seeing it, stared too and demanded:

"What is it? What's the matter?"

"Her voice—" Heather stammered.

"My voice? What's the matter with my voice?"

"My dear Judith." It was James Vail, out of his chair. "This was bound to happen sooner or later. Miss Gladd is speechless with astonishment because of the remarkable resemblance of your voice to that of her sister. You can judge of how remarkable the resemblance must be by the shock it gave her. Isn't that true, Miss Gladd? It is an amazing resemblance, isn't it?"

Heather nodded. "I can't—it's unbelievable—"

Judith was frowning at her. "You mean my voice is like your sister's?"

"Exactly like! If I shut my eyes—it's incredible!"

"Then that's why!" Ross said excitedly. "Heather! That's why! About that sonograph plate! You thought it was your sister's voice and I thought it was Mother's!" He stared at his mother, and suddenly seized her arm. "By God! That's why I thought you were out there! I heard her talking and thought it was you!" He pumped the arm up and down. "And it wasn't your voice on that sonograph plate at all! It was Heather's sister! It wasn't you talking with Vail, it was her! It was Heather's sister who—"

He stopped.

He looked at Heather, stunned, incredulous.

"My God," he said in a wilted voice.

"Precisely." Vail said in a dry harsh tone.

Ross confronted him. "You can go to hell, you. I've knocked you cold once and if you want some more—"

Judith spoke incisively: "Behave yourself, Ross. If you mean the sonotel record—"

"You know nothing about it, Mother. If you heard it—"

"I have heard it. Mr. Hicks kindly brought it—"

"Hicks? For God's sake! When?"

"No matter when. I've heard it. And if it was Miss Gladd's sister having that conversation with Vail—"

"My sister never had any conversation with Vail!" Heather put in. "She never knew him! She never heard of him!"

"Didn't you hear that plate?" Ross demanded.

"No! I only heard the first few words of it! And if it was a conversation with Vail it must have been your mother—"

"Please," Judith Dundee interposed. "You children know less than I do about it, and certainly less than Vail. His conversation on that plate wasn't with me, because it wasn't. And it wasn't with Miss Gladd's sister, because he called the lady Judith."

"Are you suggesting," Vail inquired dryly, "that by a double freak of nature there is a third lady, not only with the same voice, but named Judith?"

"No. I'm not suggesting anything." Mrs. Dundee surveyed him stonily. "I have nothing to suggest, and if I had I wouldn't waste my breath on you." She walked to the divan, sat beside Heather, and reached for the girl's hand. "My dear, I am ashamed of myself. I knew there was a girl out there at my husband's place who was having it hard, and if I had been human I would have gone to you. I wasn't having it any too easy myself, but that's all the more reason, and anyway I'm twice your age. Now we'll stick it out together. Won't we?"

"I think," Heather said shakily, "I'm going to throw my arms around you and kiss you. Your voice—you have no idea, Mrs. Dundee—"

"Indeed I haven't. You poor kid. I have no idea about anything, but I think that man Hicks has. His voice sounded like it—"

"Hicks?" Ross demanded in astonishment.

"Yes. That's why I was expecting Miss Gladd. He phoned and said she would probably come here because he had told her to—"

"When did he phone?"

"An hour ago. More. He should be here any minute." Mrs. Dundee took Heather's hand again. "My dear, he told me what happened today—your being there and hearing the shot and finding your brother-in-law dead—and I think you're amazing. A child your age! I expected you to look like a hard-boiled female sergeant, and here you're as lovely as a dream! I'm bitterly ashamed—"

"Do I understand," Vail interrupted, "that Hicks is on his way here?"

"Yes."

"Is Dick with him?"

"No."

"I'm glad of that. I came here, Judith, to give you an explanation of this business, at least what I know of it—"

"I don't care to hear it." Mrs. Dundee didn't look at him. "I don't even ask how you came to arrive here with my son and Miss Gladd. The whole thing is so utterly incomprehensible that I have ceased to pretend I have a mind capable of functioning. I wasn't even surprised when I entered and saw you here. I am no longer capable of surprise. Apparently my son has knocked you cold, as he expressed it. When or on what provocation I have no idea. If you have an explanation to give you can give it to Mr. Hicks—"

A buzzer sounded.

Ross went to answer it. Vail scowled at the young man's receding back, stuck his thumbs in his vest pockets, straightened himself, and breathed deeply and audibly. Voices sounded in the hall, and a door closed, and in a moment Hicks entered, followed by Ross. As Hicks crossed to the divan a glance was all he had for Vail; a corner of his wide mobile mouth curved upward as he saw that Judith and Heather, sitting, were hand in hand.

"You were right about her," Judith said. "She came all right."

"Sure she did." Hicks patted Heather's knee. "Good girl."

"What happened to you?" Heather demanded. "I got a message—"

"I know you did. We'll get around to that." Hicks seated himself on the divan beside her and looked up at Vail, at Ross. "Sit down, everybody. Let's have a little talk."

Vail blurted aggressively, "I came here to—"

"To explain things?"

"Yes. To tell Mrs. Dundee—"

"Fine. Sit down and make yourself comfortable. I'd love to hear you explain things. Go right ahead."

Twenty-two

JAMES VAIL, AS WITH DELIBERATION HE TURNED A CHAIR to face the divan and sat on it, and leveled his gaze at Judith Dundee, was not a particularly prepossessing object. His visage, with the broad insensitive nose, the thin selfish mouth, and the cold shrewd eyes, had never been intended to excite admiration, even when, well-groomed and fed and rested, he moved in the congenial orbit of a top-flight business executive; and now, not too clean, not combed, not in any respect jaunty, with an enormous disfiguring lump on the side of his head above his left ear, he was simply ugly. Under the enveloping fat folds of his lids it was difficult to tell where his eyes were focused in that light, but as he leaned back and stuck his thumbs in his vest pockets it was Mrs. Dundee he spoke to.

"I want to assure you, Judith," he began, "that I am willing to do everything possible to limit the damage in this business, even at considerable risk—"

"You're not talking to me," she snapped. "Talk to Mr. Hicks."

"Oh, but I am talking to you. As you will see. I am willing to take considerable risk, but not to the extent of exposing myself to the danger of being arrested as an accessory to a murder. Two murders. So talking here to four of you, I shall have to be—uh—somewhat discreet regarding what I know and what I surmise. Some things I can tell you. Some I can't. But I can tell you enough to show you the vital necessity of a very careful and very rigorous discretion on the part of all of us."

Hicks grunted. "New paragraph. It's late."

Vail ignored him. "In the first place, I have known for over a year that Dick had a sonotel installed in my office. I knew it the day after he did it. No matter how. I am not a greenhorn in business, and I'm not a novice in the application of plastics to the science of sound recording. I amused myself by conveying to him some hints on formulas that I don't think he found very helpful. Dick was enraged by Republic's success, and he got so he was little better than a maniac. His suspicions that I was getting his formulas were completely unfounded, but it was no use talking to him."

"If you want to rest a minute," Hicks put in, "maybe I can go on with it. You went to a play and heard an actress with a voice exactly like Mrs. Dundee's, and decided to have some fun. You got the actress to come to your office and do a little dialogue with you for the sonotel—"

"No," Vail said. His eyes did not shift from Judith Dundee. "I can do this better without interruptions. I have to be a little cautious about it, for as I said, there is at least one risk I don't care to take. I hope I don't need to persuade you, Judith, that I would not regard it as fun to involve you in such a mess. The first I knew that you were involved was Thursday last week—a week ago yesterday. I got a phone call from Herman Brager, saying he wanted to see me. Naturally I was interested in such a call from the second-best plastic research man in the world, so I made an appointment and met him that evening. I was hoping that perhaps he was ready to quit Dundee. but quite the contrary. He was after my blood, figuratively speaking. He told me that Dick had a sonotel record from a machine picking up from my office, with a conversation between you and me, showing that I was getting Dundee formulas from you."

Judith, frowning, spoke. "Herman Brager told you that?"

"He did. I gathered that he—uh—admires you, a sentiment in which of course he has no monopoly. I gathered that, because he seemed to resent, not so much my getting his formulas, as my getting you involved. He had formed the same theory that Hicks here has advanced, that, knowing of the sonotel, I had found someone to imitate your voice and put on a performance, and he demanded that I should clear you by telling Dick the facts. I denied it, naturally, since it wasn't true. His admiration of you must be extreme, for I was impressed by his vehemence. If he were a man of violence, his being after my blood might not have been merely figurative."

Vail took a breath, audibly. "Well. Since there had been no such conversation between you and me, I concluded that although I had staged no performance, someone certainly had, with an imitation not only of your voice, but of mine also. I tell you frankly that my guess was that it had been done by Dick himself, because I couldn't imagine who else would have a motive for doing such a thing. Why Dick wanted to put it on you I had no idea, but there are many things between husbands and wives of which their friends have no idea—and, as I said, I was already convinced that Dick was little better than a maniac. Strictly speaking, I had every right to take a hand in the matter, since the fake sonotel record Brager told me of was a damaging attack on my business ethics, but I—"

Judith said, "You didn't mention it when I called at your office yesterday."

"I know I didn't. I hadn't seen or heard the record and didn't know where it was. It concerned more than business ethics and Dick's idiotic jealousy of me and my company; it also involved his relations with his research man and his wife. I didn't want to mix up in that. So I told you I knew nothing about it and there was nothing I could do.

"Not that I intended to drop it. It isn't my habit to drop things that affect my interest, business or personal. I would certainly have done my best to get hold of that record with a voice on it supposed to be mine. I did in fact take certain steps. But a different face was put on the matter when I read in the paper this morning that a beautiful young woman had been murdered at the Dundee place at Katonah. It seemed to me there were three possibilities. It might have nothing to do with Dick or you. Or it might have been the woman who had imitated your voice and she had tried blackmail. Or it might have been the woman for whose sake Dick was framing a case against you—"

"My sister never knew Mr. Dundee!" Heather cried. "And she had only just got back—"

She stopped when Hicks squeezed her arm. "Let him finish," Hicks said. "He's doing a swell job."

Vail paid no attention. "As I say, there were those possibilities. At any rate, I intended to find out if I was likely to be involved, however indirectly, in anything as unsavory as a murder. When this man Hicks called at my office yesterday to try some kind of a trick with my help, I had foolishly ordered him out. This morning I made inquiries about him and decided to go to see him. While I was there George Cooper came in—I recognized him, of course, from his picture in the paper—and demanded that Hicks tell him the whereabouts of a phonograph record with his wife's voice on it! Not only that, he repeated the first words of the record, and they were the same as those which Brager had told me began the sonotel record of the conversation between you and me! Hicks denied any knowledge of such a record, and Cooper left."

"And then you left by request," Hicks muttered.

Vail ignored him. "So I knew beyond question that the murdered woman was the one who had imitated your voice, and undoubtedly her murder was connected with that fact. Since an imitation of my own voice was recorded along with hers, it was up to me to do something. My first impulse was to go to the police, and I drove to White Plains. On the way there I decided it would be desirable to see what I could find out before going to the police, and with that in mind I intended to phone Brager and arrange to have a talk with him if possible, when by a stroke of luck I ran into him on Main Street in White Plains."

Vail stirred in his chair, paused, appeared to hesitate, and then went on. "I'm being careful here. I'm telling this to four of you. I had a long talk with Brager, and found that his opinion of the matter roughly coincided with mine. He didn't know where the sonotel record was, but suspected that Ross Dundee had sneaked it out of his father's office to protect you. The first thing to do was to get hold of that record, and since Cooper had evidently heard it, he was the man to go for. He had left Hicks's place with the expressed intention of going to Katonah. Brager being completely ineffectual outside of a laboratory, and not wishing to put in an appearance at Katonah myself, we arranged that Brager should return there, get Cooper aside, and persuade him to go to meet me at a spot not far off. Brager decided on the spot, a secluded roadside beyond a place called Crescent Farm. He left to return to Katonah, and I drove to the spot, arriving a little before five o'clock. I waited there, keeping out of sight, for nearly six hours, having no idea, naturally, what was happening. I got damned impatient, and I got suspicious. When it fell dark I got a pistol that I carry in my dash compartment and put it in my pocket. When a car approached, which happened only twice on the deserted road, I concealed myself—after all, the woman whose voice was on that record with what was supposed to be my voice had been murdered. Finally a car came from the direction I expected, and stopped just behind my car. I crouched in front of the hood, and when their footsteps came up alongside my car, I stood up with the pistol in my hand. One of them came at me right over the car, and the next thing I knew I was on the ground with my head buzzing."

Ross said to his mother, "That's when I knocked him cold. I grabbed the gun and beaned him with it."

"D'Artagnan," Hicks grunted. "Where's the gun?"

"Right here." Ross took it from his pocket.

"Let me see it."

Ross hesitated.

"Don't be silly," his mother told him. "Give it to him. Is it loaded?"

"I don't know, I didn't look."

Hicks did look. "It is," he announced. He put the muzzle to his nose and sniffed several times, then slipped the pistol into his pocket. "People who jump over cars at men with guns," he stated, "are too brave for this world, so they usually get sent to another one. Continue the explanation, Vail. It's fascinating."

Vail spoke as before to Mrs. Dundee. "So far, Judith, I have told you facts. I have not gone into theory. But I ought to, I'll have to, to make you understand what I meant when I spoke of the vital necessity of a very careful and very rigorous discretion. Only before I do that I need some information myself. Doubtless Hicks can give it to me."

"It's yours for the asking," Hicks declared. "What, for instance?"

"First about Cooper. He was shot?"

Hicks nodded. "While you were waiting there on the road for him but keeping yourself concealed. At six thirty-five Brager and Miss Gladd were in the office of the laboratory and heard a shot. They went outdoors and found Cooper with a hole in his temple, dead. Brager thought he heard movement in the woods, but saw no one."

"Where were the rest of you?"

"Mrs. Dundee was in New York. So was I. Father and son were around the place somewhere. Outdoors."

"Together?"

"No."

"Then . . ." Dundee paused, and shook his head. "Where is that sonotel record?"

"Safe."

"In whose possession?"

"If I say it's safe. whose do you think? Mine."

"Good," Vail said approvingly. "I was afraid the police had it. Did you get it from young Dundee?"

"I got it by a combination of ingenuity, intrepidity, and dumb luck. From whom or where is for the present my business."

"It doesn't matter so long as you have it. I was afraid the police had got hold of it. Another item of information I need, Miss Gladd seems to have received a message that took her to the place where I was waiting. She seems to think I sent it, but young Dundee seems to think you did. Did you?"

"No."

"Who did?"

"That's a question," Hicks said judiciously. "Miss Gladd and I conversed in her room and agreed to sneak out of the house separately and meet down the road where I had a car. While she was sitting in the car with Ross, who was apparently already in training for the role of D'Artagnan, a boy came with a message that had been phoned to his home, which was near by. It was signed ABC, meaning me, I suppose, and told her to drive to a certain spot and find me in a car with the license JV 28."

"Ah," Vail said.

"Right. Ah."

The fat folds of Vail's lids were leaving him no eyes at all. He murmured, "The message was phoned to a near-by house."

"Correct. You may have time out to reflect on that if you—"

"I don't need to reflect. The conclusion is obvious. You didn't send the message, if for no other reason, because you didn't know I was there in that car. I couldn't have sent it, because I didn't know where Miss Gladd was. Who did know where she was besides you? You say you conversed with her in her room. Could Brager have overheard you?"

"Brager?" Hicks's eyes glittered. "Now you're putting on speed. I didn't see that one go by. Why Brager?"

"Could he have overheard you?"

"Well—his room is next to Miss Gladd's, but there's a wall between them and we kept our voices down."

"Bah," Vail said contemptuously. "Brager probably has that house wired like a central for experimental purposes, and a sonotel mike the size of a prayer book will pick up a whisper at twenty feet. Unquestionably he heard you, and he telephoned the message."

"Say he did." Hicks's brow was creased. "For the sake of the argument. I still can't see you. What put that playful idea into his head?"

"I don't know, but it isn't hard to guess. A double motive, I should say. Cooper was dead. Brager thought I might possibly get from Miss Gladd the information I had hoped to get from Cooper; and he wanted to be sure Miss Gladd got away, not only from that place but also from Dundee—and from you who were in Dundee's pay. He knew she was in danger, because she was dangerous. She might at any moment, by any chance, meet Mrs. Dundee and hear her voice, and that could not be permited to happen."

"Oho!" Hicks ejaculated. "Now I get you! Brager and I would make a good team. The same thought struck me."

"Do you mean," Mrs. Dundee demanded, "that Brager wanted to get her out of reach of my husband? Of Dick?"

"I do," Vail asserted. "Dick was desperate because he was in deadly peril. If anyone learned of the amazing resemblance between your voice and Martha Cooper's—if the police ever got that tip and got started on that trail—they were sure to get him for the murder of Mrs. Cooper and her husband. And they still are. That's what I'm here to tell you. They still are!"

Twenty-three

THE REACTION TO VAIL'S STARTLING PRONOUNCEMENT, while not violent, was noticeable. Heather gripped Hicks's arm and stared at his face inquiringly. Ross stood up and uttered a word not in common use in the presence of women. Judith gazed directly at Vail, if not in complete disbelief, in scornful incertitude.

"Nonsense," she said sharply. "Dick might have trumped up something against me. I've refused to believe it, but I admit it's possible. But he did not murder—"

"Please!" Hicks said peremptorily. He was cocking an eye at Vail, his head sidewise. "This is really a very fine theory. Beautiful! As I understand it, Dundee prepares to explode a mine under his wife by concocting this phony sonotel record. No sooner does he touch it off than the whole scheme is endangered by the unexpected return of Martha Cooper from abroad. Ross has heard the record. If he meets Martha Cooper and hears her speak, with a voice so amazingly like his mother's, he is bound to smell a rat; and there is Martha, right there on the place. So Dundee seizes a lucky opportunity and kills her."

"Bosh!" Judith said incisively.

"No, no," Hicks protested. "Not bosh at all, as a theory. Dundee having acted impulsively and impetuously, which is in character, finds upon reflection that he is still in a hole and even a deeper one. He not only reflects, he probably hears things. With wires and sonotels and God knows what all over that house, he almost certainly hears things. He may have heard Ross and Miss Gladd discussing that sonograph plate. He may have met Cooper and talked with him when Cooper went there this afternoon. He knows that his wife may show up out there at any moment, especially since she has heard the sonotel record, and he knows I have the record. At any rate, as Vail has said, he knows that if either Cooper or Miss Gladd meets his wife and hears her speak, he is in for it. So he kills Cooper."

"This is absolute—" Judith began.

"Don't do that," Hicks told her. "We're working on Vail's theory, and it's a beaut. It's the only one that fits the known facts. Vail is intelligent enough to realize that. He also realizes that if we all keep our mouths shut, if we give the police no hint of all this shenanigan about the sonotel record, Dundee is safe. They'll never even seriously suspect him, let alone hang it on him. Isn't that it, Vail?"

"Certainly. It's obvious—"

"It sure is. I never saw anything obviouser." Hicks glanced around, and back at Vail. "But I don't know if you can make it unanimous. Ross won't blab, not caring to see his father convicted of murder. Mrs. Dundee won't. Of course I won't, because I'm getting paid. You won't, for friendship's sake. Your old pal, Dick Dundee. But I don't know about Miss Gladd. How are we going to silence her?"

Heather and Judith spoke at once:

"If you mean you believe—"

"That's utterly ridiculous—"

"Please, ladies! Never get mad at a theory! Have I stated the situation correctly, Vail?"

"You have."

"And you sort of rely on us to bring Miss Gladd into line?"

"I rely on no one. I merely present the problem. I admit that I wouldn't like to have all this gone over in a courtroom, but the Dundees stand to lose a good deal more than I do. Maybe you do too, I don't know."

"I do indeed," Hicks agreed heartily. "Therefore I'm going to poke around in the ashes before I commit myself. You can't object to that."

"I'm not objecting to anything."

"Good. Then take that sonotel record. The theory is that Dundee faked it by using Martha Cooper for Mrs. Dundee's voice, and getting someone to imitate yours. You seem to have read the paper this morning, so you must know that

Martha Cooper went to Europe with her husband nearly a year ago and only came back Monday. So please tell me how Dundee used her when he faked that record."

"I don't pretend to know exactly when and where it was done."

"I know you don't. But theoretically?"

"It could have been done before she left."

"A year ago?" Hicks's brows went up. "He kept it around a whole year before he decided to use it? That's possible, of course, but I don't like it. It's not neat. I'd like to suggest an alternative." He turned to Heather. "Your sister visited you at Katonah a couple of times before she went to Europe, didn't she?"

"Yes," Heather said. "I told you."

"And there was a sonotel installed in that house at the time, for experiments?"

"Yes."

"Did your sister come by train, or did she drive?"

"She drove. She had a little convertible—"

"And might she not, on one of those visits, have said something like this to you? Quote: 'Good lord, let me sit down and gasp a while! I know I'm late, but I had an awful time getting here. I never saw such traffic.' Unquote. Might she not have said that to you?"

"Yes. She might." Heather was frowning. "I think I re-member—I'm not sure. Of course she might."

"Might is good enough. For that, but not for this. This is more important. Did she, on either occasion, bring you some-thing? Some kind of a gift?"

"A gift?" Heather looked blank. Then suddenly her face lit up. "Oh, of course! A dress! My tan—" Her eyes went down. "I have it on! She brought me this dress!"

"That's a nice little coincidence." Hicks patted the dress where it curved over her knee. "Nice dress. Then of course it was natural that she should say that she hoped you'd be pleased with what she had brought you. Did she say that?"

"I suppose she did. Of course."

Hicks nodded, and turned to Vail. "So there you are. That's on that record, Martha Cooper saying that she hoped the person she was talking to would be pleased with what she had brought. That's about all she does say of any sig-nificance. Most of the material items of the conversation— for instance, a reference to carbotene—are in your voice—I mean the imitation of your voice. So I suggest this. The

174

sonotel records from that machine installed experimentally in the house at Katonah were sent to Dundee. Among them were some of the conversations between Miss Gladd and her sister, and the remarkable resemblance of the sister's voice to that of his wife was of course noted by Dundee. He got—no matter when, possibly only recently—the notion of faking a record. He found someone to imitate your voice, and for his wife's part of it he used selected items from the records he had in Martha Cooper's voice. He knew, undoubtedly, that Martha Cooper was in Europe, or he wouldn't have risked it. What do you think of it?"

Vail emitted a noncommittal grunt.

"You don't like it?"

"It's ingenious," Vail admitted. "But it seems unnecessarily devious."

"On the contrary. It's far more plausible than your suggestion that Dundee faked the record nearly a year ago and kept it all that time before using it. As you know, he's an impetuous man. What I want to know, is it technically possible? Could a sonotel record be faked by using—only for parts of it—scraps from other records?"

"Certainly. Any good technician could do it."

"Fine." Hicks looked pleased. "That settles that detail. That was the chief thing that bothered me, though there are one or two other little points—"

Judith cut in, "This is perfectly absurd! I don't believe it and I never will believe it."

"Nobody expects you to," Hicks told her. "We are theorizing."

"Then why go on with this crazy—"

"We go on because it's interesting. Very interesting. Also because I'm expecting a phone call from District Attorney Corbett and this is as good a way to pass the time as any. Better than any. I don't believe you appreciate the exceptional beauty of Vail's theory, especially since we've established the possibility that the sonotel record was faked by using another record or records of Martha Cooper's voice. It will stand more wear and tear than any other theory I've ever met. Say, for instance, that your husband could prove, somehow or other, no matter how, that he didn't fake that record, and he didn't kill Martha Cooper, and he didn't kill George Cooper. Under such a blow as that most theories would totally collapse, but not this one. It would remain intact. All you would have to do would be to substitute someone else as the murderer, either your son or Vail himself."

Ross, scowling, blurted truculently, "Look here—"

Hicks waved him away. "Forget it, son. I'm not going to pick on a tough baby like you, leaping over cars at armed men. I'll use Vail instead, to show what I mean. If you don't object?"

A corner of Vail's thin mouth had a twist to it. "It seems to me that we're not here to pass the time. You say you are expecting a call from the district attorney. I want to say, I must warn you, all of you, that if my name is dragged into this, if I am brought into this in any way, I shall be compelled to give the authorities the whole story. Omitting nothing."

"Sure," Hicks agreed. "We understand that." He went back to Mrs. Dundee: "To show you about that theory. Let's say Vail faked that record and did the murders, for example. You'd hardly have to change a thing, only a few details. Why did he fake the record? To lead suspicion away from the individual in the Dundee organization—a confidential secretary or assistant—from whom he had been getting the Dundee formulas. How did he fake the record? The confidential secretary noticed that among the experimental records from Katonah were some with a voice exactly like Mrs. Dundee's, and that gave him the idea, which he passed on to Vail. They didn't even have to find someone to imitate Vail's voice, Vail did that part himself. In that detail, at least, it's an improvement on Vail's original theory. How did they plant the fake record? Simple. The confidential secretary merely inserted it in the case of records that had been delivered to Dundee by the detective agency as coming from Vail's office."

Vail stood up. "If this is a display of virtuosity—" he began contemptuously.

"Sit down," Hicks said.

"I don't intend—"

"I said sit down! If Ross could knock you cold, all alone, and you with a gun, you can imagine what we could do if we went at it together. I listened to you expounding your theory, and as a matter of courtesy you can listen to my variation. When that phone call comes I'll get practical. Good God, look at you. Do you want an ice bag for that bump?"

Vail, not replying, went back to his chair. His gaze, presumably, was fixed on Hicks; there was no way of telling. Hicks resumed to Judith:

"Last Monday, Monday morning, Vail got bad news. He saw in the paper that Mr. and Mrs. George Cooper had returned from Europe. That was awful, since the trap had already been baited and Dundee had taken the bait. If Dundee or his son met Martha Cooper, as they well might, since her sister worked for them, their suspicion would be aroused and the whole thing would certainly be exposed, and both Vail's business and his reputation would be ruined. From there on my variation pretty well follows the original. Vail, who has plenty of sand and daring, not only proceeded to remove Martha Cooper, he did it at a place and in a way to throw suspicion on the Dundees. And this afternoon, at my room, he learned that Cooper knew about that sonotel record and had actually heard it, or part of it, and intended to investigate it. Of course that wouldn't do. Cooper had announced that he was going to Katonah, so Vail went there too. From where he left his car on that deserted road, it's only a fifteen-minute walk, cross-country, mostly woods, to the Dundee place. No doubt his report of his conversations with Brager is true to fact—it must be, since he is expecting Brager to corroborate it. So after he shot Cooper he went back to his car and waited there, ostensibly, for Brager to send Cooper to him."

"You know," Vail said quietly, "this is interesting. But I'm wondering why you're wasting time with it, or even passing time, because you certainly haven't given it much thought. For instance, Martha Cooper. According to the account in the paper, she was killed between three and four o'clock. From three to six yesterday afternoon I was in my factory in Bridgeport. That of course would make it difficult—"

A bell rang.

Everybody jerked around. Hicks arose, saw that Ross too was up and crossing to a cabinet against the far wall, and was there at the young man's elbow as he swung out a phone bracket and lifted the receiver. Ross spoke into the phone, turned and said, "For you," and handed it to Hicks.

If Vail, or anyone, expected any elucidation from Hicks's end of the conversation, they were disappointed. It was brief, and his contribution was chiefly a series of yesses. At the end he said, "We'll start right away," replaced the instrument, and turned to the group:

"Okay, folks. We're all set. Off for Katonah."

They looked at him in astonishment. Then they all spoke at once, but Vail's voice dominated:

"I warn you, all of you! This man's a fool! Get Dick here! I'll have it out with Dick face to face! Judith! Ross! I warn you—let go of me, damn you!"

Hicks had his arm. "Listen, brother," Hicks said grimly. "Your warning days are over. We're going to Katonah and that includes you. On the hoof or in a package?"

Twenty-four

AT A QUARTER TO THREE IN THE MORNING ALL LIGHTS WERE on in the office of the Dundee laboratory, at the apex of the meadow triangle surrounded by woods. The night was sultry and oppressive, not a foretaste of the frosty month to come, but rather a left-over from the one supposed to have departed weeks ago; and the cricket and katydid concert, entering through the open windows, was desultory and disheartened, irritating to weary and nervous ears in its feeble stridency. No less irritating to tired and nervous eyes was the glancing of the lights off the slick surfaces of the pink desk and the purple one, the gray and yellow table, the chairs and various gadgets in all conceivable colors.

The only person in the room who was manifestly not sharing in the general atmosphere of fatigue and tenseness and vexation of spirit was the man in the Palm Beach suit and battered Panama hat, who was on a chair in a corner with his head resting against the wall, fast asleep. At the other extreme was Manny Beck, chief of the Westchester County detectives, who was striding up and down, glaring at every one implacably, his massive jaw fixed in a forward thrust of obdurate pugnacity; and three state policemen and a couple of men in plain clothes were keeping out of his path.

James Vail, Ross Dundee, and Herman Brager were on chairs which they had pulled out from the row along the wall. Heather Gladd sat at her own desk, with her elbows propped on it and her face covered by her hands, and seated at the end of the desk to her left was Judith Dundee, her back straight and her shoulders up, but her face drawn with strain and apprehension.

No one was talking, except the crickets and katydids outdoors, and their fretful and querulous exchanges were not calculated to soothe anybody's nerves.

Eyes jerked to the inner door to the laboratory when it opened and three men entered. R. I. Dundee, in front, glanced around, took a step toward his wife, changed his mind, and sat on the nearest chair. Hicks crossed to Heather, muttered something to her, and propped himself against her desk and folded his arms. District Attorney Corbett with no sign whatever of joviality either on his pudgy face or in his voice, spoke to the room:

"Mr. Hicks is going to say something. Not as my representative. He is in no sense speaking officially. I want that understood. Manny, will you cut out that marathon? Sit down or hang yourself on a hook!"

Beck stopped in his tracks and glared.

"If Hicks represents no authority," James Vail demanded, "what is the purpose—"

"We've had that out," Corbett snapped. "I've told you, Mr. Vail, that you are not under arrest, you are not being detained, and you are at liberty to go or stay. I've told you that after a private consultation by Hicks and Dundee and myself there would be a statement by Hicks. If you were brought here by him against your wishes, your redress—"

"Baloney," Hicks said impatiently. "You know darned well, Vail, what I'm going to do. I've got the label ready for the guy who murdered Martha Cooper and George Cooper, and I'm going to paste it on him. What are you chewing the rag about? You wouldn't miss it for a dollar."

Vail, ignoring him, spoke to Corbett: "I have explained to you that it is ridiculous to suppose—"

"He's not doing the supposing," Hicks said acidly. "I am. If it will make you feel any better, I'll begin by explaining that in the discussion at Mrs. Dundee's apartment I was merely theorizing, just as you were. Your suggestion was that Dundee was the murderer, though you knew he wasn't. My suggestion was that you were the murderer,

179

though I knew you weren't. It didn't do any harm, since we were just waiting for a phone call anyhow. But now I'm ready to talk turkey."

Vail arose, walked deliberately across to R. I. Dundee, and gazed down at him. "Look here, Dick," he said ominously. "This Hicks is a madman. You still have a slim chance to pull out of this with your hide on. For the last time I ask you, will you listen to me? Will you talk with me privately?"

"No, damn you," Dundee said harshly.

"You won't?"

"No."

Vail, with his thin mouth compressed until there were no lips at all, returned to his chair, stuck his thumbs in his vest pockets, and addressed Hicks. "Go ahead. I've done my best."

"I know you have." Hicks smiled at him. "You see, you're handicapped. Not only do I know more than you think I do, but Dundee and the district attorney do too. When I went to that spot on Crescent Road and found it unoccupied, I was fairly certain that you had all made a beeline for Mrs. Dundee, because I had told Miss Gladd to go to her if anything went wrong, and I knew that both you and Ross would go along—though for different reasons. So I came here and had a little talk with Dundee and the district attorney. In passing, I wish to pay a deserved tribute to my old friend Manny Beck. With his usual thoroughness and foresight, he had kept men stationed in this building after he was summoned here to investigate the killing of Cooper. True, he had no idea what it was the men were guarding—"

"Go to hell," Manny Beck snarled.

"But their presence made it impossible for the murderer to return and remove a vital piece of evidence." Hicks, propped against the desk, kept his eyes on Vail, whose chair was between Ross Dundee's and Herman Brager's. "It will be valuable evidence in a courtroom, but it is even more valuable for the effect it will have on you here and now. First, though, I ought to ask you, are you sure you know what an accessory is? An accessory after the fact?"

Vail made a contemptuous noise.

"I guess you do," Hicks smiled. "You began, there at Mrs. Dundee's apartment, by saying that you didn't intend to expose yourself to the danger of being arrested as an accessory to a murder." Suddenly, unexpectedly, Hicks's eyes darted to the man at Vail's right. "You see, Brager, that was your worst miscalculation. You figured that Vail would stand for anything, even murder, to prevent disclosure of his own dirty work, but you might have realized that there was one risk he wouldn't—"

"What is this?" Brager's eyes were popping with indignation. "Dirty work? I am aware you are paid by Dundee—"

"Wrong again," Hicks cut him off. "You're about the wrongest guy I've ever run up against. Your alibis were absolutely childish. Take Thursday afternoon. I came in here—will you help me out with this, Dundee?"

Dundee got up and disappeared through the door into the laboratory, closing the door after him. Hicks went on:

"I came in here and found Miss Gladd here at her desk, tears running down her face, typing like mad, with a man's voice filling the room—Miss Gladd, will you please switch on that loud-speaker?"

Heather looked at him blankly.

"Turn it on. Not the machine, the loud-speaker from the laboratory."

Heather reached to a switch at the end of her desk and flipped it, and instantly a man's voice, Brager's voice, came from the grill in the wall:

"Twelve minutes at five one oh, nine minutes at six three five! Vat two at three-ten, less tendency to streak and more uniform hardening! Shrinkage point oh three millimeters. . . ."

Hicks, moving to the end of the desk, turned it off.

"Foolishness!" Brager blurted. "That is merely—"

"It is merely," Hicks snapped, "a demonstration of the method by which you got in on a three-way alibi with Miss Gladd and me at the time Martha Cooper was being killed. It's a new twist on an old gag. Because your voice wasn't supposed to be coming to us directly, but over a loud-speaker system, and therefore it worked. All you had to do was start a bunch of records on that machine you have in there, connected with the mike, with the proper intervals of silence, and you could go out the back way and take whatever time you needed for your errand. And you had to hurry up about it, since Ross Dundee had gone to the house, and Miss Gladd had just learned on the telephone that her sister was there, and Dundee himself was expected—"

"Foolishness!" Brager repeated. His eyes went to Corbett. "This is an insult you permit—"

A shot rang out, shattering the air.

Brager started from his chair, then sank back into it. Heather was on her feet, rigid, staring at the window. Judith Dundee and her son were both halfway across the room toward the door to the laboratory, but they were intercepted by policemen in their path and by Hicks's sharp command:

"Ross! Okay! Hold it!"

They turned, staring at Hicks.

"My husband," Judith said determinedly.

"What was that?" Brager demanded hoarsely.

The door to the laboratory opened and R. I. Dundee was there. Ross backed up. Judith dropped onto the chair her husband had formerly occupied, and he stood beside her.

"That," Hicks said grimly, "was the shot that killed George Cooper. You ought to recognize it by this time, Brager, since you fired it and also reproduced it."

"I—" Brager gulped. "I will say nothing. Nothing! But you will see! These tricks! They will be paid for!"

"They sure will," Hicks agreed. "You've used the right word for it. Foolishness. You've insisted all along that everyone but you is a fool, and you've certainly proceeded on that theory. I admit you were right up to a point, but you carried it too far. Don't you think so? Now?"

"I will say nothing!"

"Do you mean," Judith Dundee demanded, "that he did it all? That sonotel record—"

"It started long before that," Hicks asserted. "Whenever it was that he began selling Dundee formulas to Vail. That was a good trick, nothing foolish about that. He got big money from your husband for discovering the formulas in this laboratory, and then he collected from Vail for them too."

"He actually—did that?"

"He actually did. Of course I can't prove it, but that's where Vail will be a help. Yes, you will, Vail, don't think you won't! This, Mrs. Dundee, is my final report on the job you hired me to do. I'll leave off the embroidery—for instance, I suspect that the police will find upon investigation that the coin Brager was raking in was being used for Nazi propaganda in this country, but we'll leave that to them. Anyhow, he was getting it coming and going. But it began to get a little complicated. First, Dundee naturally got wise to the fact that he was being diddled by someone, and Brager had to watch his step. Second, Brager got captivated by your charm. Being emotionally a mixture of an ape and a sentimental ass, as Germans of a certain type always are, that led first to his abasing himself, and then to a boundless and barbarous fury when he found that his affection wasn't returned. I make a guess. Didn't you humiliate him by re-rejecting his advances?"

Judith shivered. "Yes," she said succinctly.

Hicks nodded. "So he hated you. Plenty. And he had a miraculous bit of luck. Through a sonotel that he had installed in the house here for experiment, he found himself in possession of a batch of records with a woman's voice on them exactly like yours. That was nearly a year ago, but the use he could make of them probably didn't occur to him until recently. He could kill two birds with one stone: divert any possible suspicion in Dundee's mind from himself, and get revenge on you. He knew that Martha Cooper was in Europe, and figured that it would all be over, and you disgraced for good, before she returned. He knew, of course, that Dundee had a sonotel in Vail's office, and had informed Vail."

Vail snapped, "I told you I knew that sonotel was in my office. But I didn't learn it from Brager."

"No?" Hicks smiled at him. "We'll see. Let me finish my report." He continued to Judith: "So he faked that sonotel record, using excerpts from the records he had in Martha Cooper's voice, and Vail collaborating with his own voice. You heard Vail himself admit that any good technician could do it. Then Brager found an opportunity to plant the faked record among those delivered by the detective agency, in a case in the testing room in the Dundee offices in New York.

"But it began to get gummed up right from the start. Ross, thinking to protect you from what he suspected to be a plot, made off with the record and brought it out here and hid it, and your husband had to postpone the showdown until he could find it again. That was bad enough, but it was nothing compared to what happened Monday evening, five days ago. George Cooper suddenly appeared, arriving here Monday evening to see Miss Gladd, and his wife had returned with him from abroad. That was worse than a nuisance, it was a threat of disaster. Martha was apt to show up here any minute, and if Ross met her and heard her speak, good-bye. So Brager made preparations. When Martha did come, Thursday afternoon, he was ready with a batch of records that would place him ostensibly in the laboratory while he

183

sneaked through the woods to the house and took whatever action the circumstances offered. His luck seemed to have turned again. He was able to get into the house unseen, wield the candlestick through the open window without appearing on the terrace, and leave again and return to the laboratory still unseen. Also, I was here in the office with Miss Gladd, making his alibi that much better."

"You gave us that alibi," Manny Beck growled.

Hicks ignored him. "But still, even with Martha's voice quiet for good, everything was far from rosy. Brager had plenty to worry about. Where the devil was the record? He had to find it and destroy it. Also Vail, learning of the murder, would know who had done it, and Vail might be hard to handle. Friday morning Brager phoned him from White Plains and arranged to meet him. They met, and probably it was an unpleasant session, but for his own protection Vail agreed to keep his mouth shut. Also he decided to take steps of his own, and as a starter he called on me. At my place he saw Cooper, and learned that Cooper knew of the sonotel record—had actually heard it, or at least part of it.

"Of course that was bad. Very bad. On leaving my place Vail got in touch with Brager—probably phoned him by prearrangement to some number in White Plains—and told him about Cooper. Undoubtedly he urged him to make every possible effort to find that record. For Vail's voice was on that record."

Hicks turned to Vail. "This raises the question, naturally, whether you were an accomplice in Cooper's murder. I doubt it. I think you were already as close as you ever wanted to be to murder, and a good deal closer. I think you merely warned Brager of Cooper's knowledge of the record, and urged him to sidetrack Cooper if possible, and above all to find the record."

"I'll thank you when you're done," Vail said in a tone of controlled fury.

"Don't bother," Hicks told him, returning to Mrs. Dundee. "Also Vail arranged for a rendezvous with Brager, Brager designating the spot on a deserted stretch of road not far from here. I wouldn't be surprised if they had used that spot before during the three years that Brager was selling Vail the Dundee formulas. Anyhow they used it today. Vail drove there at once, and waited. It was getting hot for him now, entirely too hot for comfort. In fact, he was scared stiff.

"But I doubt if Brager was scared. He's too cold-blooded to get scared. Look at him now, he's not even scared now, though God knows he ought to be. What he did, he beat it back here as fast as he could come and prepared to receive Cooper by getting his revolver from wherever he kept it, and by getting the recording machine in the laboratory in readiness so that all he had to do was turn on the switch. Since no one else saw Cooper when he arrived, I suppose Brager met him at the entrance and took him around by the road here to the laboratory. You may think I don't know what he said to him, but I do. No question about it. He told him he had that record he was looking for, and he took him into the laboratory to prove it by playing the record. Cooper wouldn't know the difference between a recording machine and a playing machine. Brager started the machine going, and while Cooper was gazing at it, waiting to hear the record, paying no attention to Brager, Brager shot him in the temple, with something—his handkerchief—over the muzzle of the revolver to prevent powder stain. So I do know. It couldn't have been any other way."

Hicks glanced at Brager, and back at Judith. "But he's not scared yet. Okay. There was no blood, or very little. He dumped Cooper's body out of the window, maybe went outside to arrange it in a good position, removed the record of the shot he had made and put it on the playing machine, and placed the playing machine against the open window. Then he went to the house to get an audience. It didn't matter much who the audience was, but the one he had the most plausible excuse for was Miss Gladd, so he took her. They arrived here and found Cooper not present, to Brager's pretended astonishment. He went into the laboratory to see if Cooper was there, the real reason he went, of course, being to switch on the playing machine. He scooted back in here to rejoin Miss Gladd, and in a minute bang went the shot. Since that partition is soundproof, and windows were open, it sounded as if the shot was outdoors. Naturally they ran out—"

Heather blurted incredulously, "Then George wasn't—it wasn't that shot that killed him?"

"Sure it was," Hicks assured her. "He was killed by the shot you heard, only you didn't hear it until half an hour or so after it was fired. And you've just heard it again. So will the judge and jury when the time comes. It's an extremely convenient arrangement. It will be the first time in history that the sound of the shot itself is used as evidence in a murder trial."

District Attorney Corbett spoke for the first time. "If it is admissible," he squeaked.

"Pooh," Hicks admonished him. "Found as it was right there in a cabinet? That was the biggest blunder you made, Brager. I admit it presented a problem, since Miss Gladd was here with you until the police came, and that plastic is indestructible, but it does seem you might have done better than merely stick it in among other records in the cabinet. I suppose you figured that no one would have brains enough to look for it, and of course you would have had a chance later to remove it if Beck hadn't kept men here. It took them only an hour to dig it up after I tipped Corbett off. If I were you I wouldn't build any hope on Corbett's misgiving about its being admissible as evidence. Take my word for it, that shot will be heard by a judge and jury. And still you're not scared?"

"That shot," Brager said contemptuously. "That record of a shot was made for experiment many weeks ago. I will say that one thing. Beyond that I say nothing."

"I'm surprised you say that much," Hicks declared. "I expected you to go dumb on me. One other thing, your phoning that message to Miss Gladd that sent her to where Vail was waiting. I'll bet you thought that was slick as grease. You thought it would drag Vail out into the light, and then he would have to stand by you no matter how many murders you committed. But you were wrong. There's one risk Vail won't take. At least I don't think he will."

Hicks's eyes darted, stabbed at Vail. "How about it? Where do you go from here?"

Vail sat motionless, frozen. It did not appear that he was aware that Hicks was looking at him or had spoken to him, for his own eyes, narrowed to nothing by the drooping fleshy folds of his lids, were directed only at space.

"It's a question," Hicks went on to him, "of throwing out the baby to appease the wolves. If Corbett can convict Brager of murder without your help, he can convict you as an accessory. Knowing Corbett, I can assure you he will do just that, if you hold out on him. That's the risk if you play it pat. If you come clean and help Corbett, Brager is a pushover. His conviction is a cinch, and you're out as far as murder is concerned, but you'll have to settle with Dundee about the formulas, and you may have to find a new place to eat lunch. It's six of one and about three dozen of the other. And you choose now. If you talk now and sign a statement, you go home. If you don't, you go along with Brager. That is official. Is that official, Corbett?"

"It is," Corbett declared. "That's about the size of it, Mr. Vail."

"Damn you!" Vail said through his teeth; and his eyes, malevolent still but no longer wary, aimed at Hicks, left no doubt as to whom he was damning. "If he had killed you too it would be worth it!"

"Ah," said Hicks, "I see you prefer to go home."

Not even then did Brager, staring popeyed across at Judith Dundee, look scared.

Twenty-five

SINCE IT WAS AFTER SIX O'CLOCK SATURDAY EVENING, Rosario Garci should have been attending to his duties in the kitchen, but for the fifth time in half an hour there he was, pretending he had an errand in the dining room. His wife, moving among the tables of customers with dishes, cast amused but nevertheless heedful glances at him out of the corner of her eye.

To one of the customers Rosario was speaking:

"Excuse me, Mr. Heecks, but you know what? If you want my opinion."

"Shoot, Rosy."

"This lady." Rosario was gazing with the frankest admiration at the face of Hicks's companion. "I say this with my heart. Of all the ladies you have brought to eat here with you, this one is the flower! She is the Queen! Absolute! So do you know what? I own this building. I can do anything I feel like with this building, tear it down, build it up, anything I want! Okay. I have been thinking. That floor where your room is, there are four rooms on that floor. One I can make a beautiful bathroom. I can make doors. In the little room, a window. New paint everywhere—"

"No, Rosy. It's a swell idea, but no go."

"Why no go?"

"Because the lady is in love with another man. God knows why. If you could see him—you can see him! Turn around and look at him. Here he comes."

"This," Heather Gladd said, coloring, "is simply ridiculous."

Whether it was Rosario's suggestion, or Hicks's statement, or the sudden arrival of Ross Dundee, that was simply ridiculous, was not clear. Rosario backed off a step, and looked both astonished and disappointed when the newcomer was received amicably by Hicks and invited to a chair at the table. Mrs. Garci approached, and was asked to bring another set of utensils and the antipasto. Rosario retreated to the kitchen, shaking his head.

"This looks like a nice place," Ross Dundee said. "I like this kind of a place."

"How's your mother?" Hicks asked. "Have you seen her?"

"No, but I phoned her as soon as I got up, around three o'clock. She and Dad were getting ready to go out to Litchfield, a little place they have there. Right now they're probably playing badminton and fighting like fiends. They always do when they play badminton. Mom beats him."

"She may let him win this time to quiet his nerves."

"I doubt it." Ross surveyed the antipasto. "It looks wonderful, but I'm not hungry." He forked two or three onto his plate. "I ate like a horse when I got up." He looked at Heather. "Did you eat?"

Heather met his eyes. "Look here," she said determinedly, "we might as well settle this now. You've got to stop following me around. Last night you followed me, and you wouldn't get out of the car, you insisted on going along, and that was all right, I mean I admitted that at the time, you know I did, after you jumped at him and took the gun away from him. But your following me into town today, and following me here—"

"I didn't follow you here."

"Certainly you did! How could you—"

"He didn't," Hicks said.

Heather gaped at him. "He didn't?"

"No. I invited him here." Hicks broke a piece of bread.

188

"For a purpose. But before I go into that I'll answer the question you asked a minute ago. You asked how I knew it was Brager. The answer is, I didn't."

They both stared. Ross demanded, "What do you mean, you didn't?"

"I mean I didn't know it was Brager until last night. I thought it was Vail. He had an alibi for Thursday afternoon, but I supposed it was phony. But as soon as I learned of that fake message phoned to Mrs. Darby, I knew Vail was out. He couldn't have sent it, because he didn't know you were there in that car, and besides, there was no conceivable reason why he would want to bring you to him in that way."

"In what way?"

"In a way that involved him. Even giving the license number of his car. How could he know Mrs. Darby wouldn't give the message to the police instead of you? It was obvious that that message was sent by someone who wanted to tie Vail up by getting him involved, and that couldn't be anyone but Brager. So after I went there and found Crescent Road deserted, I thought it over and decided two things. I decided that you would go straight to Mrs. Dundee, because you had said you would, and I decided that Brager's alibis for both murders were frame-ups. So I went and enlightened Corbett and he started a search of the laboratory. Manny Beck had kept a man on guard there—but I don't want to bore you. You're not listening."

"I am too listening!" Heather protested.

"Nope. You've lost interest. Since Ross came. You're probably so mad at him for coming that you can't get your mind on anything else." Hicks took a sip of wine. "So I'll proceed to the purpose I invited him for, and then he can go and you'll feel better." Hicks turned. "Nedda!"

Mrs. Garci came trotting.

"Will you please ask Rosy for the package he's keeping for me?"

Mrs. Garci went.

"A package?" Heather inquired suspiciously.

Hicks nodded, wiping sauce from his plate with a chunk of bread. "I didn't want to leave it in my room, for fear Vail might take it into his head to look around while I was away. As for my inviting Ross, I didn't want to make myself liable to a lawsuit. In England, the letters a man writes and sends remain his property, not that of the recipient. In this country the question of ownership is still more or less up in the but I didn't want to take a chance—Thank you, Nedda, that's it. So I thought it best to return these things with both of you present—"

"Don't open that!" Heather clutched his sleeve. "Don't you dare—"

"What is it?" Ross demanded. "From its shape, it looks—"

"Its shape does rather give it away," Hicks admitted. "It's sonograph plates that Miss Gladd was preserving. Seven of them. There were eight, but one—no you don't, I'm hanging onto them until you folks decide—"

Heather was glaring at him, speechless with fury. Ross was gazing at her, also speechless, though not with fury.

"Why, you—" he stammered. "You s-s-said you d-d-didn't keep them!" He swallowed. "You darned little liar! You d-d-doggoned liar! Heather!"

Hicks chewed on the luscious chunk of bread and sauce.